The
WRIGHT
MISTAKE

Also by K.A. Linde

AVOIDING SERIES

Avoiding Commitment
Avoiding Responsibility
Avoiding Intimacy
Avoiding Decisions
Avoiding Temptation

RECORD SERIES

Off the Record
On the Record
For the Record
Struck from the Record

ALL THAT GLITTERS SERIES

Diamonds
Gold
Emeralds
Platinum
Silver

TAKE ME SERIES

Take Me for Granted
Take Me with You

STAND-ALONE

Following Me
The Wright Brother
The Wright Boss

ASCENSION SERIES

The Affiliate
The Bound

The WRIGHT MISTAKE

K.A. LINDE

Visit my website at
www.kalinde.com
Cover Designer: Sarah Hansen, Okay Creations.
Photographer: Eric Battershell Photography
Editor and Interior Designer: Jovana Shirley,
Unforeseen Editing, www.unforeseenediting.com

ISBN-13: 978-1635760996

To Staci Hart,
for allowing me to accidentally fictionalize you.

One

Julia

"Don't try to blame this shit on me. Just face it, Julia," Trevor spat, "You'll never be happy."

"Fuck you," I spat as I slammed the door shut in Trevor's face as the nasty words he'd uttered cut through me like a knife.

Not because he was wrong, but because he was right.

I couldn't be happy—not with him or anyone. Not with my past looming over my shoulder. The truth was a guy like Trevor couldn't handle the real Julia Banner.

My phone started ringing from the other side of the room. With a sigh, I picked it up and saw Heidi was calling.

"So, did you do it?" she asked when I answered.

I sighed. "Yeah. He hates me."

"Psh. Trevor from accounting couldn't hate a fly. He's hurt. He'll get over it."

"I don't know. We were together for a year. Our anniversary was this weekend. I can't believe I just broke up with him. I'm kind of the worst."

Heidi snorted. "It was long overdue. You and I both know that."

Of course, she was right. Because Trevor had been this perfect, normal, nice guy. He was the guy who came over to your place to do your laundry while you were with your friends and filled up your gas tank when he noticed you were running low and called your mom to chat every Thursday. Or he would have done that last one…if he'd thought my parents were alive.

And I was the opposite. It had been nice, but it hadn't been right.

"So," Heidi muttered, "want to go get fucked up to feel better about it?"

"Yes. Yes, I do."

Heidi laughed. "That's my girl."

"Flips?" I asked.

It was the local bar that we always went to. By anyone else's standards, it was kind of a dump. But Heidi adored the place.

"Actually…we're all heading to Ransom Canyon for Memorial Day weekend. Lake, boats, barbeque—the trifecta. You in?"

"And how exactly am I going to get laid from this plan?"

"Well, there will be a lot of alcohol," Heidi said.

"And?"

"And…a lot of hot, eligible men."

I rolled my eyes. "Like who?"

"Landon and the Wrights all invited a bunch of people to come hang out. I know your…issues with Austin, so I didn't mention it before. But I don't think that should stop you now."

I groaned. "Austin Wright is the biggest alcoholic jackass on this side of the planet! You know how he treated me when we were together."

"True," she added. "But…it was a year and a half ago when you were together. And, since you slapped the shit out of him last fall, he's kind of avoided you like the plague, which means, you should be fine."

"Heidi!"

"Just get your ass over here and bring a bathing suit. I want to see those tattoos you're sporting. I won't take no for an answer."

And then she unceremoniously hung up on me. I glanced down at it with a sigh. Maybe Heidi was right, and I just needed some girl time.

I stripped out of my work attire and into a pair of cutoff jean shorts and a black Queen tank top. I piled my recently dyed dark red hair up into a messy bun on the top of my head and admired the shaved undercut. I filled up my travel tote with enough clothes for a week away from home. Now, I just needed my favorite olive-green bomber jacket. Not that May in Lubbock, Texas, was cold by any stretch of the imagination, but the dusty, windy, and flat place I had called home for almost two years now got cool on summer nights. But the jacket was nowhere to be found. I tore my apartment apart, looking for it. I swore I'd left it hanging in my closet, but nope, no luck. Must have left it at work or in the car or something.

I finally added a black Beatles sweatshirt I'd picked up at a thrift store to the bag and headed over to Heidi's place where she lived with Landon Wright. They'd gotten together last year, and they were totally crazy in love. They'd gotten engaged practically right away, and they now lived together in a brand-new house that they'd had built together.

Landon was packing up his Jeep when I pulled up in my black Tahoe. He waved as I parked.

"Hey, Julia. I'm glad to see that Heidi convinced you to come with us."

I hopped out of the car and moved my bag into the trunk. "Yeah. She's persuasive all right. Told me to get my ass over here and hung up on me."

Landon laughed congenially. He had the goddamn Wright good looks—dark hair, penetrating dark eyes, perfect smile, and so tall that you could climb the fuckers.

"That sounds like my fiancée."

"I swear you say it just because you like the sound of it."

He grinned, not at all sheepish. "Can't blame me."

"Not in the least."

Heidi appeared then in tiny white cutoffs and her hot-pink bathing suit top. She had a huge floppy hat on her head, her long blonde hair falling to her waist, and sunglasses to cover her entire face. "I'm so fucking ready!"

She clobbered me on sight, planting a kiss on my cheek.

"You're insane," I told her.

"And you are wearing too many clothes."

"Don't say that around Emery. She might get jealous," I said about Heidi's long-time best friend.

"Can I watch?" Landon asked from where he was standing with his arms crossed, eyeing us.

"You can join in," Heidi said with a wink. Then, she smacked my ass and hopped into the front seat.

I climbed into the back, and once Landon was in the driver's seat, we were off and away.

It was only a twenty-minute drive to Ransom Canyon, and Heidi kept me from brooding too much about my recent breakup. Not that I was actually upset about leaving Trevor. I was more upset that he was right. I liked uncomplicated fun. Preferably with a lot of mind-blowing sex.

"So, who all did you say would be here?" I asked again.

"Um…" Heidi trailed off.

Landon shot her a look of frustration. "My family mostly."

"Mostly?"

"Heidi and Emery and her sister, Kimber, and her husband, Noah, and their two kids will also be there."

"And?" I added.

"And Patrick," Landon said, adding Austin's best friend as an afterthought.

"What happened to all the hot, eligible bachelors, Heidi?"

She chewed on her bottom lip, and her big blue eyes searched my face. "About that—"

"Oh, you're such a bitch."

Great. I was going to be the only single girl there who wasn't related to the Wright family. And the two single guys there were totally off-limits. *Just perfect.*

Heidi laughed and just shrugged. Clearly, this had all been part of her evil plan. *The little witch.*

Landon parked his Jeep next to a giant truck, which I vaguely recalled belonging to the eldest Wright sibling, Jensen.

Landon waved us off when we tried to help. "Go on and check out the lake. I've got this."

"Thanks, Landon," I said.

Heidi kissed his cheek, grabbed my hand, and dashed down the hill to the dock below. Ransom Canyon was a town of only about a thousand people, but the lake filled up all summer. And it was busiest on Fourth of July and Memorial Day. As in…today. Boats were everywhere with parties happening all up and down the lake. Maybe it wouldn't be such a loss after all.

We skipped to a stop when we got to the end of the dock, and Heidi laughed before peeling her shorts off.

"What are you doing?" I asked.

"Taking a swim. Come with me, lover."

"Uh, no. I do not have a swimsuit on."

"That's no fun." She handed me her floppy hat, tied up her blonde hair, and then cannonballed into the water, as if she didn't have a care in the world.

I laughed as she splashed water up on me and took a step back. "You're crazy!"

"Oh my God, get in! The water is amazing!"

"No chance in hell. I have to change first."

Heidi pouted as she treaded water. "You're missing out. Emery would do it."

"Don't care. You can't goad me into this."

5

"Aw, I just want you to have some fun. Since you finally ditched Mr. Boring."

"He was not boring."

Heidi rolled her eyes and ducked underwater. "He was so boring," she said when she came up for air. "My girl is fire and passion and tattoos and top-shelf whiskey."

"You must be thinking of someone else," I teased.

"Come on. Show me those tattoos!"

"Later! When I have a freaking swimsuit on. Unless you are just dying to see my thong."

Heidi raised an eyebrow. "I bet everyone here would die to see your thong."

"You're incorrigible."

"Would you rather talk about Trevor?"

I shook my head. "Let's go back to my thong."

"Did someone say thong?" a voice called from behind me on the deck.

I took a deep breath, closed my eyes, and then exhaled slowly. Exactly what I didn't want to deal with. I turned and came face-to-face with Austin fucking Wright.

He looked...fucking gorgeous. His almost-black hair was sharp on the sides but longer in the front. He had haunted dark eyes and a smile like a razor blade. His cheekbones were hollow and jawline chiseled out of marble. And he was fucking shirtless.

His swim trunks rode low on his hips, revealing the carefully maintained six-pack and the sexy V. I didn't know how he managed it with the amount of alcohol in his system, but he was cut as fuck. Bulging biceps and ripped pecs with a half-sleeve bleeding into his chest. Ink that I had touched every inch of.

I shook myself out of my reverie. *Fuck.*

"Shocking that you showed up right when we were talking about my underwear," I muttered.

"Good to see you, too, babe," Austin said with a grin.

"Wish I could say the same."

Patrick trailed behind him with a dopey smile on his face, carrying a six-pack of beer. They both looked loaded. But Austin always held his alcohol better than everyone else. Probably because his tolerance was through the roof, considering he drank all the time.

"What's up, Julia?" Patrick said.

"Y'all coming in?" Heidi called from the water.

"Hell yes!" Patrick dropped the beer at the edge of the dock, then ran and jumped into the water, next to Heidi.

She giggled and splashed him back when he surfaced.

"Austin, man, we need something to float our beer!"

"Oh, you're drunk already and still drinking," I snarled. "How shocking!"

Austin set his dark eyes on me, and he smiled wickedly. "Heard you broke up with that tool you were seeing."

"Not that it's any of your fucking business."

"Just trying to figure out why you're still acting like this."

"Like what?" I demanded even though I knew it was a bad idea.

"Like you've got a stick up your ass."

I narrowed my eyes and clenched my hands into fists.

"And not even the way that you like it either, babe."

He winked, and I flushed scarlet.

"Why are you such a dick?"

He held his arms wide. "Just your average Prince Charming."

I snorted. "There's nothing about you that's charming."

"Nothing about me that's average either."

Then, he looked at me in a way that made my shorts and thong melt off. That seductive, eye-fucking, take-me-right-now, all-consuming look of desire that had set me on fire and pushed me into his bed the first time. The same smile that said he was bad, bad news, and I was happy to be on the front page.

"Fuck off, Austin." I turned to leave, smoke pouring out of my ears.

But Austin latched on to my wrist as I tried to break away. "Come with me."

"What part of *fuck off* did you not understand?"

"Swimming."

"What?" I asked, realizing a half-second too late what was about to happen.

He tugged me toward the edge of the dock. I stumbled into him, completely losing my footing. Then, vertigo hit. I felt weightless, suspended in midair for a split second, with Austin's chest pressed against mine. His smile was magnetic. His lips so fucking inviting. He looked…younger, happier, freer than I'd ever seen him.

Then, we crashed into the water. I came up soaking wet in my fucking street clothes, sputtering for breath. Austin popped to the surface right after me. His hands slid down my sides and twirled me back around to face him. He yanked me tight against his body, and all cognitive thought fled my mind as I felt the press of every inch of him against me.

My body went into hyperdrive, as I imagined all the ways he could touch and lick and caress and pleasure my body. All the ways that mouth could make me come. All the ways his dick could lay claim to my body. And I didn't pull away.

I leaned in, letting my body take over for once and entirely ignoring my mind. His lips were so close.

So inviting.

So easy to forget.

"Fuck, I love getting you wet, Jules," he breathed seductively.

And then reality crashed back into place.

Austin

"You motherfucker!" Julia screamed.

She shoved me in the chest, trying to get away from me as fast as she could in the lake. I released her with a laugh.

She just glared at me. "Don't fucking laugh at me."

Then, she punched me in the shoulder. *Hard.*

"Shit, Jules!"

The girl knew how to fucking punch. *Jesus Christ!* I hadn't had the privilege of finding that out the last time we were together. No, the last time she'd just slapped the shit out of me. Two for two.

"Austin, leave her alone," Heidi said with exasperation in her voice.

"It was just a joke," I said with a shrug.

Julia splashed water at me in a huff and began to swim back to the dock. I could hear her cursing my name under her breath.

"Seriously, Jules, lighten up a bit," I said, leaning backward in the water and grinning up at her.

She climbed out of the water, and her eyes were fiery hatred when she whirled back to look at me. I could barely hold her gaze.

Not because she was so angry. Seriously, she needed to chill the fuck out. It was Memorial Day weekend. We were supposed to be having a good time.

But rather because she was dripping wet from head to toe. Her short jean shorts clung to her muscular legs, and the flimsy black tank stuck to her curves like a second skin. I could just envision the black lace bra she was wearing beneath the material, and suddenly, I wasn't thinking with the right head any longer. *Fuck*.

God-fucking-damn it, she was the most gorgeous woman I'd ever laid eyes on. There was something feral about her. Something dangerous and dark and predatory. A feeling that radiated from her that said she was a badass bitch, and everyone should beware. She had a fucking do-not-disturb sign plastered to her ample chest. And all of it had only intrigued me more and more every time my drunk ass landed in her office. I'd never admit I'd been doing stupid shit just to get sent to the head of HR.

"You ruined my shoes," Julia snarled at me before turning on her heel and stalking away from the water. Her feet squelched in her worn slip-on Vans.

Heidi smacked me up the side of the head. "Why do you have to be such a dick?"

"He really can't help it," Patrick insisted.

"Thanks, bro."

I shot him a disdainful look, but he only grinned like a fool. He was eating this up, the shithead.

Heidi hauled herself out of the lake and grabbed her discarded clothing. She was tall and thin and mouthy with eyes that looked straight through a guy. I'd always thought she was fun, and I was glad that she'd loosened Landon up. Even if she was staring down at me right now like she was going to roast me on a spit.

"I brought her here to help her get over her breakup, not so that you could be an asshole to her, like usual."

I held my hands up and laughed. "You all take this way too seriously."

Heidi shook her head. "You don't take anything seriously."

Then, she was trudging down the dock, following in Julia's wet footprints.

I turned to face Patrick and just shrugged. "Women."

Patrick laughed hysterically at me as soon as Heidi was out of earshot. "Man, you are so done for."

"Whatever, man."

"Oh, fuck off, Austin. You're so going to fuck Julia this weekend."

I shrugged. "Nothing wrong with that."

Patrick splashed me as he swam back toward the dock and pulled himself up to sit on the edge. "She's so fucking pissed at you."

I lay back, floating, and stared at the sun burning bright overhead. "She'll get over it."

"I'd almost think that you weren't totally into her."

"Whatever."

Patrick laughed again as he popped open a beer. "I can't wait to watch this play out. I sure hope you keep acting like an idiot."

"Well, look what the cat dragged in," a voice called from the end of the dock.

I righted myself and saw my sister Morgan walking down the dock. She was four years younger than me but was second-in-command at Wright Construction. We had all been born and bred to work for the company, but Morgan was the only one who really relished in it. Only twenty-seven years old and one of the most powerful women in business. She'd landed on three Thirty Under Thirty lists this year. She would have made our parents proud...if either of them were still alive.

"Morgan," I said with a grin. "Here I thought, we'd never see you out of a business suit."

"Traded it in for something cuter. What do you think the board would say if I showed up in this suit instead?" she asked, twirling in place in her white bikini.

Even though she addressed the comment to me, her eyes were fixed on Patrick. The idiot was the only person alive who didn't realize that Morgan had been head over heels for him since they were kids. But I wasn't touching that with a ten-foot pole. The thought of my best friend hooking up with my little sister made me want to stab something or vomit or both.

"Probably start a riot," I told her.

"Indeed," she said with a wicked grin, as if she were contemplating it. "Now, tell me what you idiots did to upset Julia *already*? We just got here!"

Patrick raised his hands. "Don't look at me."

"Oh, who's surprised that Austin is the troublemaker?"

"I just pulled her into the water with me."

"Fully clothed," Patrick coughed.

Morgan shot me an imperious look. "I have the power to relegate you to the couch. So, watch yourself."

"Oh no, not the couch!" I cried as I heaved myself onto the dock. "I'll make it up to you, Mor. How about a hug?"

"Don't you dare," she said, pointing her finger at me.

I darted toward her, and she took a step backward, as if we were sword fighting and she were testing her opponent. I took another step, and Patrick howled with laughter.

"I think she'll make you sleep on the roof if you throw *her* into the water," Patrick said.

"It's Jensen's house. He'll get a say."

"He always sides with me," Morgan snapped. She had three older brothers. She knew how to fight dirty if need be. "And you won't even get the roof when I'm done with you."

"Fine. Fine," I said, holding my hands up in defeat. "You win."

"Don't think I don't know your tricks," Morgan said.

"I bow to thee, fair maiden."

I dipped down low, and when I straightened, I threw her over my shoulder. She screamed and beat my back.

"If you throw me in that water, I will murder you!"

I hauled her to the edge of the dock and pretended to release her. She screamed right before I caught her and then dropped her back onto her feet.

But, when she looked up at me, she was laughing. Morgan might be Jensen's mini me, but she and I always had the most fun.

"Come on. Dinner is almost ready," Morgan said, clapping me on the back and then falling into step with Patrick, back up the hill to the house.

I grabbed the beer as I followed them, cracking one open as I went. Julia might have joked about me always drinking, but alcohol was just a part of my life. We had a special relationship. The constant buzz. The feeling of the pain disappearing.

That was what alcohol was.

Freedom.

Pure, unadulterated bliss.

If there was anything I could rely on, it was that a drink would silence everything always buzzing around in my head. It kept me numb and pleasant. I didn't even remember my life before it. And, frankly, I didn't want to.

The lake house was in chaos when I entered. Luggage everywhere. People everywhere—cooking, talking, drinking. With all four of my siblings and their plus-ones and kids, we had eleven people at the house for the full weekend. Emery's sister and her family would join us tomorrow. It made me want to get another drink already.

I finally meandered out of the house and found Jensen at the grill. He nodded his head at me.

"What's up?" I said.

"Heard you threw Julia into the lake."

"I didn't throw her."

"Semantics," Jensen said. "I don't care what you do, Austin. Just trying to make this as much of a drama-free weekend as possible. I know that's nearly impossible when we get the whole Wright family together, but don't start shit, okay?"

Jensen, the fixer, the CEO of Wright Construction, and my older brother. No one would ever guess we were only three years apart, considering Jensen treated us more like he was a father than our brother at times. Not that we'd had a good example of a father figure.

"Yeah. Sure. I'll do that."

Jensen reached into a bag on the ground and brought out a bottle of top-shelf whiskey. He grinned as he passed it to me. A peace offering.

I opened the bottle and poured the pair of us a drink. It was smooth and hot as it went down. Perfection in one little bottle.

When the food was ready, we all made up plates and took a seat around the fire pit Heidi had put together. She had schooled Landon in her fire-building skills, and he looked the worse for wear with her torment.

"Girl Scouts," she insisted with a shrug.

I got my food last, feeling more than a buzz for the first time in a while. It took a lot to get me drunk. A lot. But this shit that Jensen had bought was incredible, and we had been downing it like water.

My eyes roamed the seating at the fire pit, and against my better judgment, I decided to do something stupid.

"Hey," I said, nodding at the seat next to Julia. "This seat taken?"

Julia warily looked up at me. She'd changed out of her wet clothes, and she was in cotton shorts and an Ohio State T-shirt. "Depends."

"On what?"

"If you're done being a dick."

I shrugged and sank into the seat. "Probably not."

She laughed, short and stilted. "Of course not."

"So, you haven't gotten over me pulling you into the lake then?"

"Is this your idea of an apology?"

"No."

"You're really insufferable, you know that, right?" Her chest heaved, and she glanced away from me.

"Maybe you should have a drink." I offered her the bottle of liquor.

"That's your answer to everything. Have a drink. Drinking doesn't solve problems, Austin. It creates them."

"Your choice."

I set the bottle back down and dug into my cheeseburger. I was starving, so anything would have tasted good, but Jensen really knew what he was doing on the grill. Julia had fallen silent and was picking at her food. She was the only one here who wasn't part of the family. Emery and Heidi, unofficially. Patrick had been around since we were kids, so he hardly counted. But Julia had only moved here two years ago.

My family was overbearing at the best of times. Had to be completely overwhelming otherwise.

"Hey, you want to see something cool?" I asked.

"I've already seen your dick. It's not that interesting."

"That's a lie, and we both know it."

She arched an eyebrow.

"Look, I'd be happy to give you another look if you don't remember," I said, standing and reaching for my swim trunks.

"Austin!" she said, jumping to her feet. "Cut it out."

"Come on. Let me show you something."

"I really do not want to go anywhere with you." She pulled back her arm as I reached for it.

"Christ, just trust me, Jules."

15

"I don't."

She strode back into the lake house, and I followed her at a close clip.

"Jules…"

She whirled around. "Stop calling me that. You know I don't like it. It's Julia. You can call me Julia, like everyone else."

"Fine. Julia." I stepped up to her, as if I were approaching a wild animal. And, with her unruly red hair down, tangling around her shoulders, she gave a pretty good impression of being one. "I thought you'd like to see this."

She stumbled forward a step, as if drawn by an invisible cord that linked us together. As drawn to me as I was to her. Or maybe I was drunk and imagining things because her eyes shuttered, and that spark was gone.

"Why do you think I'd like it?"

"You'll know it when you see it."

Her curiosity must have piqued enough because she finally gave me a stiff nod. "All right. Where to?"

I grabbed her wrist, and she only glared at me.

"Follow me. It's almost time."

Three

Julia

Going anywhere with Austin Wright was a bad idea.

I'd had my fair share of bad breakups. And whatever the fuck had happened with Austin ranked up there. I was going to put it in the number two spot. The number one spot would always be taken.

Maybe I was actually following him because of my most recent breakup though. No one would blame me if I slept with Austin to forget the last year of stupidity I'd let myself go through. To let myself believe for so long that I could do nice and normal.

Except me. *Would I forgive myself?*

Austin had gotten under my skin.

Like a virus, and I was so fucking sick.

Austin grabbed keys off of a hook by the kitchen and then veered toward the exit. I glanced over my shoulder once and realized that no one else had even seen us leave. I'd been friends with Heidi and Emery for almost two years now, but the whole Wright family thing was a bit over my head. Strangely, it felt like Austin was the only one who noticed that. Or maybe he didn't, and he just wanted to get in my pants. I rarely could get a good read on him.

"Where are we going again?" I asked.

"I didn't say."

He shot me that panty-melting grin, and my frown deepened.

Warning alarms were going off in my head. I should stop this. I should go back to the party and enjoy my time with friends. I didn't have to do this with Austin to have a good time.

But I walked out the door anyway.

He jangled the keys in his hand, absentmindedly flipping them around and around on the key ring. I didn't see his shiny red Alfa Romeo. A fucking beautiful car that I had fallen in love with on sight. Not its owner, but definitely the damn car.

Austin swung me toward Jensen's giant truck.

"Um…what are you doing?" I demanded.

"Going for a drive."

"You are *not* fucking driving! You're drunk."

His face split into a smile. "I'm not driving. You are."

He threw the keys to me, and I caught them, one-handed.

"You want *me* to drive this huge truck? Does Jensen even know we're borrowing it?"

"Eh, don't worry about him. He won't care." He popped open the driver's side. "Need a boost?"

"I don't want to steal his car, Austin. Grand theft auto isn't in my repertoire."

"You want me to drive then?" he asked, reaching for the keys.

I held them back, out of his reach. "Definitely no."

"Then, get your ass in the truck."

Austin didn't give me a chance to argue; he hoisted me up and set me down in the driver's seat. I didn't even know how he'd managed it. I wasn't a small person. Short, yes. Thin, no. I'd never in a million years been Heidi's size. Not that I gave two fucks. This was who I was, and I liked it. But, damn, Austin had to have biceps for days to lift me like that.

"Austin," I said softly. My voice was a knifepoint.

"Hmm?"

"If you ever touch me again without permission, I'll gut you like a fish."

He laughed and trailed a finger down my exposed leg. "Sure thing, Jules."

I clenched my hand into a fist to keep from slapping his endearingly handsome face. "Why am I doing this?"

"Because you're intrigued. Now, let's go."

Austin jogged around to the other side of the truck and jumped into the passenger seat. I couldn't believe myself, but I turned the truck on and slammed the door shut.

All I kept asking myself was, *Why? Because, seriously, why?*

"Don't make me regret this," I told him.

I put Jensen's truck into reverse and backed out of the lake house. I was glad that I drove a giant Tahoe, or I wasn't sure how I would have managed. The roads at Ransom Canyon were narrow. Luckily, most people were inside or on the lake, and we were the only idiots driving back up the canyon wall.

The winding road cut into the mountain face made me nervous as hell. It was bad enough when Landon had driven down it. This was a whole new level of unease. We certainly didn't have canyons like this in Ohio. Truly, we didn't have much in Ohio. Not where I was from.

Austin guided me around the face of the canyon, and I was so busy concentrating on not falling off of a cliff that I hadn't noticed that we had come to some empty gravel parking lot.

"Right here," he said. "Now, turn it around and back up to the edge of the cliff side."

"Uh…how close?"

"I'll tell you when to stop."

He didn't do that until I thought I was going to drive straight over the edge.

"It's fine. There's a chain," he said when I refused to move another inch.

"A chain isn't going to stop this truck."

"Ah, come on, babe."

He hopped out of the car, and I counted slowly to ten before following after him. I couldn't believe I was doing this. *Why am I at an abandoned parking lot on the top of a canyon with Austin Wright?*

"This is what you wanted to show me?" I asked incredulously.

He'd pulled down the latch on the back of the truck and dropped a blanket over the bed. He sat down and patted the seat next to him. "Over here."

I bit back a snarl and took his offered seat. "What are we doing?"

He put his finger to his lips and then pointed out in front of him. I resisted the urge to bolt. He wasn't being a total shit even though he was clearly drunk. I didn't forgive him for pulling me into the lake or all the other stuff that had happened, but I had agreed to come up here. I could at least give him the benefit of the doubt before he fucked everything up and drove me mad.

With a sigh, I turned to face forward, conscious of his leg pressed up against my thigh and our shoulders almost touching. An electric current seemed to radiate between us as I tried to focus on everything but his body next to mine.

But what I saw was a perfect, unimpeded view of the canyon below. A crystal-clear blue lake was dotted with boats, Jet Skis, and a few tubes. From this height, we couldn't hear the screams of excitement and adrenaline, but I could sense it. Houses dotted the lakeshore, gliding evenly up the canyon walls. Some were as large as the crazy mansion on the hill, as obtrusive as the steel house that had taken decades to build, and others were as small as a tiny one-bedroom, completely hidden and tucked away in the trees.

"Wow," I whispered. "It's a great view."

"See? I thought you'd like it." His hand trailed over mine, leaving little circle eights behind in its wake. "It'll only get better."

"Why are you like this?" I asked, my voice hoarse. I couldn't look at him, but I didn't move away. I'd always loved the things that were bad for me.

"Like what?"

"Decent when I want nothing to do with you."

"Hate and love are easy emotions to feel. They're powerful. It's indifference you have to fight for," he said, gripping my chin and turning me to face him. "Not caring about someone would mean forgetting them, and we both know that neither of us are forgettable."

For just a moment, my fingers ached to thread up through his hair. My mind replayed past memories. Simpler times. My body remembered those lost hours. But my heart snagged on the rips he'd added to the shredded mess. It was a mystery how it still beat with all the damage it had sustained.

"I wish I could forget you," I told him, not caring how harsh I sounded.

But, like usual, he just laughed and faced forward once more. He didn't take my anger seriously. I never knew if it was the buzz or if he truly didn't care.

"No, you don't."

I didn't contradict him. I just huffed as I faced the horizon and watched the sun set on my first day newly single. There was nothing like a Lubbock sunset. Streaks of pink and orange and gold painted the sky like a watercolor, bleeding into the sky. The scene reminded me of a postcard—fake and full of hope.

And, for the first time in weeks, my fingers itched for my charcoals. I'd thought, when I was younger, that I would be this incredible painter, full of life and color. Then, I'd grown up. I'd realized bright colors were for other people, and shades of gray were more my speed. It wasn't often I was inspired to pick them up anymore. They brought back too many memories.

"You have that look about you," Austin said.

I'd been so focused on what the scene below me would look like on paper that I hadn't even realized he'd been staring at me.

"What look?"

"Like you're going to draw me like one of your French girls."

"Ugh! I regret the day I showed you my drawings."

"Why? You're an artist."

"I am not an artist," I said, shaking my head. "That's reserved for people who, one, have any talent and, two, are professionals. I sometimes draw on the side when the mood strikes."

"Like right now?"

"Maybe."

"I knew it," he said with triumph. "I thought the sunset would do it."

I narrowed my eyes. "How did you know that?"

"You like beautiful things," he said, gesturing to himself.

I snorted. *What an arrogant jackass!*

"Whatever, Austin."

I turned back to face the sunset. He was kind of right. I did love beautiful things. Colorful sunsets and raw emotions and crashing waves and crinkled eyes from laughter and big heaving clouds. I spent so much of my life away from all those things that, when I could soak them up, I became a sponge.

Like right now.

I bathed in the twilight and reveled in the richness of the moment.

Even if it was with Austin.

We sat there in silence for a few minutes, just watching the colors kaleidoscope the sky. It was companionable. I'd forgotten how easy it was to be with him. We were better when we weren't yelling at each other. It just didn't happen often.

Austin's arm swept across my shoulders and gently pulled me into him. I wanted to bite his head off for touching me after just telling him not to, but I didn't. Sometimes, it was easier. I'd just gone through a breakup. A little comfort, even from someone who drove me up the wall, wasn't the worst thing.

I guess. Right?

"Jules?"

I gritted my teeth and sighed in frustration. "I said—"

"Right. Fuck. Habits, babe."

"Why the fuck am I even here you with you?" I asked, straightening again.

His hand snaked up my neck before threading through my long red hair. "You know why."

"Honestly, no."

He laughed, as if I were joking. But I wasn't. Not entirely. My brain was telling me a whole other reason for being here than my body. My body wanted another taste. My brain knew it was a bad idea. Curiosity had won out, but still, this wasn't smart.

Our eyes met across the small distance, and my brain suddenly stilled. Fuck, that face and those eyes and that mouth. Possessive and commanding. Even when both of those qualities drove me mad, they filled me with desire.

A breath passed between us before he pressed forward and slanted his mouth against mine.

When we spoke, we mixed about as well as oil and water, but our bodies were another story. We were the ocean waves, destined to crash together.

Four

Julia

B*ut, God, I hate myself.*
  "Stop," I said, pushing away from Austin.

I jumped to my feet and walked to the cliff's edge. *Fuck, what is wrong with me? Sure, I'd said that I want to have sex, but Austin? Could I look more desperate?* After what we'd gone through, giving in to his advances would be so stupid. I was setting myself up to be hurt.

Austin grumbled behind me before jumping off the bed of the truck and following me. "What the hell?"

"Is this the only reason you brought me up here?" I demanded.

Fuck sensible.

I wanted an argument. At least Austin would give me that. Because Trevor sure hadn't. Now, I was picking a fight with Austin, knowing he'd provide the ammunition.

"So, what if it was?" he snapped. "You seemed plenty willing."

"Yeah, plenty willing. Even though I told you not to fucking touch me."

"Right. As if you were serious."

"Fuck, I was!"

"Then, why the hell did you come here with me in the first place?"

"I'm asking myself the same fucking question."

"Sometimes, you really make no sense," Austin said. His eyebrows were scrunched together, as if I was a giant mystery that he had yet to solve.

"It's not hard to respect boundaries."

"Boundaries?" he asked with a look of affront. "You have been eye-fucking me since you got here."

"You're mistaking my scowl for sexual attraction."

His lips quirked up. "Am I?"

"Yes." I kept my voice strong and my eyes hard.

"You're right. Why the fuck would I think to bring you up to Make-Out Point?"

"What?" I snapped.

"Where did you think we were? An abandoned parking lot?" he asked with a crisp, tight laugh, as if I were an idiot for not seeing it for what it was. "After the sun has set, this place will be crawling with teens."

I was about to boil over. He hadn't brought me here for the fucking sunset. He hadn't wanted to make me happy or convince me to draw the beautiful scenery. He'd wanted to fuck me. Plain and simple.

"You really are disgusting. You know that, right?"

"And here I thought, I was doing you a favor," Austin said, crossing his arms over his chest. "I thought you wanted a rebound."

"I want nothing to do with you, but thank you for reminding me of that fact," I spat in his face.

Then, I turned on my heel and stormed back to the truck. My hands were shaking as I reached for the door. I yanked it open and was halfway inside when Austin's hands were on my hips.

"Don't storm out of here," he said.

"Fuck off, Austin." I slapped his hands off of me and whirled to face him. "I might want a rebound. Something fun and light and easy. Something to take my mind off of things. But you're an idiot if you think that I want that from you."

"Who do you want it from then?" he asked, as if it were a challenge.

I clenched my jaw before spitting out the first name that came to mind. "Patrick."

Austin's eyes went flat and deadly. Patrick might not be his brother, but he was closer to his best friend than his own blood. I'd committed treason with one word. And it felt fucking good.

"Patrick," he repeated.

"Yeah. Have something to say about that?"

I could see all the words he wanted to say clear as day on his face. Pretty much all of them were four letters, and the rest were more colorful versions of the favorites. But I waited and held my ground, daring him to say something.

"Good luck with that."

"I'm getting out of here. You drive me crazy."

"The feeling is mutual."

I wanted to scream. *Oil and water. Christ!*

I jumped into the front seat of the truck and slammed the door in Austin's face. Everything about my interactions with him left me feeling irritated and vulnerable. *How is he able to press my buttons so easily? And not even all the good ones.*

I didn't wait for Austin to get into the truck. He just thought I was pissed and needed some space from him. But I was so done with his ass.

Without a backward glance, I peeled out of the parking lot. Through the rearview mirror, I saw him holding his hands up and cursing my name, but I didn't turn around, and I didn't stop. Served him right for bringing me up here, expecting that, just because I was newly single, I'd fuck him. Sex was never our problem. It was everything else that I had issues with.

27

All we did was argue and fuck. I couldn't have the second, and I was tired of the first. He made my blood boil—in the best and worst ways. And, right now, it was only in the worst way.

Yet I couldn't stop myself from giving it as good as I got it.

I didn't know what it was about him that brought this out in me. I wasn't this argumentative with my friends. Heidi, Emery, and I could go a whole night without a single argument. But, man, when I saw Austin, a switch flipped in my brain.

And I knew that when I'd followed him outside, when I'd driven the truck up the cliff side, when I'd parked overlooking the canyon to watch the sunset. I'd inherently known all of those things were a bad idea and, in some ways, romantic, yet I couldn't stop myself from stepping into the stupid situation with him.

It made me angrier that I'd let him have this power. That I'd let *any* man have this power ever again.

I'd told Heidi once that I was the kind of girl who attracted bad, bad boys. They couldn't help themselves. It was as if the tattoos and bright hair and nose ring were a blinking arrow pointed straight at my heart.

Then, even when I'd tried for the nice guy, when I'd tried to make it work with the Trevors of the world, I always came back to the bad boys. The ones who followed the blinking arrow and decided it now belonged to them. The ones who staked claim and fought and bit and fucked like animals. The ones who reminded me to live by bringing me so close to death. Adrenaline and fire and toxicity wrapped in a pretty, smiling package of *wrong*.

The truck skidded to a halt in front of the lake house. I killed the engine and hopped out of the cab. Patrick was standing at the front door when I tromped up. He leaned his shoulder into the door and seemed to be fighting a smile.

"Quick trip?" he asked.

I tossed the keys at him. He caught them easily.

"You should probably go get your boy."

Patrick tilted his head, as if he couldn't believe what I'd just said. "He's not in the truck?"

"Does it look like he is?" I countered.

Then, he doubled over and laughed so hard that he had to wipe tears out of his eyes. His shoulders shook, and his smile was magnetic.

"Oh, man. Fuck. I needed that." He shook his head. "You actually left him somewhere?"

"Left who? Where?" Heidi asked, striding out the front door. She gave me an innocent look, as if she weren't aware that I'd left somewhere with Austin.

"Austin," Patrick said.

"Somewhere called Make-Out Point," I told them.

Heidi's jaw dropped open. "He didn't."

"Oh, he did," I said.

"I guess I'd better go get him," Patrick said with a shake of his head. "Idiot."

"You can say that again."

Then, I brushed past him and into the lake house. I'd picked out my room earlier after Austin dragged me into the lake. Apparently, I was sharing a room with Morgan because everyone, except Austin and Patrick, were paired up. That was *fine* by me. Better to be with Morgan than someone assuming I should be with Austin.

Heidi followed me into the back room and flopped down on the bed. "Want to talk about it?"

"No," I told her as I grabbed my sweatshirt.

"This was a mistake. I didn't mean for this to happen."

"This is not your fault. This is Austin fucking Wright thinking that, just because I'm single, I want to fuck him."

"Do you?" Heidi asked.

I whirled on her, tugging the sweatshirt down over my head, and glared. "No!"

29

"Not even a little?"

I blew out a breath and released it. I wasn't angry with Heidi. I didn't need to snap at her. It was Austin who was irritating me.

I took the seat next to her with a sigh. "Maybe a little."

"Yeah. You two have this...thing."

"What thing?"

Heidi shrugged. "I don't know. It's like the air gets thicker when you two are together."

"The air gets thicker?"

"You know what I mean." She nudged me with her shoulder. "You two have chemistry. It's hard to ignore. But that doesn't mean he's for you if you don't want that chemistry."

"I want..." I trailed off.

What the hell did I want?

"Nice and normal?" Heidi offered.

"Like that worked out last time."

"You'll find someone. I promise."

I lay back on the bed and stared up at the ceiling. "I told him I wanted Patrick."

Heidi laughed and slapped my shoulder. "Now, that's just mean."

"I wanted to be mean."

"How did he react?"

"He acted like he didn't care. He acts like that about everything."

Heidi sighed. "Are you ever going to tell me the real reason you two broke up?"

"Look, I already told you," I said, averting my eyes. "He used me and then dumped me. I don't want to go back to a guy who did that to me. I don't ever want to be used. I really don't ever want a guy who makes me feel like Austin does."

"Isn't that half the fun?"

"Sure," I grumbled, picking at the comforter. "It's loads of fun. And then reality sets in. Austin is like taking a hit of cocaine and riding out the high. You feel fucking fabulous while you're on it, but then you hit rock bottom. And it fucking sucks."

Five

Austin

"Fuck!" I screamed as I watched Jensen's truck skid out of the parking lot.

Julia had fucking left me!

What the actual fuck?

I kicked the gravel, as if that would do anything. Then, I stormed back to the cliff's edge.

She was going to come back. She wouldn't abandon me. Sure, we had been fighting, but we always fought. And, anyway, she was the one who had crossed the line. That defiant tilt of her chin had told me she knew it, too.

Patrick.

Patrick!

She wanted to rebound with Patrick.

Fuck that noise.

Whatever we'd had all those months ago wasn't much, but it had been something. More than I'd given another woman pretty much ever. Until it had all gone down in flames, I'd actually considered for a second that this could be it. And she had, too. I'd even thought, now that she had seen the light with that douche from accounting, that we might have some fun this weekend. *Who am I to walk away from the best fuck of my life?*

Then, she had gone and said that shit. *Fuck!*

That woman made me want to scream.

The sun sank lower, and Julia didn't come back. I couldn't believe she had actually left me. I laughed softly at the audacity. I was pissed at her, but, God, it was still hot. That she'd treat me this way. No one stood up to me about anything. Her spunk had always been a turn-on.

But if she goes after Patrick…

I shook my head and crossed my arms, wishing I had the rest of that whiskey Jensen had given me. At least then I could drown her out of my head.

Headlights sparked in the distance as the last streaks of sunlight were noticeable on the horizon. I glanced toward the source of the light and sighed when I realized the local kids had finally arrived. Just what I didn't need.

Then, I noticed Jensen's truck following close behind the other cars. I waved my hand at Julia to get her attention. At least she came back even if it'd taken her for-fucking-ever.

The truck stopped next to me, and I hopped into the passenger seat, trying to hide my disappointment that it was only Patrick. "Took you long enough."

"What the fuck have you gotten yourself into this time?" Patrick asked.

"Nothing. She went crazy."

"You brought her to a make-out spot, you dipshit. How did you think she'd react?"

I shrugged. "She seemed into it."

"Until you told her?"

"Maybe."

Patrick shook his head and shot me a look of disbelief as he veered us back to the lake house. "You and me, Austin, we're brothers. I get you. But don't be stupid about Julia, or she'll find someone else."

"Why? Did she say something?" Curiosity got the better of me. I couldn't help the stab of anger at the thought that she might have gone after Patrick already.

"Besides telling me to get you? No." Patrick raised an eyebrow with a smirk. "Why?"

"Never mind."

I scowled out the window. She was getting under my skin. She'd said that thing about Patrick on purpose. I wasn't going to give her the satisfaction of thinking about it anymore. In fact, I was determined to pretend like she didn't exist for the rest of the weekend. I'd made her an offer. If she didn't want to hook up, then there were plenty of other hot girls on the lake this weekend.

Julia Banner means nothing to me.
Nothing.

———

Our arrival back at the lake house was duly noted. Morgan was standing at the front door with her arms crossed, looking livid. Patrick and I hopped out of the cab and approached her.

"Were you driving?" she asked Patrick, her voice low and commanding. The tone she used in the boardroom that said she was about to bite someone's head off.

"Uh…yeah?" Patrick asked, as if he didn't see the oncoming tongue-lashing.

"Are you out of your mind?" she snarled. "You have been drinking!"

"Chill out, Mor." Patrick slung his arm around her shoulders. "I didn't drink with dinner, and I wasn't drunk to begin with. It's all good."

"All good?" she asked with a shake of her head. "You were driving down canyon cliffs! You could have gotten hurt, or worse, hurt someone else."

"I appreciate the worry, but as you can see, we're fine."

He laughed and ruffled her hair, like she was still a little kid. I cringed inwardly for her. It was lucky the light was dark out or else everyone would have seen the blush coating her cheeks.

"Right. Fine," she muttered as he walked away.

I pretended not to see her wistful glance and ducked inside before I got the next bout of anger from her. When she went on a tirade, she was unstoppable. I wish I'd seen the shit that had gone down last year with Morgan and Miranda, Landon's ex-wife. Heidi had insisted it was one for the record books.

"Hey, hey, hey," Morgan said, diving in after me.

"I'm fine. Nothing happened. All is well. Feel free to yell at someone else."

"I wasn't going to yell at you." She rolled her eyes and swatted my arm. "Family meeting. We were waiting for you."

"What's it about?" I asked as I followed her.

"You'll find out with everyone else. But get ready; it's pretty kick-ass."

I blew out a breath. "Oh, good, you're not pregnant."

She rolled her eyes. "Who do you think I am? Sutton?"

"Hey!" a voice said, coming up behind us. "I heard that."

My youngest sister trotted up to us and flashed us a feisty smile. She was only twenty-two and had dropped out of college at Texas Tech after she got pregnant by her now-husband Maverick. The name was the real deal. Their son, Jason, was pretty adorable, and even Maverick was turning out to be an A-OK guy. We'd all thought he was in it for the Wright money, especially after he had taken the Wright last name in the marriage, but he'd surprised me by being upstanding and really loving Sutton. Somehow, she'd found her happiness before anyone else...even though there was an eleven-year age gap between she and Jensen.

"You were supposed to," Morgan quipped.

"Y'all can keep being jealous of my awesome fucking life." She flipped the classic Wright dark hair, though she'd died the ends blonde for the summer, and then barged between us.

I always wondered what would have happened with Sutton if she'd finished college and worked for the company. I suspected she'd have been a force to be reckoned with.

"She's got me there," Morgan said.

"I've got an awesome fucking life."

Morgan laughed. "Yeah, I bet you do, Austin."

Her laugh haunted me as she walked away toward Jensen at the front of the living room. Everyone else had made themselves scarce. For the first time in a long time, it was just the five of us again. Jensen and Morgan looked like two peas in a pod. Bonded over their love and dedication to the company…and overall sarcasm. Landon was tilted back in a recliner and offered me a beer. I willingly took it and plopped down next to Sutton on the couch. She had her legs crossed underneath her and was staring down at her phone.

"Is this going to take long?" Sutton asked.

"Have somewhere to be?" Jensen said, crossing his arms.

"Besides enjoying my vacation?"

"You don't even work," Morgan pointed out.

"Um…hello? I have a one-year-old," Sutton said, looking like she was going to toss her phone at Morgan.

"It won't take long," Landon said.

"You don't even know what it is," Morgan said.

Landon shrugged. "We can't all be in the same room together without ripping out each other's throats. So, I'm assuming Jensen is having this meeting for a reason and will get on with it."

I popped open my beer and took a long drink. *This is going to be fun.*

"I can't believe you're enabling him," Sutton muttered to Landon.

"Not you, too," I said.

Everyone needed to get off my back about drinking. This was who I was. *Fuck.*

"Can the meeting be about that?" Sutton asked. "I'm supposed to be the party animal. I'm the age to constantly be fucked up. You're…not."

"Yet you're the one with a kid, and I'm not. Seems to have worked out better for me than you."

Sutton glared and straightened. "Austin, I might be little and not give a shit about a lot of stuff, but if you insult me again, I will kick your ass."

"Enough," Jensen spat. He had his fingers on the bridge of his nose and sighed heavily. "I love you all, but can we have peace for five minutes?"

Sutton looked at Jensen, as if to say, *He started it,* but one look from him, and she kept it to herself.

Fine. I'd have it out with Sutton later. She, like Morgan, could shove her pretentious, preachy bullshit up her ass.

"Are we all done?" Jensen asked.

"Can I ask a question?" Landon said, raising his hand with a giant grin on his face.

Jensen looked up to the heavens for help. "What is it?"

"Are you and Emery getting married?"

"Oh!" Sutton gasped, sitting up. "And babies? God, please say there will be babies."

"You are so gross," Morgan muttered under her breath.

"Look…normal women like babies, Mor!"

"Thank God I'm not normal. Everyone else here is baby crazy, except me."

This time, I raised my hand. "Um…me either."

"Could we all please stop?" Jensen asked with an exaggerated sigh. "Emery and I are not getting married."

"This seems like an egregious oversight," Landon offered.

"Just because you rush into things doesn't mean that I do," Jensen said. "Marriage and…babies are high on your priority list. I've already done both of those things and…not that I need to explain that to any of you, but Emery and I want to wait."

"Well, can we cut to the chase then?" I asked.

"Yes. Back on track," Morgan said with a barely contained smile.

"The real reason we're here today has nothing to do with my marital status," Jensen said. "It's because…I'm stepping down as CEO of Wright Construction."

Austin

The silence in the room was deafening. Vicious.

What the hell?

Jensen isn't going to be CEO? My brain couldn't logically wrap itself around that concept.

Our father had died when Jensen was twenty-three years old. I was twenty and had been in college at Tech, partying and living the life. Then, with one phone call, everything had changed. Our father was apparently dead of alcohol poisoning. The newspapers had reported it as a suicide. I still wasn't sure. But, with our mother dead from cancer when we were kids and our father gone, Jensen had taken over the company. He'd been successfully running it for a decade. He was the face of Wright Construction. He was what people thought of when they saw the motto, *What's Wright Is Right*.

"What?" Sutton finally gasped out. "What the fuck?"

"Yeah. What she said," Landon said. Slack-jawed, he pointed his thumb at Sutton.

I just stared. It was as if everything in our lives had fit into this perfect little bubble, and then suddenly, Jensen had gone and burst it.

"I know this might come as a shock to you all," Jensen said.

"Understatement," I muttered.

"However, I feel like this is the best move for all of us going forward. As you know, I studied architecture in college and worked in New York for some time, focused on that. It wasn't what…our dad wanted from me, but it was what I loved. After much consideration, I've decided that I should follow my dreams and work in architecture again. I might be good at what I do, but I don't love it, like when I was designing and building things. It isn't the same."

"Wow. That's really awesome, Jensen," Landon said.

"I love it!" Sutton said.

I nodded. I was happy for him. If he was going to start his own architecture firm, then by all means, he should do it. *But what's going to happen to the company?*

"Am I the only one wondering where the hell we'll go from here?"

Jensen frowned. "I'm sure you're not."

"Okay. Then, where the hell do we go from here?" I set my beer down and leaned my elbows against my knees. I was interested now.

"I've spoken to the board about my decision," Jensen said, "but I wanted to talk to you all about what was happening. You are Wright Construction as much as I am." He cleared his throat and continued when it seemed no one had anything to say about that, "With that said, I've put Morgan's name forward to be our next CEO."

All eyes shifted from Jensen to Morgan, who had been standing next to him with her hands behind her back this whole time. She beamed at the statement. Twenty-seven years old and set to be the CEO. *Badass!*

"The board approved the decision," Morgan added.

She didn't seem shy or nervous about the decision. She looked ready. Poised and fucking ready to take on this huge responsibility. She was going to dominate.

"Hell yes!" I said, standing and pulling my sister in for a hug.

She startled a little at my enthusiasm. *But how could she be surprised?* Morgan was second-in-command. Everyone knew she loved Wright Construction more than Jensen and that she had trained for this moment. It had maybe come a little earlier than expected.

Landon and Sutton jumped up next and were quick to give hugs and congratulations. Morgan looked relieved. As if she had known that she was ready for this step but still worried about what we would think, which I thought was fucking dumb. The board had agreed. They thought she was legit. And they were right. The company was lucky to have someone like Morgan run it.

"I'm really excited to take on this new challenge. I think it's going to be a whole new step for the company," Morgan said.

"It's going to be great," Jensen said. He placed his hand on her shoulder and beamed. "Of course, it won't be immediate. There will be a transitional period while we slowly move Morgan into this key role. But this was step one, and we wanted you to know."

"Who is going to take Morgan's job?" Landon asked.

And then a bell seemed to go off in my head.

If Morgan was CEO, that meant that her position was up for grabs. *Holy shit!* That was *my* position. Sutton didn't work. Landon had golf. That meant, I was next in line. It made just as much sense as Morgan stepping into Jensen's shoes.

I was a Wright.

I deserved this position.

"We're, uh, still working that out," Jensen said.

"What does that mean?" I asked.

"It means that the board is still in consultation about how to transition Morgan's position."

I narrowed my eyes. *What the hell did that mean? How hard was it to say that another Wright would take over?*

Jensen pushed past the rest of the family and tilted his head toward the kitchen. "Can we talk somewhere more private?"

"Sure," I said in confusion. I couldn't seem to grasp what was going on.

We veered out of earshot of the rest of the family, leaving them alone to congratulate Morgan. Jensen shot me a pained expression, as if what he was about to say was something he was really not looking forward to.

"What's going on, Jensen?" I demanded.

"Look, I put your name up to the board to take Morgan's job."

"Great!"

"And they declined you."

My jaw dropped open. "They did what?"

"I don't know how to say this gently, Austin, but they don't think you'd be a suitable replacement for Morgan. You…give off the wrong image for the company."

"But I'm a Wright!" I spat, raising my voice.

"I know, I know. Trust me, I pleaded your case. I told them that you would be the right person for the job. I believe in you."

"And they just didn't give a fuck."

"It's not that exactly. They worry about your…drinking habits."

"What about my fucking drinking habits?" I snarled.

"They think…you are…" Jensen stumbled over his words and then shook his head and straightened his shoulders. "You're an alcoholic, man."

"So, I have a few drinks here and there. It's not the end of the world."

"You have a few drinks with breakfast. Legally, I don't know how you drive anywhere. You're a mess."

"Fuck off, Jensen."

"I'm serious, Austin. We've all let it slide up until now. But you're going to miss out on this if you don't sober up. Maybe if you went to rehab to show you were serious—"

"Seriously, Jensen, go fuck yourself! I don't need rehab."

"I'm trying to look out for you, Austin."

"No, you're trying to parent me. But guess what? Our parents are dead, and you can't replace them."

Jensen winced. "Come on, man."

He reached out for me, but I brushed him off.

"I don't need any of this shit."

Then, I turned on my heel and walked out of the lake house.

My mind was whirring to life at all the goddamn accusations. I loved drinking, but, fuck, I didn't have a problem. Jensen had a fucking problem. Everyone had a fucking problem. This was more bullshit to pile on me because they wanted to give the position to someone else. *How fucked up is it that they want someone who isn't a Wright to run the company behind Morgan? How could they even be okay with that?*

I stumbled down the hill to the dock and the pitch-black lake beyond. Clouds obscured the sliver of a moon in the sky overhead. A fitting vista for betrayal.

My stomach lurched as the anger boiled over. Jensen had recommended me, and the board had said no. Just like that. I hadn't even gotten to defend myself. They had made that decision with no other consideration than my name.

The Wright name, of course, always had. But *my* name had never made any splashes. Jensen was the oldest. Landon was a professional golfer. Morgan was the prodigy. Sutton, the baby. I was just…me.

Now, they had a name for me. Not exactly flattering to be known for my *drinking habits*. Or, as Jensen had so eloquently put it…an *alcoholic*.

Fuck!

I wanted to scream.

Jensen had joked that I was following in our father's footsteps. Morgan had scolded me when I jokingly brought a flask into church. Landon had eyeballed my Bloody Mary in the morning. It was never a big deal. I was responsible. I wasn't getting into car accidents. I didn't have a DUI. I still did all my fucking work. I showed up to work on time, church every Sunday, all planned family events. They had lost their fucking minds if that wasn't enough to be the right kind of Wright.

And if it wasn't enough, then why the fuck was I doing all this shit?

If they didn't respect me, then what I did in my spare time didn't mean anything. I could be off at a fucking bar this weekend, picking girls up, instead of getting left on a cliff side by Julia and verbally harassed by my family. But I was here. Not that it fucking mattered to anyone.

I stomped onto the dock and noticed a figure seated at the end with their feet dangling off the edge. Just what I didn't want to deal with—another person.

I was about to turn around and find somewhere else to be alone when the person turned around, and I saw Julia's beautiful face.

"What are you doing?" she asked defensively.

"I know it's a shock, but my world doesn't revolve around you, babe."

"I didn't say—"

"Didn't have to," I interrupted.

"Jesus Christ, I wasn't trying to argue with you."

"That's a shock. All you seem to do when you open your mouth is yell at me."

I knew I was picking a fight on purpose, but I couldn't have the one I wanted with the board. So, this would have to do.

"As if I'm the only one!"

"You left me up there."

"You were being a prick," she said with a shrug. Totally unapologetic.

"I'll add it to my fucking tally."

"Do whatever you want." She turned back to face forward, ignoring me once more.

Fuck, she wasn't giving me what I wanted. I wanted to argue. I wanted her to scream at me. I wanted to feel something. I wanted to stop thinking about what I was fucking dealing with.

So, I plopped my ass down next to her. She gave me a nasty look.

"What the hell are you doing?" she demanded.

"Sitting down. Is that a fucking crime now?"

"It is when you do it. I thought I'd made myself clear when I left you up there," she said, pointing upward. "I don't want to deal with this."

"You made yourself clear when you said you were interested in Patrick," I spat.

She rolled her eyes. "I can do whatever I want."

"Yeah, and I can fuck half of the lake if I want to."

"Then, do it," she challenged me. "See if I fucking care!"

But the expression on her face mirrored the one I had given her earlier. Her eyes were as flat as the lake water and her mouth pinched. Yet I couldn't stop admiring the way her hair blew in the breeze and the flash of the ring in her nose and the ease of her body as it tilted toward me. God, I wanted her. Even with this anger that sizzled through me, I wanted to fucking lay her back on this dock right here and now and fuck her brains out.

"Stop looking at me like that," she whispered. Her fire had dissipated in a second.

"Like what?" I asked hoarsely.

"Like you're going to kiss me again."

"Going to do more than that, Jules."

She swallowed hard but didn't avert her gaze. "What's going on with you? You're hot and cold and then hot again. I can't get a read on you. I thought you wanted a fight, and now, you're wanting to fuck."

"Two things we're best at," I said with a gruff laugh.

"Well...I don't want to do either," she lied, finally glancing away from me. "If there's something going on, you can tell me. Otherwise...I'm going to go back in. It's getting cold."

Did I want to tell her about the shit going down? She'd eventually find out, but right now, I wanted to drown myself in alcohol and forget everything Jensen had ever said. Probably wouldn't help my case, but at this point, who even cared?

It was my turn to lie.

"There's nothing."

She narrowed her eyes, as if expecting me to say more, but when I didn't, she got up off the dock and strode away from me.

I probably deserved the solitude anyway.

I lay flat on my back and stared up at the stars as I wondered how the fuck my life had gotten to this point.

Seven

Julia

Going back to reality on Tuesday morning had been a slap in the face. Despite the bullshit with my breakup and then Austin, the rest of Memorial Day weekend had been pretty much amazing. Heidi and Emery had gone out of their way to make sure that I enjoyed myself. Between suntanning, taking out the Jet Skis, and getting pulled behind the boat on tubes, it had been awesome.

It'd probably helped that Austin left Saturday morning with no explanation. Jensen had been pissed that Austin disappeared with his truck, but all the Wrights had been tight-lipped about his reasoning. Even Heidi had just shrugged it off.

I'd given him the chance to explain himself on Friday night. It wasn't my fault if all he'd wanted was a distraction I wasn't willing to give.

Whatever had happened, it didn't matter to me. I'd had a better time without him there. Or at least...I thought so.

I didn't have much time to think of it the rest of the week. With an extra day off for the holiday, I was swamped at work. To be honest, I was always swamped at work. Being the head of HR for a company as large as Wright Construction meant that things never slowed down. Not ever.

"Did you get the memo that was just sent over?" Heidi asked, popping her head into my office.

"Uh…" I pulled up my inbox and clicked the refresh button. "I don't have anything."

Heidi huffed and plopped down into the seat in front of my desk. "It should be there."

Heidi was a lead civil engineer for the company. The first woman ever in that position here at Wright. How she still had time to come harass me when she had so much work to do was beyond me. Not that I minded. We worked on the same floor, which was how we had become such good friends.

I refreshed again, and there it was. I clicked the latest email that had hit my inbox. My eyes scanned the document.

"Meeting upstairs for the whole company at three o'clock? Attendance mandatory for all staff?" I asked, my brows knitting together. This was the kind of memo that I was supposed to send. I didn't know what the fuck was so important that I wasn't even informed about it in the first place. "What's this about?"

"It's super exciting. I can't believe I was able to hold in this secret all week."

"You didn't even share it with me," I said with mock offense.

"I know. I'm legit the worst."

"Indeed. If you're not going to tell me, get the hell out of my office."

Heidi laughed and stood. "Are you still on for the First Friday Art Trail tonight?"

I nodded. "It sounds awesome. How have I never been before?"

"You lack culture. That's obvious."

"That's clearly it." I rolled my eyes and pointed my finger at the door. "Out, Martin."

She held her hands up in surrender. "All right, but meet me for the meeting."

"Done."

I grinned at her retreating back. Heidi, like everyone else in my life, save for Austin, had no idea that I had an artistic bone in my body. They probably should have guessed it from the artist's flavor I put into my tats and makeup and, God, the incredible things my hairstylist, Lisa, did with my red mane. But art was a secret I kept close to my heart. My charcoals were for healing purposes only. I no longer used them to bring myself joy, like I once had. Too much had changed in my life. And they held too many memories of the old Julia that it hurt to pull them out.

But I was dying to see the Art Trail. I had a minor in art and a healthy appreciation for all artistic endeavors. As long as it wasn't my own art.

The rest of the day flew by as I had a dozen one-on-one meetings to help people with various functions of their jobs—from new training to various coaching methods to disciplining troublemakers to hearing and resolving the latest fight on the job. Every day was a new challenge.

I packed up right before the meeting and met Heidi outside of my office. She was bouncing around, as if she were on a pogo stick. I had no idea what this new announcement could be or why she was so freaking excited. But she wouldn't explain, and I silently followed the rest of the company upstairs.

The top floor of Wright Construction was an incredible restaurant with a panoramic view of the skyline, overlooking the Texas Tech campus. It was used for the annual Christmas party among other events and apparently had closed down from lunch early so that all of the Wright employees could have this meeting. I didn't know why they wanted to get everyone in one room instead of sending the reason for the meeting in the email. Would have saved everyone a lot of time.

I surveyed the crowded room and snagged on Austin, as if I had a radar for him. He must have felt my eyes on him because he shifted and glanced over at me. I blushed. *Shit.* I'd been caught. He smirked and nodded his head, signaling for me to come over toward him. I bit my lip and then averted my gaze. Austin was bad news. *Why can't my brain grasp that?*

"So…you and Austin?" Heidi asked with a pointed cough in my direction.

"No."

"Are we going to go stand with him and Patrick?"

"Nope."

"Oh, come on."

"Trevor could see," I said lamely.

"And so what? You broke up, and you're not interested in Austin. Right?"

I grumbled under my breath. Wow, I'd backed myself into a corner.

"Heidi, no," I whispered as she tried to drag me across the room.

I tried to put up a resistance to her, but Heidi was the kind of girl who always got her way. I had no idea why she was trying to push us together, but even if I still found him hot as sin, I wasn't interested in him. I wasn't. Seriously.

Heidi wove us through the crowd to where Austin and Patrick were standing near the front of the room. Austin arched an eyebrow at my approach. Patrick was grinning like a fool.

"Babes," Patrick said.

"Hey," I said, shifting from Patrick to Austin on instinct.

He had on a suit. A black suit with a white button-up and a pink tie. He looked sharp as fuck and made me feel like a total sucker.

His eyes swept over my knee-length black skirt and V-cut blouse. I was showing off cleavage today—well, more like every day if I wasn't wearing a turtleneck—and he appreciated it. In fact, he came away looking thirsty.

"Jules," he said with a head nod.

I silently scolded him, and he only smiled broader. I swore he called me that just to irritate me.

"You're looking good today, Julia," Patrick said with his own grin.

Austin shot him a look of anger, which only made Patrick laugh. I wondered if Austin had told Patrick about what I'd said.

"Thank you," I said to him.

Heidi held her hands out. "Anyone going to say how nice I look?"

"Uh, Landon?" Patrick asked. "Last time I told him you were hot, he threw me into someone else's truck. I'll stay on his good side."

"He did what?" Heidi cried.

Austin laughed. "I don't think that was actually what happened. Or at least…you said something worse."

"What the hell? He never told me that!"

"I bet he didn't," Patrick said. "Y'all weren't dating yet."

Heidi moved over to Patrick's side and started grilling him on everything that Landon had said and done in that conversation last year. That meant, Austin and I were somehow alone together even though we were in the middle of a roomful of people.

"So…do you know what this meeting is about?" I asked. "Heidi wouldn't say."

His eyes went distant and unfocused, as if he were very far away. "Yeah."

"Not good?"

"No. I mean, yes. It's a good thing. Smart decision."

"But you don't like it?"

"Do you care?" he asked.

53

"Just making conversation," I said defensively. "Why do you always have to make it an argument?"

He shrugged. "I like the way it makes you flush all over."

I shivered at the intensity in his eyes but refused to look away. I was sure he'd said it in an attempt to disarm me. And it'd worked, but I couldn't show that. I had to remain stoic and unaffected by him. Otherwise, things would devolve quickly.

"Unless that's what you want," he said, taking a step toward me.

"I don't," I told him firmly.

He leaned forward until his lips nearly brushed against the shell of my ear. "I know every one of your tells, Jules. Say whatever you like, but I know the truth."

I roughly jerked back. Patrick and Heidi must have noticed that things weren't going that well because they both whipped their heads over toward us. My hands were balled into fists, and I shot him a look filled with venom. He might think he knew my tells, but he sure as fuck couldn't tell when he'd crossed the line. Or he didn't care.

"Oh, look, Jensen is on the stage now," Heidi said, placing her hand on my elbow. "Come on, Julia."

I turned my back on Austin, still wired with energy from our brief altercation. He was the only person I'd ever met who could do that to me. Who could make me so freaking angry… yet turned on.

"Thanks so much for joining me here today," Jensen said into the microphone. He was in a crisp suit and looked ever the part of the perfect Wright brother. "I'm sure you're all wondering why I asked you to be here today. It's not every day that I'm letting you all out of work early on a Friday afternoon."

The room chuckled. But I could feel the relief in it. Whenever this was all over, we would get to leave. I was pumped.

"I'll try to keep this whole thing short. I know everyone would rather get their weekend started. So, there are three main things on the agenda. I'll start with the good news."

I glanced around at the rest of my coworkers. Austin had said that it was a good thing, and Heidi seemed excited, but I didn't like change. Bad news usually meant change. I was still frustrated after the Tarman Corporation merger that had happened six months into my job here. From an HR standpoint, it had been a nightmare to deal with. I was *not* looking forward to something like that again.

"The good news is…we got the new Disney contract for Walt Disney World! Construction starts next summer, so we have our work cut out for us. But I know that, the last time we had a major project like this, we all knocked it out of the park. I'll expect nothing less this time around."

"Plus," Heidi whispered to me, "Disney perks! I bet we'll be able to get some discounted tickets."

"I've never been," I admitted.

Heidi's eyes bugged out of the sockets. "You've never been to the most magical place on earth?"

I shrugged. "Nope."

"Uh…we're going to have to fix that."

Having a friend like Heidi was a whole new experience for me. I'd never really had girlfriends before I moved to Lubbock. And what a culture shock it had been for me, coming from Ohio. It wasn't a small town or anything, but it had the small-town vibes. The everyone-knew-everyone kind of feel. Plus, the flat, dry, dusty aspect still felt foreign to me. Maybe it always would.

"But the main reason that I brought you here was because I wanted to announce that I'm stepping down as CEO of Wright Construction," Jensen said.

My jaw dropped. "What?"

Heidi bounced up and down on the balls of her feet.

"What is happening?" I hissed at her.

"This was a very hard decision to make, but after careful consideration, I have decided to follow my passion and move back into architecture."

He smiled wide, and it was clear that he was excited about the change, but holy hell! What did this mean for Wright?

"And, without further ado, I would like to introduce you to your new CEO, my sister, Morgan Wright."

The applause held a split second of hesitation, as if the room wasn't sure what to make of this new change. I sure as hell didn't know what to make of it. Morgan was awesome, totally amazing really. I didn't know her that well, but she seemed to know her shit. But Jensen had run Wright Construction for nearly a decade. It was hard to believe that anyone else could take over when he was still so young.

"Thank you all so much," Morgan said, raising her hand to silence the applause. "I'm deeply honored to move up as the CEO of this company that I have loved my entire life. I know that it will be a big change for everyone, including me. I hope to be able to fill my brother's shoes." She grinned. "Who am I kidding? His feet are huge."

I laughed along with the rest of the crowd as Morgan lulled us into a sense of security. I didn't like change, but I did like Morgan.

"My spot as the CFO will be vacant at the present time as we work with the board to find a suitable replacement. In the meantime, we'll have an open search to try to bring in someone new and fresh to take this company into the future."

My eyes split from Morgan's at the news that…they hadn't filled the CFO position. *Second-in-command hadn't gone straight down the Wright line?*

I turned in my spot and found Austin's eyes glued to Morgan, but he was distant. He'd already known about this. But…I didn't understand. *Shouldn't Austin be next in line for this position?* Landon was too busy with golf, and Sutton was raising her baby. It seemed to make perfect sense to me for them to just move Austin up.

But, when his eyes shifted to me, the realization dawned on me.

They weren't going to give him that position.

Part of me wanted to laugh, wanted to feel good that he hadn't gotten what he wanted. But I didn't. I felt awful. He was a Wright after all. Even if he was kind of a fuckup.

I opened my mouth to ask all the questions floating through my head. But he shook his head and broke eye contact.

My heart sank. No wonder he'd left this weekend. It hadn't been me. It'd been this. I was sure of it. Heidi had known. They'd all known. And none of them had gone after him. None of them had tried to stop him.

He might be an asshole, but this was harsh. I couldn't imagine what he was going through. And I had to remind myself...it wasn't my business. He didn't want to confide in me. He didn't want me to console him. He didn't need to be fixed.

Austin Wright was broken...and I wasn't about to try to fit the pieces back together.

Eight

Julia

"I really, really wanted to tell you," Heidi said with a sheepish grin a few hours later.

We were at Emery and Jensen's house before we were going to head out to the Art Trail. It was still strange that Heidi and Emery didn't live together. I was used to showing up at their little apartment and finding them both being ridiculous. Their love affair was legendary. I was just lucky to fit in with their tight bond.

Though, at first, when Emery had come back from college, I'd felt a bit like a third wheel. Not anymore…at least not for the most part.

"It's fine," I muttered. "I cannot believe that Jensen is stepping down."

"I'm so glad," Emery said, appearing in black shorts, a black tank, and black Converse.

Sometimes, I swore, she and I had been separated at birth.

"Oh, look, you match," Heidi singsonged, glancing between Emery and me. "I'm so shocked."

"Okay, Barbie," Emery said, smacking Heidi's ass as she passed.

Emery really wasn't far off. Heidi's favorite color was hot pink, and she wore it all the time. Though Emery had tried to convince me that this was a step back for Heidi's color choices…I found it hard to believe.

"Oh, do it again." Heidi winked and bent over at the waist.

Emery laughed. "I love your face."

"And my ass?"

"What ass?" I asked with a laugh.

"Don't be jealous of my ass," Heidi said.

"Oh, she's not," Emery said. "Julia has it all."

"Anyway, like I was saying before I was interrupted," Heidi said with an eye roll, "Morgan is so up for the task, and this will make Jensen happy."

"So much happier," Emery added.

"Right…but why don't they have a CFO already?" I asked.

Heidi and Emery exchanged *the* glance. The one that said they both knew more than they were supposed to tell.

"It's not really our place," Emery said softly.

"It's stupid really," Heidi added. "They just want a broad search."

I wanted to ask the obvious question—why not Austin? But I couldn't seem to get the words out. Asking about Austin was like opening a can of worms.

"Okay," I said with a shrug, like I didn't really care. "Are we ready to go then?"

"Yep!" Heidi crooned. "We're picking Morgan up along the way?"

"We are?" Emery asked.

"Oh, didn't I tell you? I invited her to have girls' night with us to celebrate her promotion."

"So, we're a foursome," I said.

Emery raised her eyebrows at me. "Now, you're talking."

I laughed and followed them out to Emery's Subaru Forester. We all jumped into the car and drove out to Morgan's apartment complex. It was downtown and nearly walking distance to the office. A really ritzy, upscale kind of place with gates and a doorman. Heidi buzzed Morgan down and grinned when she realized that Morgan lived on the top floor. Because...of course, she did.

Morgan moved into the backseat, next to me. "Hey, Julia."

"Morgan," I said with a head nod.

"Thanks for inviting me, y'all," Morgan said with a genuine smile.

I wondered if she had many girlfriends that she could do this kind of thing with. She didn't really seem like the type. Maybe because I knew Jensen was kind of a loner, and Morgan was a smaller female version of her older brother.

But what did I know? I'd never been like this before either. Though...truth be told, it hadn't all been my fault in the past.

"We're super glad to have you with us," Heidi said. "Now, let's go hit up food trucks and wine."

"Wine!" Emery cheered.

"Is there actually art to look at?" I asked.

Morgan cocked an eyebrow at me. "Have you never been to a First Friday Art Trail?"

"Nope."

"Plenty of art to see," Morgan told me. "But, first, wine."

"That should be on a T-shirt," Heidi said. "But, first, wine."

"And they all said, *Amen*," Emery muttered.

We parked in a parking lot with a big sign that said they were going to tow us if we parked there. I shot Heidi a look of unease, but she laughed at me. Apparently, all parking lots downtown were free game for the First Friday Art Trail. Where I came from, if we'd parked there, we wouldn't have a car when we got back. *Lubbock, man.*

The weather was overcast and a little nippy as we meandered down the street to the main center where the food trucks were set up. I wish I had my bomber jacket, but again,

I hadn't been able to find it. If I'd lost it for good, I was going to be really pissed at myself.

We all bought some wine, and Heidi got an ice cream cone as well from the Blue Oasis food truck. Then, I finally got to walk into my first gallery.

A sigh escaped me. This was pure joy. Canvas after canvas was covered in beautiful paint, capturing an emotion, a person, a new discovery. Art was insight and power and passion. Art didn't lie. It didn't cheat. It didn't hate. It just was. You took out of it whatever message you saw in it, but it was all beautiful. From the smallest photograph to the largest mural from a solo street dance performance to a symphony from a haiku to a full-blown novel. If art made you feel, then it had done its job.

I was so engrossed in the amazing work an artist had done with growing intricately designed plants in pots and creating an elaborate mural with tiny flora with soft, velvety green leaves that I'd almost completely forgotten that I was with a group. And I'd somehow downed my entire glass of wine. I couldn't even remember putting it to my lips.

"I think I need another wine," I said, catching Morgan's eye nearby.

She held her empty glass up. "Same. I'll walk with you."

We waved our empty glasses at Heidi and Emery, who were arguing over a circular terrarium at the center of the room. They waved us off, and Morgan and I set off to refill our glasses.

"That was a cool exhibit," Morgan said. "I'd never seen anything like that before."

"Me either. I don't have a green thumb whatsoever. I'm pretty sure I would kill every plant imaginable."

"You and me both."

"Are you excited about your new job?"

Something in Morgan shifted at that question. She stood a little taller. She smiled a little wider. Her eyes glittered.

"I'm ready to take over the world. It's time."

I laughed. "What are we doing tonight, Brain?"

"The same thing we do every night," Morgan said with a grin.

"Drink wine?" I offered.

"Hell yes. I deserve some celebratory drinks. Like, ten at least."

"Are you going to be able to stand?"

"God, I hope not."

This was probably the most one-on-one time I'd ever spent with Morgan, and I was kicking myself, wondering why I'd never done it before. Probably because Morgan was a bit intimidating. She really had her shit together. She knew exactly who she was. And she showed no fear. It was enviable. Especially for someone like me.

"We should do this more often," Morgan said. "How do you feel about trashy magazines and bad reality TV?"

"Um…guilty pleasure?"

"Great. We're going to be best friends. Can we get matching tattoos?" she said with such a serious face that I had no idea if she was joking.

"I'm covered in tattoos. I'll hold your hand."

She sent me a secret little smile. "How do you know I don't already have one?"

"Touché."

We grabbed another glass of wine and were on our way back to the exhibit we'd left Heidi and Emery at when someone started catcalling Morgan's name. Her eyes widened, and she shot around. I followed her in a circle, only to let my stomach drop to the concrete.

Austin.

"Morgan! Whoop!" Patrick called, whistling suggestively at her.

Her face bloomed a perfect shade of pink at the attention. But I could see that she enjoyed it. What got me was…Patrick was most certainly not alone.

"I'm not a dog. Stop whistling at me," Morgan said.

Patrick laughed and threw an arm around her shoulders. "Ah, Mor, come on. Have a little fun."

"Hey," I said to Austin.

Austin's dark eyes met mine, and I shivered.

"Hey."

He looked sexy as hell. A light cotton button-up with the sleeves rolled up to reveal the tattoos hidden underneath. His hair was tousled, as if he'd been running his fingers through it. I envisioned myself gripping the longer strands on top and had to visibly reel it in. His stormy eyes seemed to sense where my thoughts had headed, and they sparkled with amusement. But I could also tell that he was loaded. I wasn't surprised, especially after the announcement this afternoon. I would be, too.

"So," Patrick said, leaning heavily on Morgan, "y'all coming to Louie Louie's with us?"

"Dueling piano bar?" Morgan asked. "I'm in."

"Jules?" Austin asked.

I gritted my teeth. *Stupid fucking nickname.* "We're with Heidi and Em. We'll have to ask them."

"They're in!" Morgan said. "Heidi already promised to get me wasted."

"You're getting wasted, and you didn't call me?" Patrick asked, affronted.

Austin was unusually quiet. He and Patrick usually went back and forth, as if they were brothers more than best friends. But he was letting Patrick take the lead on his usual instigating, antagonistic personality, hardly saying a word.

I wondered what was going on up there. *Is he pissed or resigned? Had he gotten over not being chosen for CFO? Or is he still in the running?* Fuck, I didn't know. And I couldn't ask because asking would only cause an argument. Another one.

"Cool," Austin said. "We'll see you there then."

"Let's snag Mini Wright and our resident tatted up HR girl," Patrick said while Morgan deflated at the choice nickname, "and have the Wright wifeys meet us there."

"We've barely seen anything yet," I said.

I was torn between wanting to look at all the exhibits and wanting to find out what had happened with Austin. Plus, Morgan obviously wanted to hang out with Patrick.

"I'll walk the exhibits with you if y'all want to head to the bar early," Austin offered.

Patrick's head turned so fast that I thought he might have pinched a nerve. "You're skipping the bar?"

"I'm meeting you there later," he corrected. He held up his beer. "It's not like this whole place isn't open container."

Patrick held his hands up. "All right, all right. We'll save a table. Get the wifeys and meet us there. You up for that, Mor?"

She nodded vigorously. "I want to be thoroughly trashed by the time they meet up with us."

"Challenge accepted," Patrick said.

Austin punched him in the arm. "Hands off my sister."

But Patrick looked back at him like he was totally insane. As if he had never thought of Morgan as anything other than his *own* sister. In that moment, I felt a bad for her. The girl was on top of the world, and her crush didn't even know that she wanted to be on top of him instead.

"Dude," was all Patrick said before walking away with Morgan.

"Dear God, he is oblivious," I muttered.

"Tell me about it."

"Oh my God, did we just have a conversation without arguing?"

"You look fucking hot," he said in response.

I rolled my eyes. Well, that was close. "You're a pig."

"Really? Because I think I just got you more time to look at all the art you're dying to see. Otherwise, you would have been dragged away to see drunks singing Bon Jovi and Journey at the tops of their lungs. A simple thank you would suffice."

I bit my lip to keep from snapping that he hadn't done me a favor. Everything Austin did was self-motivated. I just didn't know what his motivation was here.

"Fine," I settled for instead.

"Fine," he said, nudging me toward another exhibit.

"Let me tell Heidi and Emery first."

I jogged over to the landscape exhibit and informed them as to what was going on. They did another one of their all-knowing looks and then told me to have a good time. It was not a date. It wasn't. No matter what their sly grins said.

"This one is my favorite," Austin admitted.

"This one has been here before?"

He shrugged. "Once or twice."

I narrowed my eyes in his direction, wondering how this was going to be a trick, but still, I followed him anyway. It might be stupid. I still hadn't figured out what the fuck he wanted from all of this. But my feet carried me up the few steps and into the next building.

But what I saw on the inside stopped me in my tracks.

This is Austin's favorite? This is the one he wants to show me?

Did I even know him at all?

On all the walls in perfect little picture frames were children's artwork. Unicorns and robots and horses and rainbows and a Technicolor burst of color from every frame. Under each piece of artwork was the child's first name and age.

Katherine, seven.

Jimmy, twelve.

Aiden, four.

But what really got me, after I passed the first wall in awe of all the little boys and girls who had created something important to them, was the sign proclaiming where the art had come from. Not an elementary school, as I had expected.

"They're foster kids?" I whispered, my eyes glazing over, as I turned to face Austin.

He nodded. "They're supposed to draw something that inspires them. I hate that there are so many kids in Lubbock without a forever home, but I'm glad we have programs like this that help kids in need by getting donations from the local community."

He dropped a few bills into the donation box at the front of the room and then continued to look at every *single* picture with perfect care.

This man. *This* man. My argumentative, drunken, narcissistic asshole. The one who caused me so much pain and anger and lust. The person who I'd thought I had completely figured out. He was the one who had just confided in me about this.

My heart melted.

Just a sliver, for him.

Nine

Austin

This was not how I'd thought the night would go.

Not at all.

I'd thought I'd be waist-deep in booze before the sun officially set, so I could happily forget the last week of my life. No matter that it was apparently the whole problem anyway.

And then there was Jules.

Standing there in tiny little cutoffs, her pale and perfect thighs revealed in all their fucking glory. Her All Time Low tank top straining at her chest and showing a slice of her stomach. She'd slid her red hair off to one shoulder. Her nose ring complemented her studded ears…and there were tattoos for days. There was nothing fucking sexier than a woman with ink. And I wanted nothing more than to trace every line on her curvy body.

But I knew that I probably shouldn't want her.

I'd fucked up my first chance. We'd both fucked up.

Still, I was sitting next to her at Louie Louie's, listening to the dueling pianos battle and trying not to stare at her. I wasn't successful.

"What?" Julia asked, catching me for the third time since we'd sat down with our beers.

A girl who liked beer. *Fuck me*.

"Just you."

"Me?"

I shrugged noncommittally. Yeah, she looked fucking hot. She had to fucking know it. She might think I'd been a pig earlier, but it was the truth.

"Can you two make out already or something?" Patrick joked, nudging Morgan. "Right?"

Morgan slipped forward. Her long dark hair curtained the front of her face, and she giggled. Oh, she was fucked up. "Yes. Make out. Everyone should make out."

Heidi put her hand on Morgan's shoulder. "You all right?"

"I'm amazing! Dream job, here I come!" she said, tipping backward and nearly falling off of her barstool.

"How much did you get her to drink?" Emery asked.

Patrick shrugged. "We did a couple of shots. She was fine before you got here."

"We did eight shots!" Morgan said. "I'm great at counting."

Julia snickered and then covered it with a cough.

"CEO material right there," I said with a shake of my head. It was hard not to be bitter even though I knew Morgan truly deserved the job…and this time, right now, to kick back and relax. She didn't do it enough.

"Oh my God!" Morgan screamed. "I love this song!"

I widened my eyes as she jumped up and started singing, rather poorly, to Britney Spears's…"Baby One More Time." Heidi jumped up and started singing with her. And, eventually, she grabbed Emery and Morgan and pulled them out to the dance floor. Patrick realized pretty quickly that he was now alone with Julia and me. Then, he hightailed it out to the dance floor. *Smooth*.

Julia snagged her beer and took a long drink. I didn't take my eyes off of her.

We were in a packed dark bar, alone at a table in the back. All of our friends had miraculously disappeared out onto the dance floor, acting like fools. I might be a bit drunk, but I wasn't a fool. I wasn't going to let this opportunity pass me by.

"You want to go out with me?" I asked point-blank. No point in beating around the bush with her.

She nearly spat out the beer at my question. "What?"

"A date. You, me, together. I'll pick you up. We'll do normal human things instead of running into each other over and over on accident."

She went from confused to amused to angry in the seconds it took to finish my sentence. It was sexy as hell.

"Are you out of your mind?" she asked with round eyes.

"Not that I know of."

"Austin," she groaned. "We tried this. We broke up. We're *awful* together."

"Maybe things have changed."

She snorted. "They haven't."

"Sometimes, I really don't get you."

"Sometimes?" she asked with raised eyebrows. She leaned forward toward me and poked me in the chest. "I'm pretty sure you *never* got me. Ever! If you understood me at all, then we wouldn't have gone through the *shit* we went through two years ago."

I eased into her personal space. Our faces were mere inches apart, and she didn't back down as I met her gaze.

"I do get you, Jules. I get you better than anyone you've ever met. I see you. I know you. And that's why this didn't work. You can blame me all you want, but the truth is that you won't open up."

"I won't open up?" Her voice was low and deadly. "You think that's the reason? So, you're blind and stupid."

"I think that you'd rather have someone safe in your back pocket than have someone who challenges you."

I ran a finger down her exposed arm. She shivered under my touch, but her eyes were still hard.

71

"And you think that you're a bright ray of sunshine? You're completely open and honest? What happened Memorial Day weekend, Austin? Why didn't you tell me about the CFO position? You had the opportunity, and you fucking choked. You might think that I can't open up, but if that's the truth, then you're just as bad."

She huffed and jerked her arm back. But I remained immobile.

Is it that obvious, what had happened? Of course, she had looked at me at the meeting this afternoon. She'd known something was up. I just hadn't talked to anyone about it. After blowing up on Jensen, I'd wanted to get the fuck away from the whole thing.

Now, Julia was expectantly looking at me. Her eyes were searching, waiting to see if I'd explain…or if I was exactly like she'd said. I didn't like to back down from a challenge.

"The board didn't approve me," I finally admitted to someone other than my family. I hadn't even told Patrick, but I was sure someone else had.

"This fast?"

I sighed. "Jensen put my name up for CFO when he moved Morgan up to his job. The board had some…concerns about my behavior."

"That shouldn't be reason enough not to give you the job. You're a Wright. Maybe they'll change their minds."

I almost laughed. *Oh, how I wish it were all that fucking simple.*

"No. Jensen accused me of being an alcoholic and said that I had to go to rehab before they'd even consider it."

Julia chewed on her bottom lip, and for the first time, she glanced away from me. I knew what she was thinking. She'd made it clear that she thought I drank too much. But it was all bullshit. An excuse layered over everything else. If I gave up drinking, they'd find some other reason not to pick me.

"Maybe you should listen to him," Julia said.

Here it comes.

I pushed my chair back and started for the door. Fuck, I really just wanted to get drunk and laid tonight. Not deal with this shit.

I was outside and walking down the darkened alley toward Buddy Holly Avenue when Julia rushed up behind me.

"Why the hell did you storm off?" she demanded. She had her hands covering her arms as the late-night cold bit into her.

"Why the hell are you following me, Jules?" I snapped back at her.

She glared in my direction, and something in me snapped. I grabbed her by her shoulders and slammed her back into the brick wall outside the bar. Her breathing was ragged, and her mouth parted slightly at my movements. My body was pressed up against her lower half, and I never let her shoulders go. I held on for dear life as I stared down at those perfect pink lips, and I kicked myself for not diving straight in.

"You just up and left without explanation."

I leaned forward into her, got dangerously close. Everything in her awakened at the movement.

"You don't want to go out with me," I said. "You don't want to have anything to do with me. You abandoned me on the top of the canyon a week ago and said that all we did was argue. So, if you don't want this, then leave me the fuck alone."

"Excuse me for trying to find out why you're not getting a job I think you deserve," she spat in my face. "I guess I was wrong."

"What I deserve has never mattered to anyone."

She searched my face. I didn't know what she hoped to find. All I was feeling right now was rage. Yet my dick twitched at her nearness, and I knew that she noticed. Truthfully, I wouldn't mind unleashing all my pent-up energy on her. I could fuck her in this alleyway. We both wanted it. We were both holding back. Hanging on the edge by a thread.

"Oh, I've missed that look," I said, pushing her even though I knew I shouldn't.

"What look?" Her voice was breathy and her eyes unfocused as my hands slid down from her shoulders to her waist.

"The one begging me to fuck you." I moved my mouth to her ear. "Do you want me to fuck you, Jules?"

She whimpered softly as I thrust my hips harder against her.

"No," she managed to get out.

"You sure?"

She hesitated. "No."

"That's right. I know you do."

"You don't know anything about me," she whispered.

"I know that your body is craving mine, like an addict in need of her next fix."

Julia winced. "You'd know all about that, wouldn't you?"

"I don't do drugs," I said with disdain.

"And alcohol is…"

"Different."

"Bullshit," she spat, pushing me away. "You talk about all the other addictions out there—drugs, sex, money—yet you won't own up to your own. It's pathetic."

"What's pathetic is that you'll use any excuse to argue with me." I shook my head and pushed away from the wall. "Any excuse to put distance between us."

"Sex was never our problem!"

"Then, why aren't we having it?"

"Because *you* are the problem," she said, gesturing to all of me.

"Keep telling yourself that."

I turned on my heel and started back down the street. There were plenty of other bars. I didn't need to be in the one loaded with expectations and judgment.

"Where the hell are you going?" Julia called after me.

"Finding someone who wants to suck my dick," I viciously snarled back at her.

I heard the string of curses come out of her mouth and almost laughed. She was the one denying herself. It wasn't my problem. She didn't want to go out with me. She didn't want to fuck me. She wanted to fix me. Well, I didn't need fixing. And I didn't need her.

I glanced back over my shoulder once and saw her standing alone on the sidewalk. She looked torn between coming after me again and walking back inside.

Truth was…I might not need her, but, fuck, did I want her.

"Go on inside, Jules," I said. "The life you want isn't with me."

She opened her mouth and then closed it. Her eyes drifted back to the space we'd just occupied, as if she were contemplating how we'd gotten from point A to point B. Her eyes finally met mine, and she sighed softly.

"You push everyone in your life away. One day, you're going to wake up and realize that you don't have anyone left."

Then, she disappeared back into the piano bar. It hurt worse than I liked to admit, seeing her leave…again.

That was the other thing we were good at—walking away. Because running was easier than facing the facts. Sex was easier than feeling. Arguing was easier than communicating. A lie was easier than the truth.

Ten

Julia

I stumbled back into Louie Louie's, more pissed at myself than anything. *Why the hell had I let Austin rile me up like that?* One minute, we had been about to have sex in the alley, and the next, we had started screaming at each other.

Of course, I knew what the trigger had been this time.

Addiction.

Just what I needed was another addict in my life.

As if I hadn't been around them my entire existence. I'd come to Lubbock to be free of my past. Somehow, it always seemed to catch up to me.

I'd said that I didn't want to put his pieces back together, but the thing that pissed me off was, now that I knew the truth…I kind of did want to. I should want to run far, far away. I knew where that road would lead. I knew that the likelihood of him stopping was zilch. That him stopping because of *me* was actually zero. People didn't change because of someone else. They had to do it for themselves and no one else. Otherwise, it wouldn't stick. That was a damn fact.

Yet I still wanted to make things right. I still wanted to prove to him that it was possible. But he didn't want to hear it.

He couldn't even see right in front of his face. If he cleaned up his act, he would get the CFO position. Done deal.

What had to happen for him to see reality? Because, right now, he was drowning in liquor. He was sinking, not swimming. And what I'd told him was true…the more he pushed, the worse things were going to get.

I, of all people, knew that.

"There you are!" Heidi gasped when she stepped off the dance floor. "Where were you?"

"I needed to get some air," I lied.

Emery appeared then. She frowned at me. "What's wrong?"

"Nothing."

"You have the look."

"Really, I'm fine."

Heidi rolled her eyes. "Um…yeah, right."

"I'm tired. I'm going to go home, okay?"

"What? No!" Heidi cried. "Come on. Come and dance with us. It'll be fun!"

"Did Austin do something?" Emery asked with a worried crease between her eyebrows.

"He…yeah." I shrugged. "I don't know. He asked me out."

Heidi gasped. "That's so exciting!"

"No. I told him no. Then, he told me about the CFO position, and we got into another argument."

"You told him no?" Emery asked. She slowly blinked at me, as if she couldn't believe what I'd said.

"Yeah. I don't want to date him again."

Heidi snorted. "In what universe is that statement actually true?"

"He told me he was going to find someone else to suck his dick! I think I'm justified in saying that I'm not interested."

"He said that because you'd turned him down," Heidi said, waving the statement away.

"Well, if he wants someone else, by all means." I waved my hand at the door.

Emery smiled at me in that clever way she did. "Loving a Wright isn't easy. I can't imagine Austin is any different."

"I do *not* love Austin!"

"I wasn't..." Emery shook her head. "That's not what I meant. Simply that, if Austin got up the nerve to ask you out after your breakup, after you slapping him in the face last fall, and after you abandoning him on top of the canyon last weekend...he must be into you. No guy puts up with that much shit and sticks around for no reason."

"Oh, there's a reason," I muttered. "He wants to have sex with me."

"No guy works that hard for pussy," Heidi said.

"What about really good pussy?" I asked.

Emery coughed through her laugh. "Jensen and Landon both jumped through hoops. Wright men love the chase."

"So, what? You think I should give him a chance?" I asked skeptically. "After what he put me through?"

"Well, we don't know what actually happened," Heidi said with raised eyebrows. She looked like she was about to bounce up and down with excitement to finally find out.

But, as with most things in my life that hurt...I never wanted to rehash them.

"It doesn't matter. It's ancient history," I muttered.

"All right," Emery said, not pushing even though it was clear that Heidi wanted to. "Then, yeah...maybe give him another chance."

I ground my teeth together. This was not how I'd thought *this* conversation would go either.

"Is this what it's like to have girlfriends?" I groaned.

"We give you sage advice, and you listen to us wise women who have been where you stand?" Heidi asked with a giggle. "Yes, yes, it is."

79

"Don't listen to her," Emery said. "Girlfriends are here to cheer you on and commiserate when shit goes down. Also, for *Buffy* marathons, ice cream dates, and shopping."

"You mean, force-feeding all my friends colors in their wardrobes?" Heidi said.

My eyes met Emery's, and we both started laughing. Neither of us had a speck of color on us. We were both addicted to black, as if it were the only color choice. Heidi, as per usual, was in some bright pink color.

The girls veered the conversation away from Austin and my decision about what to do about him. They somehow managed to convince me to stay and hang out with them longer. I even danced. It really wasn't my thing, but Heidi and Emery were the two best friends a girl could ask for, and when they said dance, I danced.

I had so much to think about that the dancing helped to clear my head. I didn't need to decide what to do about Austin yet. He irritated me to no end…yet I felt drawn to him. And I'd felt an unwelcome stab of jealousy at the thought that he might actually try to date someone else.

Jealousy was an ugly emotion. I hated it.

One of my promises to myself when I'd moved to Lubbock was to be happy. It seemed like such a small thing to ask for, but from what I'd left behind…I'd thought it would be impossible. Then, I'd met Heidi, and for the first time in my life, I had a girlfriend. For the first time, I really was happy. I had a good job that paid well and a great friendship, and all my skeletons were happily buried in my closet.

But that gut-wrenching feeling I'd gotten when Austin so flippantly said he was going after someone else cut deep.

I didn't want to listen to my friends' suggestions. I wanted to tell him he could go fuck himself for all I cared. But I did care. And I didn't know what that meant or how to handle it. When Austin was involved, I was all topsy-turvy.

By the time we all piled back into Emery's Forester, my mind was more messed up than ever. I had no idea what to do and the extra shot or two I'd had with Heidi didn't really help. Luckily, Emery was the designated driver, so we wouldn't have to Uber back.

Heidi had picked me up from my apartment after work earlier today, so Emery drove straight there first. I lived the closest anyway. Both girls had moved in with their Wright men and now lived in sprawling mansions on the developing ritzy south side of town.

My apartment wasn't as fancy as Morgan's place by any stretch of the imagination, but it was good enough for me.

Heidi laughed as we pulled up. "I still can't get over the fact that Landon used to live here in a tiny one bedroom."

"That does seem crazy, considering where he lives now and the place he had in Clearwater," Emery said.

"I'm glad I opted for the two bedroom," I told them as we pulled up to my apartment building. "I took one look at the one bedroom and decided I couldn't live in a shoebox."

"Hey, did you leave your car door open?" Heidi asked in confusion.

"My what? No, why would I leave my door open?"

"I don't know, but it's open."

"Fuck!" I cried, jumping out of the car as soon as it stopped.

Heidi followed. We had both sobered almost instantly at the possibility that someone had broken into my car.

"Is the window broken or anything?" she asked.

My hands were shaking as I approached the car door. I shook my head. "All the windows are fine."

I ran my hand down the side of the door that was left ajar. There were no visible marks or anything that showed that someone had broken into it. Not that it necessarily would if they hadn't smashed any of the windows. I'd broken into my own car a time or two when I left the keys in it. It wasn't exactly rocket science.

I scrambled across the front seat and searched around. I'd grown up outside of Akron, Ohio, in a not-exactly-safe side of town. Old habits died hard, and I never kept shit in my car because there was never a guarantee it'd still be there. But I knew that I'd left my Bose headphones sitting out. Stupid of me, but I hadn't grabbed them when I got home today.

But the headphones were still there.

Why would someone break into my car and leave the only thing of value?

I drew my hand down my face and popped the trunk. I had a duffel in the back for the rare days when I went to the gym. It was still there, too. It didn't even seem to be ruffled through or anything.

"Is anything missing?" Emery asked, approaching my car.

"No. Not even my headphones."

"That's lucky," Heidi said.

"Maybe you just left the door open," Emery said. "It could happen."

"Yeah. You were in a hurry," Heidi added.

I shook my head. Had I closed the door? I honestly couldn't remember. It was possible that I had left it open, but it seemed really outrageous that I hadn't closed it—at least partway. This had been *wide* open. *Had I ever been so careless with my vehicle? My baby?*

I really didn't think so. But…the evidence was before me.

The headphones were there. My gym bag was fine and untouched.

No one had been in my car.

"False alarm, I guess," I muttered.

Heidi and Emery hugged me and walked me into my house to make sure that the house hadn't been vandalized or something. It was clear that they both thought that I'd been negligent when I got home. My house was fine. Nothing had happened. I'd panicked for no reason.

I watched them drive off and closed and locked all three locks on my front door. Sliding the chain into place gave me little satisfaction this time. Normally, it made me feel safe and secure. Like I could get through another night.

Tonight, I couldn't erase the sense of unease.

For I was certain that I'd closed that door.

Eleven

Austin

I peeled my eyes opened, squinting against the sun blasting in through the windows. My head weighed a solid ton. When I tried to sit up, my head spun.

"Fuck," I groaned, lying back down.

I didn't remember the last time I'd gotten blackout drunk. How much had I fucking drunk to get to where I was? What exactly *had* I done last night?

Jesus Christ, I must have been obliterated.

I sat up in bed again and waited until the world stopped spinning. Then, I noticed that I wasn't in my bed. Nor did I recognize anything. Not a damn thing.

I was shirtless but still had my pants on. At least that was a good sign. Maybe.

After a few minutes, I eased out of bed and walked into the living room. I cringed. I definitely recognized this apartment. I had, in fact, been here before. My eyes darted around the room as I wondered if I could make a hasty escape. I took a step further out of the bedroom and saw a skinny brunette in short shorts and an oversize T-shirt, brewing coffee. She shifted from one foot to another as she danced to the techno music coming out of her phone.

I sighed heavily. *No chance of escaping this.*

I cleared my throat, and she whirled around.

Her hand flew to her chest. "Austin, Christ, don't scare me like that!"

"Uh...hey, Mindi."

"Babe, you look horrible."

"Thanks," I said with a heavy dose of sarcasm.

Mindi was one of Patrick's many crazy exes. She wasn't exactly his ex-girlfriend since Patrick didn't do relationships, but she was pretty close. Then, she'd gone and threatened to stab him with a butcher knife if he didn't define their relationship. So...that had been the end of that.

But he'd first met her through Maggie...and Maggie was not a person I wanted to see right now.

"Uh...what the hell am I doing here? And...is Maggie around?"

My eyes darted to her closed bedroom door.

"She's out of town, but I figured she'd appreciate me saving your life," Mindi said, pouring herself a cup of coffee. "Do you want some?"

I shook my head as a relieved sigh escaped me.

"Like, what do you remember about last night?" Mindi asked.

"Nothing. It's a blur. Did we hook up?" I sure fucking hoped not.

She snorted. "Ew."

"You're so good for the ego."

"I mean...I'd be down if you could convince that golfer brother of yours. You *know* how I am about brothers, Austin." She batted her eyelashes at me.

"I'll take a pass. Landon is engaged anyway."

She popped out her bottom lip. "Shame. Mags would probably gut me anyway."

"So, why am I here?"

"You were at the bar, talking to this girl. You were going on and on about this other girl, Jules, who you're apparently obsessed with. And something about being an alcoholic and the company. I was getting off my shift and saved you from yourself. So, you're welcome."

I tilted my head back and cringed. *Great.*

"Well, thanks."

"Anytime. Now…if you could put in a word with Patrick for me," she said with hopeful wide eyes, "that would be really great."

I knew there was no chance in hell that was going to happen, but I nodded anyway. If what she had said was true, she had rescued me from a much worse situation. I was just fortunate that Maggie Hooper was not in town. She was probably the last person I wanted to deal with at the moment.

I called an Uber to take me back to my house and promptly flopped back down in my own bed. But, no matter that I needed so much more sleep, my mind wouldn't shut off. I'd gotten so wasted that I told complete strangers about my problems. All because Julia had struck a nerve. Jensen and the rest of my family and the company had all tried to tell me something, and I'd refused to listen.

I didn't want to fucking listen. But, if I had, then I might not have ended up at Mindi's apartment. I wouldn't be hungover and regretting my actions from last night. *Would I have yelled at Julia like that if I'd been sober? Would I have pushed Jensen's buttons if I'd been sober?*

For the first time in a decade, I wasn't sure what the hell I was doing with my life. Everything felt muddled. Usually, when I got frustrated, I would have a drink, and suddenly, it would be better. Today felt different.

I shook my head to clear the cobwebs. Maybe I'd know what the hell was wrong with me when the hangover cleared.

Nothing really helped.

I'd felt off all weekend.

By the time work rolled around on Monday morning, I knew I needed to do something. I stared down the bottle of whiskey after I changed into a suit for work. My mouth went dry. I reached for it and then set it back down. Then, I reached for it again. I pulled the top off, pouring myself a shot into a whiskey glass. Then, I walked out the door without it.

When I made it into work, I skipped my office entirely and went straight up to the top office floor. I knew Jensen would already be in. He was a bit of a vampire. Insomnia had always been his curse. And I wasn't disappointed when I stepped into his office. It was strange to think that, one day soon, this would be Morgan's office, and someone else would occupy the room down the hall.

Someone who was not me.

Jensen glanced up from his computer at my approach. "Austin. To what do I owe the pleasure?"

My brother looked tired. It couldn't be easy, stepping away. He wasn't the type to lay this all on Morgan and walk. He was a fixer by nature. I was sure he had been working day and night to make everything would run smoothly in his absence.

"I came to talk about the CFO position." I shut the door behind me and eased into a seat in front of Jensen's desk.

Jensen pinched the bridge of his nose. "You want the job."

"Well, of course I do," I said.

"Look," he said, finally glancing back up at me again, "I want to apologize for the conversation that we had over Memorial Day weekend. I was so excited for Morgan and disappointed about what had happened with the board in regard to you. I shouldn't have said the things I did. You know I hate when we fight."

I nodded. "Yeah, well, maybe I needed to hear it."

Jensen's eyebrows shot up his forehead. "Come again?"

"I don't know, man. I just think things aren't going how I expected them. And I didn't have a drink this morning."

"When was the last time that happened?"

I shrugged. "No idea."

"All right. So, where do we go from here? How can I help you?"

"I don't want this to be a big thing," I said, immediately deflecting.

"Does this have something to do with Julia?"

I narrowed my eyes. "Why would you think that?"

"I live with Emery," he reminded me.

"She say something?"

"She might have mentioned that y'all ran into each other at the First Friday Art Trail."

"Yeah, well, Julia wants nothing to do with me. It's probably better that way anyway."

"Who are you trying to convince?"

I flipped Jensen off, and he laughed.

"I'm here for you, no matter why the sudden change of heart. You know that we all worry about you. The last thing we want is for you to spiral and end up like Dad. I'd hate to see this damage your health and ruin any chance at a normal relationship with a girl like Julia."

"You really think I'm far enough gone that I could be like Dad?" I asked, shuddering at the thought.

"If you're talking to me about it right now, then no. And I'd like it to stay that way."

"All right."

It was a relief to hear that. Even though addiction ran through our family, I'd never once considered my drinking a problem. Even all the times my family had needled me about it, I'd never thought that I'd end up buried six feet under for it. That was a chilling thought.

Yet…I wanted that drink that I'd left on the counter this morning. I missed the numbness that came with the feeling.

Even after my troublesome weekend, it didn't stop me from wanting it.

Just another taste. One more shot.

"Austin, I think we should figure out a course of action from here," Jensen encouraged.

I slowly rose to my feet. "I think I'll just give it a try on my own. See how it goes."

Jensen frowned and clearly did not like that suggestion.

"You really think there's no chance that the board will look at me for CFO?"

Jensen stared down at his screen again and sighed. "It's not entirely out of the realm of possibility."

"But?"

"But we have already been inundated with applications for the position."

"Didn't you just post it on Friday?"

Jensen nodded.

"Well, fuck," I muttered. "Anyone good?"

"A couple," he admitted. "I've seen two that I really like— David Calloway and Elizabeth Leyton."

"David Calloway? Like, the Silicon Valley guy?" I asked with wide eyes.

"The one."

"What the hell does he want with us?"

"A Fortune 500 would be a step up for him. He brings a lot to the table," Jensen said.

"Shit. Where have I heard of Elizabeth Leyton before?"

Jensen laughed. "I think you slept with her sister in LA that one summer."

"I did? That summer is a blur."

After my dad had died, I'd gone to LA for an internship to work for a talent agency. It'd been no pay and shit work, but I'd been more interested in the process at the time and getting fucked up with every gorgeous Hollywood star who wanted an in with my agency. I'd been taking the LSAT and applying to law school at the time with the hopes of moving into the agency. Then, life had caught up with me, and I never went back.

"Anyway, Elizabeth seems to be the brains of their family. I wouldn't count her out."

So, basically I'm fucked.

"All right," I said. "Well, great."

Man, I need a drink.

"Austin, we'll figure it out. Okay?"

"Yeah. Sure. Sounds good."

I nodded at Jensen before disappearing out of his office. Somehow, that conversation had shifted so suddenly. I'd thought, if I took this step, like everyone wanted, things would improve, but again, it seemed as if it didn't matter what I did. A drink sounded really, really good right now.

I hurried into my office and closed the door. I knew that I had a bottle or two hidden in my desk. Sure, I'd gotten in trouble for it before, but, fuck, who cared?

As soon as I found the bottle of whiskey, my irritation seemed to dissipate. As if my body knew exactly what was coming.

Then, I just stared at it.

I didn't want to be my father.

Alcohol eased the pain and stopped me from feeling. I didn't know how everyone functioned without it. And, still...I wasn't sure I was functioning with it.

I put the bottle back and closed the drawer.

My stomach flipped. I could do this.

Just as I started up my computer to get to work for the day, my door opened. I glanced up to find Julia standing in my office.

Julia's here? Why the fuck is she in my office after this weekend?

And then I realized that I didn't care. Because she looked fucking hot, and her eyes were shining. I couldn't tell if she was pissed at me or nervous, but I realized I was fine with either.

"Fine," she spat fiercely.

I shot her an exasperated look. "What are you talking about?"

"Okay, fine. I'll go out with you."

"You will?" I asked in disbelief.

"Yes. Under one stipulation."

"What's that?"

"No alcohol."

My eyes landed on the drawer that I'd just shut. *Could I go on an entire date and not drink? Is it horrible that I even had to contemplate that?*

"All right. What do you have in mind, Jules?" I asked with that same cocky grin.

"Fuck if I know," she muttered.

"I'll figure something out. Friday night?"

"Fine," she said again. She seemed angry with her decision, as if she wasn't expecting to have a good time. As if she couldn't believe she was giving in.

"What changed your mind?"

"I really don't know," she said.

Then, she bit her bottom lip, which sent my mind straight into the gutter. My dick twitched at the look, and it took effort not to say fuck a date. I wanted her body.

"Glad you can admit you want me at least."

She huffed. "I did not say that."

"Don't worry, Jules. Your secrets are safe with me."

She cut her eyes away from mine, and I could see that there was so much more under the surface than she wanted to admit. To me or anyone.

"Just pick me up after six thirty because I'll be at the range until then."

"Why don't we start there?"

"Have you ever even fired a gun?" she asked with her own cocky grin.

"Wait and see."

"Good luck, Wright."

"Don't need it."

She rolled her eyes and then sashayed out of my office. I watched her perfect ass as she disappeared.

Well, fuck.

I had a date with Julia Banner. Without alcohol.

This was going to be interesting.

Twelve

Julia

*W*hat the hell did I just do?

I'd been single a total of one whole week, and already, I was jumping back into things with Austin. On a scale from one to horrible life choice, I was pretty high up there.

But I couldn't back down now. Even though I still thought slapping him sounded like the better option, I couldn't deny what Heidi and Emery had said. They'd laid it out, and plain and simple, Austin was chasing me. He had to still be interested in me to do that. And not just in the physical sense because I knew he could get it a lot easier than me.

I had reasons to run. Good reasons. But I had a hard time listening to my head when my heart and body were screaming at me. Austin ignited something in me. When we were together, we were electric. Sometimes, that was amazing, and sometimes, it completely blew up in my face, as it had two years ago.

I was rolling the dice and hoping I'd beat the house.

It made the rest of the week drag. Anticipation hit me like a sledgehammer. I swore, every day, all day, was like watching water boil. I couldn't tell if the churning in my stomach was nerves or excitement. I tried not to overanalyze it, but that was nearly impossible. Overanalyzing situations down to the smallest part was kind of my job. It made it hard not to do it in my own life.

"Really, just chill out," Heidi said on Friday afternoon as I was finally, *finally* leaving the office.

"That's easy for you to say. You're engaged. Shit all worked out."

"Yeah, but it wasn't rainbows and fucking unicorns when it all happened. You remember that."

I winced. "Yeah. I do."

Heidi sighed. "Look relationships aren't easy. Especially not with the Wrights. They have actual skeletons in their closets and, sometimes, psycho ex-wives and a legion of devoted fans." Heidi shook her head. "Anyway, what I'm trying to say is, enjoy your time. If he acts like a dick, then ditch him."

"Sage advice from my bubblegum queen."

Heidi rolled her eyes. "One day, I will get you into pink."

"I'd like to see that."

"One day, damn it." She laughed and shook out her blonde mane. "So, call me after the date to fill me in on the details. Unless, of course, you make it an all-nighter."

"Heidi!"

She held her hands up. "Then, I expect a report tomorrow or whenever you two surface."

"You're horrible."

"It's not like it's the first time. Right?"

"Well, we're starting over."

"Did you really tell him no alcohol?"

I nodded.

"You're brave. I love you."

She waved at me and then jogged over to her car to get out of the oppressive heat. This was the first week we'd hit the high nineties, and I was already dying. My pale skin was not used to these rays. It got hot in Akron, but nothing compared to Texas summers. This Ohio girl was not a fan of this weather.

I thought about Heidi's comment the entire drive back to my apartment. *Had I been brave for asking Austin not to drink on our date?* I didn't know if it was bravery or stupidity. Things had fallen apart last time because of his drinking. Maybe I was a fool to think that it wouldn't wreak havoc this time around as well. But I had to at least try.

Despite knowing that we were going out after the shooting range, I didn't put on anything fancy. Just a black V-neck tank top, a pair of shorts, and my Vans slip-ons that he'd tried to ruin at the lake. I hoped we weren't going anywhere that I needed to be dressed nicer than this.

I shrugged off the momentary anxiety. Austin didn't care what I was wearing. The last time we'd been together, we'd hardly left his bedroom. So, I knew he gave zero fucks about what kind of clothes I wore. Not that I intended to end up in his bedroom. This was not going to be a repeat of the last time we had been together.

At six o'clock, I pulled into the parking lot at the shooting range. Austin was already parked outside in his shiny red Alfa Romeo that stood out among the standard-issue Texas pickup trucks. He hopped out of the car when he saw me pull up. He was there, opening my car door and helping me out of my own damn car.

"Hey, Jules," he said with a genuine smile.

Warmth shot through me at the smile on his face and the feel of his hand in mine and the way he regarded me with a mix of adoration and desire. This was the Austin Wright I had dated two years ago. The one who had intrigued me so entirely.

"Hey."

I didn't drop his hand, and he didn't pull away. He just stared down at me, enraptured. Our bodies were nearly pressed together in the close space, and I even momentarily forgot about the Texas heat. I just wanted to be near him.

That was the hard part. We fought like cats and dogs. Yet…I missed him and what we had once had before he royally fucked up.

But I pulled back, let loose a pointed cough, and he got the message. He took a step back and dropped my hand.

"Are you ready for this?" he asked.

I laughed and reached into the backseat to pull out the carrying case for my Glock 43. "More than ready."

"You came prepared."

"I'm here two or three times a week. I'm always prepared."

His eyebrows rose. "I didn't know you came that often."

"Well, when we were last together, I didn't."

"What made you change your mind?" he asked, holding the door open for me to enter the range.

I averted my gaze and shrugged. "Can never be too prepared."

"Next, you're going to tell me that you have a concealed carry permit."

My matching grin said it all.

"Fuck," he groaned.

The word heated me from the inside out, and I hastily entered the premises.

"Julia!" Tip said from behind the counter.

"Hey, Tip," I said as Austin followed behind me.

"Perfect timing, as usual. I have you on six today."

"I'll need one nearby, too," I said, nodding my head at Austin.

"No problem. I can put him in seven."

Tip smiled warmly at us both as he got Austin a gun and both of us ammo as well as protective gear. I waved at Tip again as we left to grab our lanes.

"So, you are here a lot," Austin confirmed.

"Pretty much."

"That guy is so into you."

I laughed. "He so is."

Austin shot me a look I didn't understand.

"What?"

"Most girls don't notice."

"Good thing I'm not a girl then. I'm a woman."

Austin laughed softly. "That is a very good thing."

As Austin fiddled with the gun and began to load the ammunition, I pulled out my baby and inspected it. This was my first real purchase in Lubbock, and I was proud of it.

I might not originally be from Texas, but I'd grown up around guns. I knew my way, forward and backward, around them. From a rifle to a handgun and back. I'd gone hunting with my dad as a kid, and the shady neighborhood I'd grown up in made it clear that a gun and the ability to know how to fire one were necessary.

When I'd first been looking for a place to rent, I'd looked at a house with a legit gun safe with eight different locks and a keypad. That was the moment I knew that I'd fit right in, in Lubbock.

"All right, show me what you've got, Wright," I said, motioning for him to go first.

He shot me a cocky grin before pulling on the protective headphones and aiming at the target. He carefully and methodically unloaded into the target down the line. My heart rate picked up. Watching Austin shoot was magical. The intensity in his gaze, the perfect stance, the slight kickback. It was more of a turn-on than I had imagined. I squeezed my legs together as my lower half responded full force to him.

He laughed when he put the gun down and pulled his headgear off. "I forgot how much fun that is."

"Adrenaline rush, right?" I asked.

His eyes traveled the length of my body, and then he nodded. "Your turn, Banner."

I swallowed and slowly averted my gaze. The tension between us was thick, and I needed to concentrate. When I worked with my gun, I went completely in the zone. Nothing else existed around me in that moment. It was me and the gun and the target.

When I finished my magazine, Austin's expression said everything I needed to know. He eyes were glazed, his lips parted, his body angled toward me. Watching me shoot had done the same thing that it had when I watched him. If we kept this up, we wouldn't even make it to the second part of the date.

I cleared my throat. "So, uh, what did you think?"

"Not bad."

"Not bad? Are you joking?"

"Pretty good."

"I'll show you pretty good when we get our targets back, and I kicked your ass."

"So competitive."

"Aren't you?"

"Oh, absolutely," he said. "But watching you makes me want to get out of here, Jules."

"Does it?" I asked breathily. I placed my gun down and fully faced him.

"You know it does."

"Is that what this is?" I couldn't stop myself from asking. "Just sex…again?"

"No," he answered automatically.

"Are you sure?" I was being combative for no reason.

"I'm here on your terms. You know I want you. But I'm fucking trying. Why can't I want you without an argument?"

I held my hands up in surrender. He was right. Not that I wanted to say that out loud.

"It's hard after what happened last time."

"Living in the past is a surefire way to screw this up."

"I know," I whispered. But that was my life. I couldn't stop living in the past. "Let's start over. Hi, I'm Julia Banner."

I extended my hand to him, and he firmly took it in his own.

"Austin Wright."

He tugged me toward him so that we were between the lanes. Movement was going on all around us. It was loud as hell. And we probably were supposed to be focused on the shooting range. But none of that mattered.

My body was pressed against his, and everywhere he touched sent shivers straight through me. His hand tilted my chin up toward him. Our eyes locked, as if he was waiting for permission, making sure I wouldn't snap at him, as I had in the past. But all he saw from me was compliance. Maybe I did need to live in the present more.

His lips touched down on mine, and I surrendered to him.

For a moment, the stars aligned. The world felt right. Just the taste of his lips and the incredible feel of him against me. The memories of days spent locked together flooded my conscience. As Austin took over, I released into a free fall.

Thirteen

Julia

A throat cleared behind us.

"If you're going to make out, do it somewhere else."

I laughed and pulled back from Austin. "Sorry," I said with a shrug that showed how sorry I really was.

"We were just leaving anyway," Austin said.

"We were?"

"Yeah. Let's get out of here. We can come back another day."

I arched an eyebrow. "Already planning a second date? You're very confident."

"You can pretend to hate that about me if you like."

Cocky bastard.

Of course I didn't hate his confidence. It had always been a huge turn-on. Even when everything about him drew me crazy, I still knew it was hot. And my body was torn halfway between relishing this date and wanting to push his buttons just for fun.

"But there are so many other things to pretend to hate about you," I said, batting my eyelashes.

Austin shook his head at me. I could tell that he wanted to press his luck and inch closer to me again. That kiss had been…electric. A current of energy that had trapped us in a whirlwind. I hadn't wanted to stop…and I wouldn't have if we hadn't been interrupted.

It was so easy to be caught up in Austin. I needed to be careful, or I wouldn't make it through the night with my heart intact.

I carefully replaced my Glock in its case while Austin returned his to the front. Our targets were pulled down and handed to us as a souvenir. I grinned like a fool when it was clear that my aim was *much* better than Austin's. Not that he was bad, but I was better.

"Luck," Austin said as we left the shooting range.

"Ha! Sore loser!"

"Well, if I was there as often as you, then I'd be as good."

"Yeah, but you're not."

I popped open my Tahoe and placed the case into a carrier under my seat, so it wouldn't slip around. Then, I raised my hands over my head and stretched. I could feel Austin's eyes on the bare strip of stomach I was revealing.

"So," I said, dropping my arms, "where are we off to? Do I need to change?"

"Uh, yeah, no. You're fine." He gestured to the dark jeans and black polo he was wearing.

"Right."

"And where we're going is a surprise."

I narrowed my eyes. A surprise from Austin. I wasn't sure what that meant exactly.

"Let's drop your car off first," Austin said to keep me from arguing. "Then, I can drive you around all night."

"Sure. Sounds good," I agreed easily.

He raised his eyebrows at the ease of my compliance, but in that moment, I decided to go all in. No more hesitating at everything he did. No more second-guessing motives. I wasn't going to have a good time if I didn't relax and try to enjoy this date. Austin and I could fight like cats and dogs, but I wanted to prove to myself that we could do more than that. That we were capable of just being Austin and Julia…like we had at the art gallery. I wanted more of that Austin.

It was a quick drive to my apartment where I ditched my Tahoe and ran inside to secure my gun back in its safe in my closet. Then, I hurried back out and slid into the passenger seat of Austin's Alfa Romeo. Being in his car again brought back a flood of memories. When we had been together before, everything had been so easy. So effortless. It was as if things were really supposed to be like this all the time.

I'd fooled myself into believing it. And I didn't know why I was giving Austin a second chance. But I needed to toss the memories aside and live for today.

"So…dinner?" I asked. "I'm already starving."

"Shooting takes it out of you, doesn't it?"

"It's like I ran a marathon."

"Same. That was a total adrenaline rush though. I see why you do it so often."

I frowned and glanced away. No one really knew why I went to the shooting range that often. But it for sure was not for the adrenaline rush. That was more of a bonus.

"Food then?"

"Don't worry, Jules. I'll take care of you."

I leaned back against the leather seat, enjoying the sentiment. I'd thought he'd want to take me to a fancy dinner. It seemed like a Wright move. And, while we were in West Texas, where jeans, boots, and belt buckles were common dinner attire, I knew Austin preferred to dress up for such occasions. That likely ruled a fancy dinner out of the equation.

It felt nice, letting someone else take the lead for once. Even if nerves hit me, I liked the idea of Austin taking care of me. I had been in charge of my relationship with Trevor. One hundred fifty percent. And, already, I could feel myself handing over some of that control that I clung so desperately to. It was terrifying and refreshing.

We were past the loop and halfway out of town when I sat up to appreciate the flat farm fields on either side of us. *The country? We are going into the country?* Now, *that* was unexpected.

"Where the hell are you taking me, Wright?"

He laughed. "Well, your stipulations made it a little difficult."

"I had one stipulation."

"Sure, but I wanted to do it right."

"Right or Wright?"

He rolled his eyes at my inflection. "Both."

The first indication of where we were going was the Ferris wheel on the horizon. My jaw dropped, and I turned to face Austin in wonder. He had put some effort into all of this. I hadn't even known there was a carnival happening right now. I would have thought it would be too hot.

"I hope you like carnival rides."

"You are full of surprises," I admitted.

He parked in the open field next to the carnival and helped me out of the passenger side. I glanced at the dirt on his shiny car.

"We probably should have brought the Tahoe."

His hand slowly slid into mine, and he tugged me close. "I don't mind getting a little dirty."

"You or the car?"

"Yes."

I laughed. *Of course.*

Austin looked like he wanted to kiss me but instead locked our fingers together and walked me to the entrance. I sighed at the ease with which we were together. Hard to believe that I had been screaming at him only a couple of days ago.

Okay…it probably wasn't that hard to believe. Austin and I were only extreme highs and extreme lows. It was why those weeks we'd dated were some of the best of my life…and any time I'd spent with him after were some of the worst.

We headed straight for the heavily caffeinated, fried, and sugary foods.

"What are you in for, Jules?" Austin said.

"Funnel cake!"

"You're going for a sugar high?"

"Best high out there, trust me."

Austin ordered us two cheeseburgers, two giant Cokes, and a hand-battered, powdered-sugar-covered, deep-fried funnel cake that made me bounce up and down with excitement.

We carried our food to a wooden picnic bench and plopped down. I saw Austin look up at a sign over my head with a wistful glance. I craned around to see what he was looking at. The stand next to the burger place had a sign offering ice-cold beers.

Oh.

"Are you doing okay?" I asked, picking at my burger.

"Don't worry about me. I'm fine."

I almost believed him. Except I didn't. He might seem as if he was doing really good on the outside. Great even. But I knew better.

"You know the road ahead isn't going to be easy."

"The road ahead?"

"Withdrawal," I said in a small voice. "It's going to be really hard."

"I suspect it will be."

"You don't have to do it alone. You have people who care about you, you know?"

Austin reached forward and took my hand. "I'm doing fine, Jules. It's a slow process. I'm not going to go cold turkey. It'll take time, but as long as I'm with you, I feel like I can do anything."

I smiled shyly at him. A flush crept up my neck and flooded my cheeks. I wasn't used to feeling this way. As if everything really was going to be all right. That, even though it was a hard road, we might be able to make it through together.

The way I'd made it through all the shit that had happened to me with the help of a close friend. Maybe I could be that person for Austin.

I ignored the part of my brain that said it wasn't possible. That part of my brain was a bitch.

Fourteen

Austin

I actually believed that.

That I could change the world with Julia at my side. I'd been ignoring my feelings for her for a long time. Longer than she even knew. But, now that we were here together, that felt stupid. I wanted to keep my job, I wanted Julia, I wanted to live longer than my dad. If I had to give up alcohol for all of that…it was feasible. At least, I hoped so.

"Well, what about your art?" I asked, veering the conversation to safer territory, as she tore into the sticky funnel cake.

White powder coated her face, and she laughed as she tried to wipe the sugar from her mouth and fingers. She put one finger into her mouth and sucked it down to the end. She made a little pop sound as it left her lips. Her dark eyes met mine, and a seductive smile appeared. For a second, the carnival disappeared. All I could see was a fucking beautiful woman sucking off her own fingers like I knew she could suck off my cock. And I wanted it.

Goddamn control!

Why did I have to have some? Why did I want this to go right so bad? Fuck everything else; I would be happy to find the back of a booth or the open field or even my tiny little car. But I knew she deserved more.

"Austin?" she said in that throaty deep voice.

"Uh, yeah?" I had to shake myself out of my trance. I was glad that we were sitting down.

"I asked what you wanted to know about my art."

"Right." I picked myself out of the gutter. "What have you done lately?"

"Nothing," she said with a nonchalant shrug that I knew was anything but.

"Why not? With your talent, you could have your own studio exhibit downtown."

"I don't feel inspired."

I shot her an exasperated look. "Tell me what we have to do to inspire you. Because you cannot waste that talent."

"Austin—"

"No, Jules, you need to be in classes. You need your own studio. Practice makes perfect and all that. If you're helping me, then don't think I'm going to sit back and let you ignore something that brings you joy."

"Who the hell are you, and what have you done with Austin Wright?" she asked with a flirtatious smile.

I held my hands out to the sides. "Same person I've always been."

She snorted. "We'll see."

We finished off the rest of our food and dumped it in a trash can before walking around the carnival. I reached for her hand, and she didn't bite my head off when I took it.

"Oh, look, progress," I muttered under my breath.

Her eyes shot to mine. "Don't make me cut you."

"Well, the last couple of times I've tried this, you almost did."

"You were being a dick."

I shrugged. "Can't change the way we are together."

"So, I should be jumping down your throat."

"With your tongue preferably."

"Pig."

But her tone was light, and her eyes were sparkling. I was ready to get back to what we had started at the shooting range. As soon as I pushed, she'd pull back. She seemed determined for this to be a normal date. I thought it was interesting that she thought we could ever be normal. *Hadn't she dumped that boring douche from accounting because she didn't want that shit?*

"Take it or leave it, babe."

"I'll think on it."

I'd take that.

We spent the next hour riding all of the rickety high-speed rides that made my heightened nausea grow. This no-drinking thing was already taking its toll. I was glad when we finally gave up on the fast rides.

"Ferris wheel?"

She shook her head. "Nah, let's play games."

"What? You've been on every other ride."

"So?"

"You don't want to make out on the top of the Ferris wheel? Are you really going to deny me this?"

Julia laughed. "I'm kind of afraid of heights."

"What?" I gasped. "I thought you were fearless."

"How could you possibly think that?" she asked seriously.

"You take on everything headfirst. You're strong and smart. You kick ass."

She glanced off in the distance, and once again, I was struck with the thought that there was something Julia wasn't telling me. Something that just wasn't right. I didn't know what it was, but I wanted to find out.

"Everyone has to have a flaw," she said after a minute, flicking her hair in a way I'd seen Heidi do. It was a good imitation of nonchalance.

"I haven't found yours."

"Oh, Austin," she said with a shake of her head. "You must not be looking very hard."

"I'd be happy to look later," I said suggestively.

"Oh, I bet you would."

She grabbed my hand and pulled me toward a row of games. Her eyes ran up and down all the games before settling on knocking over milk bottles with a cheap plastic ball. I knew the game was next to impossible. They really didn't want people to win, but I paid and let her have at it anyway.

She lost miserably.

She held up a Tootsie Roll at the end. "How lucky am I? They give out consolation prizes."

"Poor thing."

"Your turn," she said, popping the Tootsie Roll into her mouth. "I want a giant stuffed animal."

I glanced up at the massive pink flamingo next to a pink-sequined unicorn and an oversize poop emoji. I had never wanted an oversize poop emoji so much in my life.

I wished that I had played baseball or football or something. Or at least that the game wasn't rigged. Unfortunately, I had been more into theater, girls, and parties—in no particular order. Landon and Sutton had always been the athletes in the family.

The guy took my money from me with a sympathetic look. Yeah, I was probably screwed. I wasted twenty dollars, failing miserably at this stupid fucking game. Julia had tears streaming down her face by the time I was ready to give up.

"You're horrible at this game," she said through her laughter.

"Can I just buy the goddamn stuffed animal?"

"Sorry, sir. They're not for sale," the guy said.

"That wouldn't be any fun anyway. Where is your consolation-prize Tootsie Roll?" Julia asked.

"I'm not done!" My competitive streak was winning out, and I was not ready to give up on that damn stuffed animal. No matter how much of a sucker that made me.

"Seriously, Austin, it's not a big deal. I don't think anyone can knock that thing down." She asked the guy behind the stand, "Does it actually even move?"

He pushed the bottles over with one hand, and Julia started laughing hysterically again.

"Oh, this is too good," she crooned.

I shot her a glare and then aimed for the bottles again after the guy set them back up again. I tried to channel the two seasons of little league my dad had forced me in as a kid. Then, I aimed and threw the ball.

And missed.

Julia was doubled over, and her laughter was music to my ears. Despite the fact that I was losing horribly, she was so happy. I'd forgotten how much her laughter affected me.

"Fuck, I suck."

"You do," she crowed. "You really do."

I finished off the rest of the balls I had to throw in a miraculously awful fashion, only managing to knock over one milk bottle despite all my throws. The guy in charge of the game shook his head and then pulled down the pink-sequined unicorn.

"I've never seen anything so pathetic in my life. You've earned this, dude."

I took the stupid fucking unicorn and held it out to Julia. "Look what I won you!"

"Oh, I'm so lucky." She wiped tears from her eyes and then took the giant unicorn under one arm. "We'll probably have to share custody of the kid."

"Nope. It's your fucking unicorn."

"Don't kill our love fern!"

I cracked up at her *How to Lose a Guy in 10 Days* reference. "You and Morgan would so get along with your bad taste in movies."

"That movie is a classic," she told me as we moved away from the game I'd sunk a small fortune into.

"So, what are you going to name it?"

"It's not a goldfish. We don't have to name it."

"Why do you hate your new unicorn?"

Julia shook her head at me. "If I name it, it'll probably be Glitter Sparkles Sprinkles V."

My eyes bugged out. "Yeah. I am not sharing custody on a unicorn named Glitter Sparkles Sprinkles V."

"Why do you hate my new unicorn?" she said with mock seriousness.

"How about we compromise with something that doesn't sound mildly edible?"

"I'm thinking Waffle."

"Waffles are edible, Jules," I said in exasperation.

"For some reason, I can only think of food."

I threw my hands up. "Waffle the Unicorn it is."

"Don't worry, Waffle. You'll have two great parents who will love you."

We packed up Waffle into the tiny trunk of my Alfa Romeo since it was only a two-seater. Julia petted Waffle on the head before slamming the trunk shut with vigor.

"You're going to be crazy about this damn unicorn, aren't you?" I asked when she got into the car.

"You're the one who wanted joint custody," she said with a laugh, swishing her red hair to one shoulder.

My eyes were glued to her. I couldn't seem to process that we were supposed to be heading out of the carnival and back to reality. I didn't want this date to end. My hands shook on the steering wheel, and I quickly covered the movement by dropping them. I needed Julia more than I needed a drink. I needed her like nothing else.

"Austin?"

"Yeah?"

She didn't respond. She threw herself across the stick shift and crushed her lips to mine. My hands went up into her hair. She had her fingers wound around my shirt, clinging to me for life.

Her kisses held no hesitancy. She explored my mouth, relearning everything about me. She dragged my bottom lip between her teeth. I groaned into her mouth and lightly licked across her lip. She completely opened to me. My tongue slipped inside and massaged across her tongue in a game of hockey. My heart was thrumming in my chest. My body forgot all the early signs of withdrawal that had begun to set in, bursting with adrenaline at the taste of this gorgeous, unbelievably amazing woman.

"We should get out of here," I told her breathlessly.

She nodded, barely able to pull herself away from me. I zoomed out of the carnival parking lot and back onto country roads just as the sun began to set on the horizon.

Julia seemed impatient, leaning over the center and trailing kisses down my neck and over to my shoulder.

"Fuck, Jules," I muttered.

Her hand slid to my shorts, making lazy circles in the material. My dick responded in turn at the contact. She hesitated a second as she inched closer and closer to the exact spot where I wanted her to be. Then, with purpose, I picked up her hand and placed it on my hard cock.

A sigh of desire left her lips. All I could think about was her lips on me. Her lips fucking me.

Her fingers flicked the button of my shorts open. I slightly leaned back and slowed the car down. I was suddenly in no hurry at all.

"We shouldn't," she said softly.

"You don't want to?"

"That's not it. I just…wanted this to be different."

"Does it feel the same?"

"Yes, and no."

I put my hand on hers. "Then, we can wait."

"But I really fucking want to taste your cock," she nearly whispered into my ear.

My dick throbbed painfully at her words. She could feel it twitch under her hand, and she released a throaty gasp.

"Fuck," was all I was able to say before she drew the zipper down and removed my erection that was so hard, it was almost painful.

She palmed it in her hand, stroking it up and down from base to head. As she wrapped her lips around my dick, I slowed further, absentmindedly remembering that I was driving a seventy-five-thousand-dollar car with a fucking stick shift.

She moaned as she eased the entire shaft into her mouth. I swerved as she bottomed out at the base of my dick, and then I hastily righted the car. Thank God no one else was out in the country right now. She dragged her lips back up to the head, and she released me with a soft pop. Just the way she had sucked off her fingers earlier.

Jesus Christ!

Her finger smeared the pre-cum on the tip around in a circle, and I gasped.

"Jules," I groaned.

"I'm a tease. I know."

She lapped up the come and then went back to long, deep strokes into her mouth. My vision was nearly blurry. My body struggled not to lose complete control and crash the car.

But I was an idiot if I thought I had any control.

Julia owned me.

My balls tightened, and I tapped her head, letting her know that I was about to come. She hummed against my dick, and I lost it. I came hot and explosive up into her mouth. Still, she didn't move, clamping her lips around me and taking it all.

She pulled back when I finished jerking into her mouth. Then, she swallowed masterfully. Our eyes met. She looked mighty pleased with herself. And, fuck, she had every reason to be.

Julia wiped a little come off her lips. "I've always wanted to do that."

"Fuck, woman, feel free anytime."

"I think you're going to have to reciprocate."

"It would be my pleasure."

She brushed a kiss against my cheek and leaned back in her seat as I revved the engine and took off for home.

Fifteen

Julia

After what had happened in the car, I supposed I shouldn't have expected there to be any shyness between us. This right here had never, ever been our problem. *Damn Heidi for being right.*

I'd had every intention of giving Austin a spectacular kiss good night and sleeping in my own bed. Not blowing him in his smoking-hot car. Not racing to his home to be together. Not doing every single dirty thing that I had running through my head.

Fuck expectations. This is way better.

Austin skidded into his garage, closing the door behind him. Butterflies rattled around my stomach with anticipation. He casually exited the car and then popped the truck.

"Can't forget Waffle," he said, picking up the enormous pink unicorn.

I snort-laughed. "You are ridiculous."

"I take my custody very seriously."

We moved into his house, which was located a couple of blocks off of Texas Tech's campus in Tech Terrace, a subdivision that had been growing since the '60s. Austin had bought the house a couple of years ago, gutted the interior, and started over. The property itself had been worth more than the house sitting on top of it. But, now, it was gorgeous, rustic, and a total bachelor pad.

Austin put Waffle on the couch with care. "There you go, buddy."

"I wish you were like this all the time."

Austin's head snapped to me. "I am like this all the time."

"Uh, no, you're not. Most of the time, you don't give a shit about anything."

"All this time, you've thought that I don't care about you, Jules?"

"What else am I supposed to think with the way you act? Every time we are together, you make some snide remark about getting me in bed. You didn't care that I had a boyfriend, which I suppose shouldn't have been a surprise, and you are generally a jerk."

"Truth is, I don't know how else to act around you."

He took a few steps away from Waffle, pinning me in place with his heated gaze.

"So, you go with antagonistic?"

"Yes. It's easier than telling you that I've thought about you every day since you left."

"That was almost two years ago," I said a little breathlessly.

"It was."

"You could not have been into me this whole time. You were the one who fucked up. You were the one who pushed *me* away."

"I know. I'm not going to make that mistake again."

I read the sincerity on his face before he pressed me back against the wall, his mouth covering mine. I gasped as we collided. He took advantage of the movement and moved his tongue into my mouth. My body shuddered under his with all those months of pent-up sexual tension between us.

His hand slid down my thigh and hoisted it up around his hip. We shifted together a fraction closer, thrusting our hips together. I threw my arms around his shoulders, and he took that as indication to go further. He grabbed my other leg, pulling me completely against him. I locked my legs behind his back.

"Jules," he muttered like a prayer.

"Hmm?"

"Want to fuck you, babe."

I pulled back from his lips as he grasped my ass roughly in his hands. "That a question?"

"Statement."

"Good. That's what I thought."

He grinned. "Could you be more perfect for me?"

"Yet to be seen."

He kissed me again. This time, it was soft and gentle. Not at all like a kiss I'd ever gotten from Austin. He leaned me into the wall, caressing my lips with a tenderness I hadn't known he was capable of. This wasn't a quick, desperate kiss. This was passion, and in some way, it almost felt like an apology.

"What was that for?" I whispered against his lips.

"Just wanted to do it once before we went back to yelling at each other."

I laughed. "You're so confident that we will."

He winked at me as he started walking me through the living room and the kitchen, and then he kicked open the back door.

"Austin…"

"Yeah, babe?"

"What the hell are you doing?"

One hand slipped between my legs and stroked me. I groaned at the intimate motion.

"Getting you wet."

He slipped his shoes off, and before I could protest, he threw us both into his pool. My head went under with a giant splash. Austin released me as we went under, and I kicked away from him. I might have even kicked him in protest. I resurfaced, gasping, with him a quarter of the way across the pool.

"What the fuck?" I sputtered.

I pushed my soaked red hair out of my eyes and found Austin coming back toward me with a mischievous look on his face.

I held my hands out and shook my head. "Stay back, Wright."

I grabbed both of my shoes and tossed them over the edge. Those Vans were seriously dead now.

"Ah, come on," he said, stepping close to me again.

"Oh no, you've lost rights to all of this." I gestured to my body.

"Don't think so."

"You ruined my shoes. Again."

"Can't ruin something twice."

"You just did."

He finally reached me, and his hands slipped, wet and full of confidence, down my sides.

"Austin," I said warningly.

"Babe."

His lips brushed mine once before he tasted his way down my neck. I wanted to stay pissed at him for throwing me in the fucking water *again*. But, somehow, I just arched my back and gave him better access. His tongue trailed up my neck, sending shivers down my body. He tugged on my earlobe with his teeth, and my lower half throbbed with desire.

Damn him!

Austin reached for the bottom of my T-shirt. I halfheartedly smacked his hand.

"You're a pain in the ass. You know that, right?"

Austin laughed as he ripped my shirt up and over my head. "I'd be happy to oblige that, too."

I flushed from head to toe, which only egged him on.

"God, I love that."

His fingers skimmed the underside of my bra, enjoying every inch of milky-white skin before cupping the breast and squeezing.

"I have dreamed about these tits."

He unhooked the bra and let them spill out before him. His mouth was hot on my nipple, teasing it with his tongue and sucking it to a peak. My head tilted back, and I arched into the side of the pool.

Austin Wright knew exactly what to do with this tongue. I was already shaking from the attention to my tits.

My fingers gripped his shirt, as I ached to see the six-pack underneath. He tugged it off, and it squelched as it dropped to the ground.

"Fuck," I said, running my fingers over every taut inch.

"Yes, please."

"I sure hope your neighbors can't see into your backyard."

"Eh, let them have a show."

I laughed at him as he backed me into the shallow end. Only Austin would be so cavalier about anyone seeing us half-naked in his pool.

"I still can't believe you threw me into this pool."

He snapped the button on my shorts and dragged the zipper down to the base. His eyebrow quirked. "Are you complaining?"

I squirmed as he striped me fully naked, picked me up—as if I weighed nothing, which was far from the truth—and laid me out on the side of the pool like a feast before him. Yeah, no complaints from me.

"Jules?" he said, his fingers inching slowly up the inside of my thighs. "Do you want me to stop?"

"No," I spat out.

"You sure, babe?" He reached the apex of my legs and found out exactly how wet I was.

"Austin," I squeaked.

"Fuck. You do want me," he said, like the arrogant bastard he was.

He moved one finger into my pussy before spreading me open and inserting a second. I moaned at an indecent volume and could give two fucks if anyone heard. As he stroked me, he leaned forward, teasingly blowing on my clit.

"Yes, I want you!" I gritted out at the wonderful torment.

His answering laugh was muffled as he lowered his tongue to my clit and ravished me. My hips came off of the ground. My back arched. My entire core trembled as he licked, bit, and sucked my clit. He consumed me. I forgot where we were and nothing else mattered, just the feel of him.

I felt myself letting go. I writhed under him as the pressure mounted. But he wasn't letting me get away. He wrapped his loose arm across my hips and pressed me into the ground. I was completely trapped by his tongue, and when I came, I completely released. I screamed into the night as Austin drew out my pleasure with a few gentle strokes into me.

Austin stepped out of his soaked shorts and boxers as I recovered. I eased into a sitting position, just now feeling the burn across my back from the ground. *Oh well. Worth it.*

"Come here," Austin said.

He crooked a finger at me as he took a seat on the top step. I moved over to him, towering over him in a way I never could regularly.

"I think you might have liked that as much as I did." My eyes drifted to his cock, standing up and waiting for me.

"I enjoy watching you come."

His hands gripped my hips and drew me onto his lap. I straddled him, teasing the tip of his dick with my wet pussy. It was his turn to shudder.

"I enjoy this more," he said before roughly pushing me down.

His cock thrust into me deep and without warning. It was a good thing I was soaking wet as I wrapped all around him.

"Jules," he groaned. He leaned his head forward into my shoulder and kissed across my collarbone.

I didn't want this to end. This feeling. This energy between us. The way we seemed to fit perfectly together. As if our bodies were two pieces of a puzzle, destined to match.

His hands on my ass guided me up and down on his dick. The motion was slow and building until he got impatient. Then, he picked me up and slammed me back down. My tits bounced in his face. All worries left my head.

The past was the past. Our future was a blurry haze on the horizon. All we had was the present. This very moment.

No matter where we went from here, there was one certainty. Austin and I were as addictive as heroin and as combustible as gasoline.

I just hoped we didn't go down in flames…again.

Sixteen

Austin

"So, you and Julia again?" Patrick asked the next week after work.

"Yep."

"And it's going well?"

I shrugged nonchalantly. "She screams at me in much better ways now."

Patrick laughed. "Good for you, man. I knew no one else would ever really do it for you after Julia."

"You never said anything."

Patrick shrugged. I gave him a skeptical look as I poured us both shots of whiskey from the stash in my office.

"I told Julia I was going to give up alcohol. I should probably get rid of all this shit."

"That's...a big deal, Austin."

"Yeah. I know."

Patrick took the shot I'd handed to him, and we each knocked one back. I'd been feeling like absolute shit all day. Withdrawals were a horrible, horrible fucking thing.

"Clearly, you're not going cold turkey," Patrick said, setting the shot down.

"No. I'm cutting back. Try to wean myself off of it. Not drinking around Jules. It's easier being sober when I'm with her."

"Harder at home, I'd imagine."

"And work."

"Well, let's trash this shit on the way to Jensen's office then."

We gathered up the last of my supplies and took them to the restroom. I felt a horrible pang go through me as we dumped the whiskey down the sink. The clink of the bottles in the trash can made my nerves shake. I knew I could do this. I was strong enough. *But, fuck...*

"So..." Patrick said as he pressed the button for the elevator, "I was talking to Mindi—"

I punched Patrick in the arm. "You are not seeing her again, are you?"

"She's a really good lay, man."

"She threatened to stab you with a butcher knife!" I cried in exasperation.

Patrick might be my best friend, but he was such an idiot sometimes.

"Okay. Well, that was...unfortunate."

"Unfortunate," I said with a snort.

"Anyway, Mindi said you stayed at their place."

"I got wasted and crashed there. Mags wasn't even around."

Patrick shot me a look that said, *I've been your best friend your whole life. I'm not an stupid.*

"She wasn't," I insisted.

"All right, dude. I believe you."

"Believe him about what?" Morgan asked, appearing at our side as we passed her office.

"That Austin isn't going to fuck up with Julia."

"You and Julia are back together?"

I nodded, as it was obvious. We'd spent all weekend together, getting reacquainted with each other's bodies and talking through the night. I'd felt like absolute shit on Saturday morning. Cold turkey had not been an option for me, but I had significantly reduced the amount of alcohol I was drinking. It was a start at least. And, if I didn't get wasted, then I couldn't do something stupid like end up at Mags's apartment again.

"Great!" Morgan said with enthusiasm. "I actually like her. She's not a dipshit or fucking crazy."

"I'm so glad I'm being met with Her Majesty's approval," I said sarcastically.

"Hey, dickface, don't make me kick your ass."

"Bring it, Mini Wright."

She glared at me. I knew she hated the nickname that Patrick had bestowed upon her.

"I will end you."

"Oh, Jesus, what trouble are you two getting into?" Landon asked. He had his arms crossed and was leaning against the closed door to Jensen's office.

"Austin started it!" Morgan cried.

"What are you? Twelve?" I asked.

She stuck her tongue out at me as Jensen's door opened. Landon stumbled back into the empty space.

"Calm down, children," Jensen said sarcastically.

"Austin's dating Julia!" Morgan said.

"I didn't realize I needed to make an official announcement."

Jensen stuck his hand out, and we shook.

"Congrats, man. I really like Julia."

"Thanks."

I laughed. I didn't know what to make of all this attention. No one usually gave two shits about who I was dating or not dating. I glanced between Jensen and Landon and realized... fuck, they'd probably already known. Heidi and Emery had

129

probably spilled the beans about the last week Julia and I'd spent together. They'd been waiting for me to say something.

"Is she going to come to Fourth of July with us?" Morgan asked just as Sutton, Maverick, and their son, Jason, appeared upstairs.

"What did I miss?" Sutton asked.

Maverick held Jason while still keeping a protective arm wrapped around Sutton.

"Family meeting," I said. "There's always something new going on."

"Julia and Austin are dating," Landon said.

"Knew it!" Sutton cried.

"You did call that one," Maverick said, staring down at her with adoration.

"I so did."

They shared a kiss that wasn't exactly PG, and Morgan made a gagging noise. Sutton laughed as she pulled back and smacked Maverick's ass.

"Don't be jealous, Mor," Sutton said, leaning her head on his shoulder.

Jason reached out his arms for Sutton. "Mommy!"

"Oh, come here, honey," she said as Maverick transferred their son to her.

"So, Fourth of July then?" Morgan asked.

"I'll ask her."

"Well, if that's settled," Jensen said, "we should probably head out to the Parade together."

Every year in Lubbock, a bunch of the construction companies and specialty builders erected over thirty homes in four of the biggest, most expensive subdivisions in town. For two weeks, the houses had an open house to showcase their talents as well as all the big features from subcontractors—interior design, shutters, fencing, and more. The event had grown over the years so that there were huge food-truck events on the weekends, and the builders and sponsors would set up raffles and private events at their locations.

Wright Construction had had a home in the Parade of Homes since its inception over six decades ago. Tonight was our big night with catering, an open bar, and, of course, our entire family on display.

I'd always thought that the idea of the parade was fun, but our part in it kind of sucked. I had never been the kind of person who liked to be on display. Small talk sucked, and it was always impossible to stay sober around all the cling-ons. Tonight would be a different night.

We piled into two cars to head over to the mansion that had been constructed for the parade. Unlike many of the other houses in the parade, the Wright home hadn't been built to spec—where the home was purchased ahead of time and then built to their specifications. We liked to showcase the best of the best, and by the end of the parade, it always sold anyway. Everyone in the process got to have more fun with the designs that way.

Maverick parked down the street from the Wright home, and the rest of us exited his Lexus SUV. There was already a line waiting to get into the house. I knew most people were probably here for the free booze. How could I blame them? But it felt silly, waiting in line to see a finished house that you weren't going to buy.

Jensen and Morgan smiled and shook hands with some of the people in line. I knew that, if I wanted to make an impression about the CFO position, I should be up there with them. But they couldn't actually be enjoying this part of the job, could they?

Sutton took one look at my face and cracked up. "I hate this part, too."

"It's the worst."

"The absolute worst," she agreed. "Maverick and I have plans to try to christen a bedroom and then leave."

I cracked up laughing. "You would."

"I think we have enough time before people get into the house."

I glanced over at my other siblings and saw that Sutton had already handed Jason off to Landon. *Sucker*.

"Hurry up," I said. "I'll cover as best I can."

She grinned like a fool, grabbed Maverick's hand, and then ran through the house.

"Where are they off to?" Landon asked.

"Just checking out the rest of the house," I lied.

I heard a laugh behind me that I recognized immediately. I turned around to find Julia entering the room with Emery and Heidi. She was glowing and dressed in a short black dress. I considered grabbing her hand and finding another bedroom. There were at least five in this house. Surely, we had time, too.

Julia caught my eye, drawn to me like a moth to a flame. Heidi and Emery exchanged a look between them and then nudged her toward me.

"Hey," she said, eyeing my suit.

"You look stunning."

I wrapped a possessive arm around her waist and bent in for a kiss. She was wearing some kind of cherry-flavored lip gloss. I flicked my tongue against her bottom lip to get a better taste. She moaned softly into my mouth and pulled back.

"Careful."

"Never with you."

Pink bloomed in her cheeks, and I thought about all the other places I'd made her flush all week. I really, really wanted to cut this entire event short.

"Heidi and Emery are excited we're together again."

"I noticed that. Jensen and Landon seemed to already know."

"Oh, yeah. I hope that's okay." She gave me a look of pure innocence. "I didn't think it was a secret."

"It's definitely not a secret."

"Well, good."

"Morgan wants you to come to Fourth of July with us."

"Oh? What are you guys doing?"

I laughed and put my hand in hers. Then, I brought our clasped hands up to my lips. "One day, we're going to get you to say *y'all*, babe."

"Not likely."

"For the Fourth, we go to the marathon downtown at the ass-crack of dawn. Then, there's a parade, we grill out, and there are fireworks at night."

"Count me in," she said with a giddy bounce to her step.

"Oh, also, I kind of got you something."

She glanced around uncomfortably and then back up at me. "Why?"

"Because I care about you."

"But…I didn't get anything for you."

"That's okay. This is to help with your promise."

"My…promise?" she asked skeptically.

I pulled out the paperwork I'd been carrying around all day to give to her. She took it out of my hand and read the headline.

"Austin, you didn't!"

"I did. I signed you up for the summer art class at one of the studios in the Art District."

"You can't do that."

"Well…I just did. And it's paid for you, so you can't back out."

She sputtered in confusion, looking down at the paper and then up at me and then back at the paper. "Austin!"

"Babe, I'm finding you inspiration. I said I would. Plus, I'll be there. So, consider it a date."

She shook her head in disbelief. Her eyes were looking up at me, as if it was the first time she'd ever seen me. "Why will you be there? You don't art."

"I know."

"And you're really going to come to a painting class all summer?"

"I really am."

"Damn you, Wright."

Then, she threw her arms around my neck and kissed me again with that sweet cherry flavor.

It was torture, letting her go. I could have disappeared, like Sutton and Maverick, and been really fucking happy. Julia might even be up for it. She was adventurous in bed, but I wanted to prove that I was in this for good. If I could give up alcohol…eventually…then I could hold off on sex in a public place. At least…this time.

"Go hang with Heidi and Emery. I have to do this for a while, and then we can head out," I told her.

"All right." Her eyes darted to the open bar. "Are you going to be okay with all the alcohol?"

"Yeah. I'm fine."

She frowned. "You say that, but I do want to help."

"You're helping, just being here."

It was true. When she was around, I was much less tempted to dive face-first into a bottle.

"Okay. Text me if you need me. I'm going to look around this house because, holy fuck, Austin."

I laughed. "Yeah, Jensen likes to go all out."

"That he does."

She kissed me one more time before running back to Heidi's and Emery's sides. Heidi hip-checked her, and they burst into laughter. Emery stuck her finger in Julia's face, and she held her hands up. Then, she pushed Emery and Heidi together, as if to say, *Don't worry; I won't break up this love affair.* Heidi slung her arms over both girls' shoulders, and then they disappeared into the next room.

Patrick appeared at my side. "Don't panic."

"Panic?" I asked in confusion. I tore my eyes from where Julia had disappeared to look at Patrick. "Why would I panic?"

"I didn't know they'd show up."

"They?"

But Patrick didn't have to tell me. I could see clear as day who he was talking about as Maggie and Mindi walked into the house. Maggie caught my eye with a characteristic smirk before walking straight to the bar.

"What the hell are they doing here?" I asked.

"I don't know. You said nothing was going on."

"Nothing *is* going on!"

"Okay. So then…she probably won't even come talk to you."

"Aren't you talking to Mindi again?"

Patrick frowned. "Define talking."

"I hate you."

Of course, Maggie steered directly toward me with Mindi hot on her heels as soon as they had drinks in hand. Maggie was tall with chestnut brown hair that barely brushed her shoulders, and she was wearing her standard-issue skimpy dress and heels. I'd hardly seen her in anything else. She was carrying a glass of white wine and a beer.

"For you," she said, offering me the beer. She gave me a heavy-lidded look of seduction. "Obviously."

"No, thanks," I said politely.

Her eyes expanded in surprise. "Are you turning down a beer?"

"Just did."

She laughed softly and pushed the drink into my hand. "Funny joke."

The beer was cold in my hand. The bartender had just popped the top off the glass bottle, and it was still fizzing slightly. She'd grabbed my favorite, of course. But there was a difference between having a shot to keep from throwing up from withdrawal and casually drinking a beer for no reason. I swallowed twice, hard, before passing it to Patrick. He took it without comment.

"What are you doing here, Mags?" I asked, irritation lacing every syllable.

She shot me a quizzical look. "Enjoying the parade, like everyone else."

"Uh, hey, Austin," Mindi said, trying to crack the tension.

"Mindi," I said with a nod.

"Why do you seem so offended that I'm here? Mindi was the one who told me that you were at our place. If you wanted to see me, all you had to do was ask."

"Well aware of that. Not interested," I said point-blank.

"What's with you?" Maggie asked. "First, you aren't drinking. I've never seen you without a drink in your hand. And, now, you can't even carry on a civil conversation with me?"

"I'm dating someone."

"So? That suddenly makes you unable to have any fun?"

"You should leave," I told her.

Just being in her presence was making me furious. I never felt like I had to have a drink to have a good time with Julia. Maggie was making it sound like I was a crazy person for stopping when every other person in my life was insisting that I had to.

"I'm a paying customer," Maggie said defiantly.

"Whatever."

I turned to walk away from her and nearly ran right into Julia. I grabbed her by her shoulders to steady us both.

"I was just coming to look for you," I said earnestly.

Her eyes drifted over my shoulder. "Before or after you talked to Maggie?" she bit out.

"She…I…that isn't what it looked like."

"I bet." Julia shook off my touch. "God, I am such an idiot."

"Jules," I called as she shook her head and then walked out of the house.

Seventeen

Austin

I dashed after Julia as she disappeared through the back door. This was the exact reason that I hadn't wanted Maggie to be here. I hadn't had contact with her in weeks. I'd had no clue she would be at the parade event. And I certainly hadn't wanted for Julia to see me talking to her. *Fuck. Fuck. Fuck!*

"Jules!" I called after her.

She didn't stop walking. She opened the gate to the fence and started down the driveway in the back and out into the alleyway. I followed her as she paced down the alley.

"Leave me alone," she called over her shoulder.

"No way in hell."

She finally whirled around and put her hands out. "I need space. Just leave me alone to process."

"Can't do that, Jules."

"Stop calling me that!" I cried. "I hate that nickname."

"You didn't have a problem with me calling you that when I was inside you."

"Sex! Is that all it's going to fucking come back to with you?" She ground her teeth together and kicked a stray rock.

"This isn't about sex. This is about you jumping to conclusions and getting pissed at me."

"I'm *not* pissed at you!"

I raised my eyebrows in question as she nearly shouted at me. "Sure sounds like you are."

"I'm mad at me."

"What? Why?" I asked in frustration.

I really, really did not want to be dealing with this shit right now. Julia and I were finally back together, finally in a good place again. It had seemed too good to be true. Seemed like the saying was right. If it looked like it, it probably was.

"God, don't you see it?" she asked. Her eyes met mine, and she looked ready to sprint away all over again. "This is the reason we broke up, Austin!"

"I know why we broke up."

"Really? Should I give you a refresher? Because you must have forgotten if Maggie was here."

"I didn't even know she'd be here!"

"Yeah, and last time, I had to find out that you had a fuck buddy the hard way! When I found her at your house, naked!"

"I know," I said softly.

"And then to find out that not only was she there, naked, as if this were some stupid mistake you had gone through, but she was also your fuck buddy! You had been together for a couple of *years*. On and off and on again. Apparently, whenever the other one gets bored."

"Jules, I know," I ground out.

"Yeah, well, it was wonderful to find out that the only reason you hooked up with me was because she was out of town for the holidays. You *used* me, Austin. You were *my* mistake. A Wright mistake. How ironic."

The memory of that night two years ago hit me fresh all over again. Julia and I had been together for the best six weeks of my life. The girl of my dreams. And then something had happened. I'd choked. I'd totally freaked out about my feelings for her.

It was stupid. I knew that now. I'd had a long-ass time to think about it. But catching real feelings for someone made me vulnerable. It made Julia vulnerable. And she didn't even know that loving me was as good as putting her Glock to her head and pulling the trigger.

I couldn't let that happen to her. And I hadn't been able to tell the truth. It was easier to let her think the worst about Maggie than to own up to how I felt about her.

"Maggie and I weren't together two years ago," I told her.

"I *saw* her in your bed, Austin! The day before Valentine's Day!"

"I know you did. I won't deny that she was there, and she was there to seduce me. That we'd been together as fuck buddies for a couple of years. And all of that." I held my palms up in front of me. "But we didn't hook up when you and I were together, and I wasn't with her that day."

"Then, what was she doing there?" Julia asked. Her voice was still as icy as a glacier, but at least she was listening to me.

"Exactly what you suspect she was doing there. She showed up as a surprise for me for Valentine's Day. Mags doesn't really care who she hurts when she wants something. She was dating someone then, too."

"Don't call her Mags," Julia snapped.

"I'm not going to try to justify what happened two years ago. I was an ass. I let you believe the worst about Maggie and me even though nothing was going on."

"You *let* me believe it." She snorted and glanced off at the horizon. "You didn't even tell me about Maggie. You let me find her!"

"To be fair, I didn't know she was going to be there when we showed up at my place."

"That's not fair! That's bullshit. We dated for six weeks and not one word about any ex-girlfriends. Not one!"

"Did you tell me about any of your exes?" I shot back. I ran a hand back through my hair in frustration. "We didn't exactly have the who-was-the-last-person-you-fucked conversation. We were too busy enjoying our lives and moving on."

Julia didn't meet my eyes and seemed to be contemplating what to say. Eventually, she just shook her head. "I hate this. I hate arguing with you."

"You do?" I asked skeptically.

"I hate it when it's about this shit. It was two years ago. I'd thought I was over it. But then I saw Maggie standing there so casually while you talked to her, and I just lost it. I'm not over Maggie. I don't like seeing you two together. I'll never be okay with that."

"I think that's totally understandable. I was telling her to leave. I don't want her there."

She sighed. "But she's always going to be there. Lubbock isn't small, but it's small enough. With my luck, we're going to run into her again."

"I can't guarantee that you'll never see her again. Unfortunately, Patrick is talking to Mindi again, and that's her new roommate."

"Maggie and Mindi?" Julia asked with an exaggerated eye roll. "Great. Now, I'm going to hate M and Ms."

I took a step forward and reached for Julia. She yanked her arm back and shook her head. Things were not good.

Once again, I had fucked up.

The first time had been when she found out about my drinking. She'd gone home to Ohio for Christmas, pissed at me for not revealing my bad habits. I'd shrugged it off, like it didn't matter, and she'd gotten irrationally pissed at me.

When she'd come home, she'd decided to give us a try again. Then, Maggie had happened.

Now, here I was again, with my old issues hindering me from moving forward all over again.

"I don't care if you hate them both. I'm telling you that, two years ago, I was so afraid of my feelings for you that I let you believe that Maggie and I had been together rather than admitting how I was feeling."

"That doesn't even make sense!"

"I know," I said. I couldn't tell her why it made sense to me in my fucked up head. But it did. It had at the time at least. "But I told you I wasn't going to make the same mistakes. I want us to work, Jules."

"And you haven't seen Maggie since we've been together?" she asked hesitantly.

I shook my head. "That was the first time I'd seen her in weeks."

"Sounds familiar."

"It's not the same. I don't want Maggie. I want nothing to do with her. She doesn't understand the first thing about me. She tried to offer me a beer, for fuck's sake."

Julia leaned toward me, as if the very thought of tempting a recovering alcoholic made her visibly nauseated. "She didn't!"

"Well, she doesn't know that I'm not drinking like I was before. She thought I was joking."

"That's shitty."

"You get me." I reached out and took her hand this time. "You help me. We work together. I'm not afraid to admit how I feel now. You have to believe that I wouldn't let Maggie come between us a second time."

I threaded our fingers together. She stared down at our clasped hands. Mine were so much bigger than her small, delicate hands. I was just relieved that she hadn't pulled away.

"I don't know how to explain this, Austin. I feel like a crazy person for getting so worked up, but I'm so worried about the future. I want a future with you. I want to believe that's possible."

"It is," I insisted.

"And it's not so much that Maggie is here. It's a public place. She could show up anywhere, I suppose. It's more the trend. My fear is that the past will repeat itself. Then, I'll be the idiot for falling for it twice." She stroked her thumb up my hand. "Seeing her brought all my old fears to the surface. I don't want Maggie to be a backup plan."

"She's not."

She took a deep breath and then expelled it. "I'm sorry I freaked out like that."

"No need to apologize. If I saw you with Trevor, I'd probably blow a gasket, too."

She wrinkled her nose. "You cannot be jealous of Trevor. He's so…Trevor."

"Insanely jealous."

"No way."

"The thought of putting my fist through his face did cross my mind every time I saw him."

Her big brown eyes rounded. "I never would have guessed. You always acted like you didn't care."

"I pushed you away. I hurt you. I figured seeing you with someone like that was my punishment."

"What about the times you came on to me?"

I shrugged unapologetically. "Usually, I was drunk enough to let my feelings show."

"You have a funny way of showing that you like me."

"I do." I nodded my head back toward the house. I was glad that this conversation hadn't completely dissolved. There was no fucking way I was going to lose her over Maggie again. Not when things had been going so well. "Want to head back in?"

She sighed. "Is she going to still be there?"

"I can get Jensen on it. He's the fixer."

"I don't know. Maybe I should just go."

"Jules…"

"It was a wake-up call. I don't trust her. I don't trust her motives. I think, if she feels threatened, she'll do stupid shit. I've known other girls like her. I don't want any part of it."

I slipped my hand up to her cheek and memorized every inch of her beautiful face. "Then, I'll leave with you."

"Don't you have family stuff?"

"Screw family stuff."

"No, Austin," she said with a resigned sigh as she disentangled herself from me. "I think I want to be alone."

"Are you sure?"

"Yeah."

"Are we okay?"

"We're fine," she said, repeating the mantra I'd said every time she asked about my drinking.

I didn't realize how hollow it sounded until that moment.

Eighteen

Julia

We weren't fine.

Or at least…I wasn't fine.

Maggie made my skin crawl. Seeing her stupid, flawless face made me go berserk. And, for the last two years, I'd believed that Austin had used me for sex while Maggie was out of town. If he couldn't get it from his fuck buddy, why not make a new one when she was gone? Easy enough.

I'd been crushed.

It was the first time I had opened my heart since I left Ohio and all my baggage. For a long time, I'd never thought I'd be interested in letting someone else in. Then, Austin had happened. And then Maggie.

It hurt my head to think about what he had revealed to me in the alleyway. *Why wouldn't he have just broken up with me if he didn't want to fall for me? Why had he let me believe that he and Maggie were together?*

In my experience, if something seemed to make perfect sense, like Maggie and Austin, then it was usually true. But he had been so sincere that he'd used Maggie as an excuse. There had been no waver in his eyes. No flick off to the right. No shifting of his feet.

He had explained the situation in such a calm and collected manner that it seemed as if it was a huge relief to him. That maybe he had been waiting a long time to tell me the truth. Why he had concealed it all in the first place was a mystery to me. I didn't usually piss off and push away the people I cared about. And he'd claimed no excuse for his actions.

Had he really caught feelings for me and scared himself off?

Either way, I felt stupid for leaving. Heidi would have barged back into that place and put the smackdown on Maggie. I just didn't want to deal.

So, I drove home and crashed down on the couch after carefully locking the door back up. A text dinged on my phone from Heidi.

Where the hell did you go?

I never told Heidi about what had happened with Austin two years ago. She probably wouldn't even know who Maggie was. And, if I told her the truth, she might actually find Maggie and do exactly what I'd envisioned.

Austin and I got into a fight.

Again?

Yeah. I think we're okay. Just…shit with our last breakup.

And that is?

I really don't want to talk about it.

Okay. Girl time. Emery and I will be there in ten.

Heidi, you don't have to!

Want to. See you in a minute.

I walked into my room and stripped out of the black dress I'd put on for the event. I was hanging it back up on a hanger when my eyes snagged on olive green amid the layers of black. I grabbed the bomber jacket I'd been looking for, for weeks.

"What the hell?" I grumbled.

Had I overlooked it this whole time? That pissed me off. I couldn't believe it was here all along. I shook my head. I was seriously losing my mind.

Replacing the jacket, I changed into shorts and an oversize T-shirt. Then, I pulled my hair up into a high pony. Heidi and Emery were prompt. It only took ten minutes to get across town, but they must have booked it.

"Hey," I said, unlocking the door and letting them inside.

"What the hell happened?" Heidi asked.

Emery patted me on the shoulder, and Heidi pulled me into a hug.

I methodically locked the place back up before turning to face them. I knew it was time. I had to tell them what had happened. And they were going to hate Austin as much as I had for the last two years. Though I was more confused than ever.

So, I spilled the beans. I started at the beginning and didn't leave anything out. Heidi and Emery were rapt listeners. Both angry and disgusted in the right parts. Both agreeing to go find this Maggie girl and make her regret her decision.

"Okay. So, all this time, you thought that Austin had used you for sex until Maggie got home? Then, he'd cheated on you as soon as she was back?" Heidi asked.

"Yep. Pretty much."

"Why the hell didn't you tell me this? We could have hated on him together."

"I hardly knew you at the time," I finally said, sinking into the chair opposite where Heidi and Emery sat on the couch.

"That's true, Heidi," Emery cut in. "Even you said you liked to wait a year to make serious friends because so many people leave Lubbock."

Heidi waved her off. "Okay, fine. But then later?"

"I don't know. I was embarrassed." I shrugged off their looks filled with pity. "Do you think he's telling the truth about Maggie now? That he lied about what had happened and only let me believe that something had happened because he was basically scared of his feelings?"

"That actually sounds like Austin," Heidi said.

Emery nodded. "Classic Wright behavior."

"Well, what do I do? I cannot deal with Maggie again."

"Honestly? I know it's hard, considering what he put you through in the past, but maybe you should trust him," Heidi said. "I know; I'm the worst to give this kind of advice. I didn't trust anything Landon said. I didn't ever believe he'd divorce Miranda. Not until the evidence was directly in my face. But Austin's bachelor life is pretty legendary. If he's willing to try to be with you, I think it's worth it."

"To be honest, Julia," Emery said, "the reason we've been so excited about this is because Austin has *never* really dated. He has flings. And he's not treating you like a passing dalliance."

"I want to believe that. I do." I tilted my head back onto the cushion and stared up at the ceiling. "My life hasn't always been easy. Trusting people is really difficult for me. After Austin hurt me, it confirmed everything that I'd thought I knew about him. Giving him a second chance was unfathomable."

"Then, why did you do it?" Heidi asked.

I met her eyes and smiled at the thought of Austin bringing me to the top of the canyon to show me the sunset and Austin walking me around the art gallery on First Friday and Austin losing so bad at carnival games that we got Waffle out of pity and Austin getting me art classes all summer.

"When we're not at each other's throats, we're perfect."

"Maybe that's enough?" Emery said.

"Maybe it is."

Despite my conversation with Heidi and Emery, a bubble had burst. A part of me had cracked when I saw Austin and Maggie together, and I didn't know how to fix it.

Austin had come over after he finished at the Parade of Homes. He'd apologized again for the situation, for the past, for everything. He'd reassured me he wasn't interested in Maggie. And I even believed him.

He could have Maggie if he wanted. He'd had Maggie for a long time. They had this weird relationship as it was. She wasn't out of town or anything, so he didn't have to find a new girlfriend to make up for the lack of sex. And Heidi and Emery were right; when I thought about it, it was clear that he cared for me.

I cared for him.

He cared for me.

Things were good.

But not right.

By the time our art class was rolling around, I wasn't even sure if I should show up. Though I adored art and people said I had a scrap of talent, I didn't ever think it was something that just came to me. Not even in college. It'd irritated my professors so much when I turned in something shitty after having no real inspiration and not wanting to draw because I was capable of so much more.

All artists were insane in one way or another. Creativity didn't grow on trees, but inspiration could strike like lightning.

With a sigh, I changed into loose-fit jeans and a black T-shirt that I didn't mind getting paint on. Because, let's be honest, I always got paint on myself.

Austin had said that he'd meet me there after the gym. I didn't know how he spent so much time there. The idea of going to a gym that often made me break out in hives. So many sweaty bodies and dirty equipment and judgment. My couch was a much better alternative.

Unfortunately, I had to leave the house and my precious couch. I shakily locked up behind me and drove downtown. The studio where Austin had signed me up was in a small brick building on the Art Trail. I parked in the same tow zone Emery had parked in then. There didn't seem to be anywhere else to park, so I sure hoped this was okay.

Nerves hit me fresh before I even got into the studio. My stomach was in my throat as I stood outside.

What if I forgot how to paint? What if I totally sucked? What if everyone else was amazing and showed me up?

It was ridiculous to even think that. Talent didn't disappear overnight. I knew that logically in my brain, but logic wasn't winning. Art was such a solitary endeavor that I couldn't help but feel intimidated as I strode into the new space.

My eyes swept the open room as a wash of familiarity swept over me. Easels were set up in a circle around a platform with a cliché bowl of fruit at the center. I couldn't even explain the number of times I'd had to draw a piece of fruit.

"Let me guess," an African American woman said, approaching me. She had kinky, curly hair that was probably the most amazing thing I'd ever seen and librarian glasses. "Julia?"

"That's me."

"Wonderful. I'm Nina. I'll be teaching this session. Grab a canvas, a palette, and some paints. We'll get started soon."

"Thank you."

I did as I had been told and found a space for both me and Austin. I absentmindedly fiddled with a paintbrush and tried not to make eye contact with anyone, so I wouldn't have to make small talk. But class time was about to start, and Austin still wasn't here.

"Is this seat taken?" a Hispanic girl asked. She had stick-straight hair and a great smile.

"Uh…yeah. Sorry."

"No problem!"

I watched the girl circle the room as I chewed on my nail. A bad habit I'd never gotten rid of. I double-checked my phone. One minute until class time. Austin still wasn't here.

I shot him a text message.

Hey, where are you? Did you decide not to come to the class? It's about to start.

I waited another minute, but there was no answer. *What the hell? Was he in the car, rushing here, and couldn't get to his phone?* He had a stick shift after all. It was feasible. You weren't supposed to text while driving. But, still, it seemed strange that he had signed us both up for this class, and now, he wasn't even going to show.

Not strange…wrong.

Like…what the fuck had he been thinking?

"Hey," the girl said, having made it back to me. "It looks like this is the only seat left. Is it cool if I sit here?"

"Sure," I huffed.

I knew I probably should have been friendlier, but getting stood up to an art class Austin had paid for was doing nothing for me. Not a thing.

"Okay," Nina said, moving to the center of the room. "Thank you all so much for coming out today. It's the start of a brand-new session, and I have a special treat for you today. Last session, we worked on portraits. We're going more

K.A. LINDE

advanced this session with life drawing, also known as figure drawing."

I sat up straight in my seat. *Figure drawing? Like...for real?*

"We're lucky to have a volunteer to sit in for this session. Please remember to give him our full respect. His job isn't any easier than yours."

My eyes were glued to the back door of the studio, as I waited to see who the hell would volunteer to sit for a figure drawing. Standing in one position for an hour, completely naked, wasn't my idea of fun.

Then, the door opened, and my jaw dropped open.

Austin took a step into the room.

Nineteen

Julia

"Oh my God!" I gasped.

The girl next to me shot me a quick look. "He's pretty cute, right?"

I laughed hysterically and then covered my face. *Oh my God! Oh my God! Oh my God! What is my life right now?*

Austin had said that he was going to be in the class with me all session. That he knew he didn't art. That it wasn't a problem. So…of course, he wasn't worried. Because he wasn't actually doing any painting. *He* was the model.

"You're bright red, honey," she said, patting my shoulder. "It's okay. Is this your first time having someone sit for you?"

I met her dark eyes and nearly lost it. "No," I got out.

She looked at me, as if I was a crazy person, but I couldn't stop laughing. Austin was going to be naked in a room of twenty people. They were all going to draw him. *Oh my God!*

He caught my eyes across the room and grinned like a fool. No wonder he'd gone to the gym and avoided my text. He must have been warming up all his sexy freaking muscles before everyone started to draw them. I could see the definition in every single abdominal muscle. All the way down to the sweet V, which trailed down into the sheet.

Nina began to explain everything we were supposed to do in the next hour, but she sounded like one of the adults from Charlie Brown. All I saw was Austin walk onto the platform, find a comfortable enough position, and then drop the sheet.

I covered my eyes with my hands. *How many times had I seen Austin naked?* Yet here I was, and I couldn't even look at him. *How embarrassing! And totally crazy! And amazing!*

He'd said that he did this, so I could find inspiration. The last time we'd been together, I'd drawn him with my charcoals as we lounged around his house. It had been a dream. The inspiration and creativity had come to me like nothing else. Austin Wright was my muse.

And, somehow, he had known that. Or at least, he had done something this outrageous to try to snap me out of the funk I was in. He cared enough to do anything to make me remember my love for my art.

I slowly peeled my hands back and stared up at him in his pose. Our eyes locked, and all I saw was desire in the lines of his face. If he wasn't careful, that wouldn't be the only place desire would be evident.

"You should probably get started," the girl next to me said, dragging me away from Austin's body. "We only have an hour."

"Thanks," I muttered.

Then, I got started.

Either Austin was a genius or extremely lucky because my hands seemed to work of their own accord. Muse, he was indeed. Everything in me that usually locked up when I looked at a canvas dissolved like salt in water.

By the end of class, I had a not-so-terrible start to a painting of Austin in the nude. I'd thought that I had perfectly inspected his body before this, but I had never looked at it quite as intensely.

"Hey," the girl next to me said. "You should totally stay after and talk to him."

"What?" I asked, distracted.

"He was staring at you the entire class. I'd be shocked if he didn't ask for your number."

"You think so?"

"Totally."

Then, she winked at me and sauntered off.

Yeah…I bet he would like my number.

Austin was covering himself up with the sheet again as Nina went over to thank him for coming in. I cleaned up my supplies and put my painting away with the others, so I could work on it next week. Once the class cleared, I walked up to Austin, shaking my head as I approached.

"Austin Wright," I said with a short laugh.

"Julia Banner," he said in a teasing tone.

"I cannot believe you just did that."

He gave me a confident smirk. "Why? I'm not self-conscious."

"That is blatantly obvious."

"Actually, it was kind of the bargain I made to get you in the class," he said, nodding his head to the back room for him to change.

"You had to bargain to get me in?"

"Well, the class was full. I had a friend who works the Art Trail and suggested that he could get you in, but they needed a model. So, I sort of volunteered to do it if it would get you in."

I stared at him, slack-jawed. "That's…I mean, why? Why did you do that?"

He looked confused. "You know why. For you, of course. Look," he said, running a hand back through his hair, "I know that things have been weird between us since Maggie."

I winced at her name. "Yeah."

"I get why you're hesitant to jump into this feetfirst. I hurt you. And seeing her brought that all back to the surface. But I'm not dipping my toe in the pool with you, Jules."

"I know, I know," I muttered.

He reached for my paint-smeared hands and brought them to his lips. He slowly kissed his way across each individual knuckle. His eyes remained glued to mine as he took his time with my hands.

"This isn't some stunt. Watching you paint was addictive. The way you looked at me, babe." He shuddered. "It was a work of restraint not to get turned on while watching you do what you love."

He nipped at my thumb. My body heated at the gesture.

"Was it that much of a turn-on?"

He moved my hand to his dick, covered only by a thin sheet. "What do you think?"

I wrapped my hand around the length of him and stroked up once. "Looks like you were into it."

"I was half-tempted to make you be the model with me. I wouldn't have minded one bit if you were naked underneath me on that platform."

"Filthy," I whispered.

"I don't think I was the only one thinking dirty thoughts," he ground out, walking me backward into the stone wall.

"I can't believe you sat naked for me. For an entire class of people so that I could get into a studio." My heart sang for him. Perhaps I should have been upset that he had shown off his beautiful body to all these people. But all I could think about was how lucky I was to have someone who cared. And how fucking hot he looked naked.

"I can sit naked for you anytime."

My hand slid back up his cock, and then, with one easy tug, I pulled the sheet off his body. He was naked before me one more time.

"Watching you naked for an hour like this was torture."

He smirked once, and then his lips were on mine. The past week of uncertainty between us vanished as quickly as it had come. I wasn't completely over what had happened, but big gestures went a long way with me. The class in and of itself was a big deal. Sitting nude to get me into the class was above and beyond. Now, I wanted every inch of that fucking sexy body against me.

Our bodies crashed together in the back room of the studio. Neither of us knew how much time we'd have before Nina came looking for us. Neither of us knew if we'd get caught. And maybe that was half the fun.

Austin snagged my jeans and ripped them down my thighs. His hand thrust up between my legs, rubbing me none too gently. I moaned louder than I probably should have. Austin pressed his other hand over my mouth.

"Shh, baby," he crooned as he wet his fingers and circled my clit until I was shaking.

My knees threatened to give out as need shot through me. "Please," I whimpered.

Austin pulled me off the wall and bent me forward over one of the art tables. I reached across the table and gripped the other side. He angled his cock to my pussy and then pressed into me. As he took my body, I bit my bottom lip so hard that I tasted the tangy rust of my own blood.

His strokes were fast and forceful, stretching me open for him and taking me. Owning me. I loved it. I loved it so much that I couldn't even think straight. I always loved my pleasure mixed with just enough pain. The line was so thin. The edge so close.

Austin swiped a finger through my wetness, and then I felt the pressure against my pucker. He didn't wait for permission or to see if I wanted it. He just pushed his finger into my ass. The sensation shocked my body, and I gasped.

It was hardly our first time doing any kind of anal play, but it still surprised me every time it happened. How good it felt. How confident he was with playing with me. How he knew exactly how to use it to draw out my pleasure.

And here we were, in the back of the art studio, with no time at all, and I was getting fucked in both holes. Bliss.

"Oh God," I moaned, clenching him as hard as I thought possible.

"Come for me, Jules."

"Yes," I said. "Yes. God, yes."

My release crashed through me like a tidal wave. I saw red as I shook from head to toe. My orgasm was so tight that I felt Austin follow in the wake of my tsunami.

I banged my head forward on the table when I finally was able to relax. Austin bent over me and kissed my neck twice before pulling out of me. I stayed there a few seconds longer before righting my jeans. Austin was hastily throwing his clothes back on just as Nina knocked on the back door.

"Everything okay back there?"

Austin and I looked at each other.

Oh, yes. Things were a hell of a lot better than okay.

Once clothes were straight, we profusely thanked Nina for allowing me to join the class. She gave us both knowing looks but chose to ignore whatever indiscretion had happened in the back.

"It's my pleasure. Thank you for volunteering to sit for us. I've been looking for someone for weeks," Nina said.

"It wasn't as bad as I'd thought," Austin said.

"Well, good. I'll see you both next week."

"Bye," I said.

Austin slung an arm around my shoulders as we walked out of the studio together. I could feel that euphoria of a new relationship settling back over us. That feeling of rightness returning. It wasn't a hundred percent better. Things like that didn't get better overnight. But, for the first time in a long, long time, I thought that maybe, just maybe, love could conquer all.

"Where's your car?" Austin asked as we approached his Alfa Romeo across the street.

I pointed to the parking lot next to the studio. Then, I took a second glance. And a third.

"Wait…where the fuck is the Tahoe?"

I jogged across the street in frustration and circled the place I knew the SUV should have been parked. But the parking lot was completely empty. There had only been two other cars parked by me. They'd probably left with the class, but where was my car?

"Must have been towed," Austin said.

"Fuck!"

"It's fine. Call the company on the sign and see if it's there. I can drive you over."

"I fucking hate tow companies," I growled.

But I did as he'd said. The guy who answered confirmed that my SUV had been impounded in the last hour, and I needed to come by and pay the fine to get it.

"Thanks," I muttered sarcastically before hanging up on the guy. "Just my luck."

Austin pulled me into a kiss. "Don't let this ruin our date. It happens to everyone at some point. It'll be fine."

"You're right. I know. But ugh!"

We hopped into his car and drove over to the towing company. There she was. My black Tahoe, sitting all pretty. I walked up to the station where the guy I'd called was working. I handed over my ID and a debit card to pay the fucking one-hundred-and-eighty-dollar fee.

"I'm here for the Tahoe."

"Sure thing," he said. He handed me a paper to fill out and ran my card.

"I can't believe you guys even towed that parking lot. People park there all the time."

He shrugged. "The company that owns it called it in. Bad luck."

I rolled my eyes. Of course the company had called it in on the day I was there. Between this and the break-in, I was totally running out of luck.

"You're all good to go," the guy said, handing me a receipt and a copy of the paperwork I'd filled out.

"Thanks."

I snatched the stuff out of his hand and flagged down Austin. "All good to go. The company called in the cars there for the art studio."

"Assholes."

"Right?"

"At least we got it all settled."

"Yeah," I said, dragging his lips against mine again. "Come over?"

"Absolutely."

"See you there."

He nodded and then headed back to his car. I jumped in the Tahoe, and before I drove away, I took a deep breath and let it out. *Just bad luck. This shit happened to everyone. It didn't mean anything. Not a thing.*

Twenty

Julia

"Why the hell am I awake this early?" I asked, squinting blearily into the hot West Texas sun.

It was only eight o'clock, and already, it was ninety-five degrees outside. The weather was hot and dry and dusty. I could already see the characteristic red haze on the horizon that meant this Fourth of July weekend was doomed.

"Maverick is in the marathon," Sutton said next to me. Her son, Jason, was passed out on a blanket on the parade line, and I seriously considered joining him. "I had to be here before seven. Be glad you got to miss the opening and all that. I barely got a kiss before he took off."

"Why would anyone want to run a marathon in this Texas heat?"

Sutton shrugged. "He's obsessed. This is his third this year. He's constantly training. He runs, like, a hundred miles a week. Ten to fifteen every morning before he goes to work."

My eyes rounded as large as plates. "Um…that sounds horrible."

"Doesn't it?" she said with a laugh. "But I like him sexy and sweaty. Jason usually naps when Mav gets back before work. Very convenient."

I laughed. "Oh, I bet."

"How long does it take for Heidi to get waters?" Sutton grumbled. "It's so effing hot out here." She fanned herself with her hand and sighed. With warmth, her eyes drifted down to her sleeping son. "At least he's happy."

"Where's everyone else anyway?" I asked. "I didn't think that I would be the first one here or else I would have slept in."

"As if Heidi would have let you sleep in."

"Truth."

"All the guys and Mor are bringing in the first interview candidate."

"For the CFO position?"

Sutton nodded. "Some guy from California."

"Why the hell would he come here for the Fourth of July?"

"No idea. I'm only half in the know since I'm not working for the company." She flipped her head over and pulled her ombré'd brown-and-blonde hair up into a ponytail. "Not that I want to work for the company."

"Well, you have Jason."

"Even if I didn't," she said swiftly.

"I didn't want to work with my family either," I said softly. Not that it was even remotely relatable to what her family did.

"It's just…they all expect it, you know?" Sutton said with a sigh. "It's not enough that Mav works there. Mor looks down on me because I want to stay home. There's nothing wrong with loving babies and wanting to raise a family!"

"I think you should do whatever makes you happy. It's your life."

Sutton grinned wickedly. "Oh, I do."

"Here you go, bitches," Heidi said, tossing each of us a water bottle.

I glanced around at all the children in the vicinity. "Language?"

"Eh, they'll hear it one day." She shrugged. "So, I heard from Landon, and he should be here soon. They just found a parking spot. And Emery is coming with her sister's family."

"Oh, Jason will be so happy that Lilyanne and Bethany are here!" Sutton said, referring to Emery's sister, Kimber's, kids.

I downed my water bottle while we waited for everyone to show up. It was supposed to get up to an unspeakable one hundred twelve degrees today. I was already melting, and it was only going to get worse.

But I couldn't stop thinking about the interviews for the CFO position. Austin had been doing so well. It was one thing to know that interviews were going to go on. To know that he wasn't going to get the job. It was another thing entirely to see the interviews happening and have the person in his space. I really didn't want anything like that to make him relapse.

Emery and Kimber along with her husband, Noah, and their two kids showed up first, waking Jason up from his nap in the process. He didn't seem to mind after he saw Bethany. She was only six months older than him, and they got along great. Lilyanne was the oldest, bossing them around like oldest siblings did.

The first marching band was coming down Buddy Holly Avenue when the rest of the Wrights showed up. Jensen was in the lead with a guy to his right, who was somehow even taller than Jensen. Didn't see many guys like that. Morgan was dwarfed on the other side of the new guy. Landon, Austin, and Patrick followed in their wake.

It was like the Cullens entering the high school cafeteria. People stopped and stared at the gorgeous, untouchable Texas royalty. They seemed oblivious to the attention. Of course, they probably were used to it.

"Hey, everyone," Jensen said when he reached the spot Sutton had been saving for all of us for over an hour. "I'd like to introduce David Calloway. He's here all weekend, interviewing with the company. You've already met Emery, but this is her family. This is my little sister, Sutton, with her son, Jason, and Austin's girlfriend, Julia."

David held his hand out and shook with everyone. "Pleasure to meet you all. Thank you for letting me crash your family holiday."

"That's all right," Sutton said. "The more, the merrier."

We all said our own welcome, and then the formalities dissipated since we were overtaken by the marching band.

Austin moved to my side and kissed me full on the mouth. "Fuck, I missed you," he said against my lips.

"I missed you, too. How are you doing with all of this?"

He shrugged and tugged me a bit further from the rest of his family. "It's fine."

"You say that, and I don't believe you."

"Okay. It fucking sucks. The entire thing feels utterly ridiculous. This guy is some big shot from Silicon Valley. What the fuck does he want to do with Wright Construction? For that matter, what the fuck does he even know about the business? He's never been in construction before. I know he's qualified, but we'd have to train him from the start. I already know the job. I've always known the job. The whole thing could be avoided so easily if they just went back to the board."

It was the first time I'd heard Austin talk so frankly about wanting the job. I knew that he had been mad and had been trying to stop drinking to make himself look better for the company. Also, for his health and me, and I was sure a million other reasons in his head. But he really sounded like he cared here.

"You really appreciate this company, don't you?"

"Yes," he said automatically. He ran a hand back through his hair and glanced off to see the kids rushing the brick-lined street to grab candy. "I feel like this was an eye-opener."

"How so?"

"Like I've just been getting by. I didn't really care what happened as long as I could continue my life the way it was. Now…that doesn't feel like enough."

It was probably because he was thinking clearly for the first time in years. With a depressant clogging his system, it was no surprise that he hadn't given two fucks about what happened in his life. And, now that he was pulling way back, he was seeing all the mistakes he'd made.

"What are you going to do about it?" I asked.

He shrugged. "What can I do?"

"Anything you set your mind to."

"I can't get the CFO position."

"Do you really want it?"

He opened his mouth and then closed it. "No one's ever really asked me that."

"Well?"

"I do want it. But I don't know if I want it because it was always the position I thought I would get or if it's because that's what I want to do with the rest of my life."

"Then, maybe figure out what you *do* want to do with the rest of your life and go from there."

He swept an arm around my waist. "What would I do without you?"

"You'd be lost," I assured him.

"Probably true."

"So, what do you think of this David guy besides the fact that you don't think he should get the position?"

"I didn't say that. I said that we'd have to train him." Austin sighed and rolled his eyes dramatically. "I kind of like the guy."

"So begrudging."

"I really want to hate him."

"But you don't?"

"Nah. He seems like a good guy, smart as a whip, and charming. It's kind of not fair."

"As if any of you Wrights know about what's fair."

"Watch it, babe," he said with a grin.

I laughed and dragged him back over to his family. We sat on a quilt to watch the parade pass us. Austin grabbed us breakfast biscuits at the halfway point. I chowed down, enjoying the ease with which I now fit into the Wright family unit. It was crazy to me to think that, during Memorial Day weekend, I had been an interloper on their festivities, and now that I was dating Austin, I fit right in. It had been a long time since I felt like I was part of a family. And the Wrights were above and beyond.

I found myself really relaxing for the first time in a long, long time. Austin made me feel safe. As if it wasn't me versus the world for once. I wanted to keep my guard up, but I couldn't seem to do it. Despite my past, I wanted to get lost in Austin. After our art classes, it was hard not to see how sincere he was about our relationship. And even better was there hadn't been any more Maggie sightings. No more room to second-guess our newfound happiness.

Once the parade finally ended, the first of the marathon runners started to come to the finish line, which had been erected only a dozen yards from where we were seated. Sutton had clearly picked this spot on purpose.

"It'll probably be another hour before Mav comes through," Sutton explained to the rest of her family. "These people are insane with their times."

"Watch out, Sutton. You might need a twenty-six-point-two sticker for the back of your car soon," Morgan teased.

"Mav already has one," she said, not taking the bait.

"I know how much you love running."

"Adore it. My favorite thing ever." Sutton gagged. "I like it as much as you like babies."

Morgan cracked up. "I like Jason."

"He doesn't count. You have to love him."

"Fair."

"You both are ridiculous," I said with a laugh.

"Truth," Morgan said. "I don't like babies. Sutton hates running. What about you?"

"Heights. I've never liked them, but a couple of years ago, I…" I trailed off. *What the hell had I been about to say? I couldn't tell them that story.* "I don't know. They just freak me out."

"Understandable," Sutton said.

"I don't mind heights. It's the falling that would bother me," Morgan said.

Sutton laughed and pushed Morgan. "They go hand in hand!"

"Yeah, they do," I said softly.

I was glad when they changed the subject.

David came and sat down on our blanket. He was dressed comfortably, like the rest of us, in khakis and a cerulean polo. He and Morgan seemed to hit it off right away. I found that most people got along with Morgan if they had a real personality and didn't threaten her family. She would cut you faster than you could blink if you did anything to her family. But seeing her with David made it very obvious that they could work together well.

"And you work for the company, too?" he asked.

I nodded. "I do. I'm head of HR."

"Wonderful to meet you. Did you grow up here as well?"

"No, I'm the only transplant. I moved here from Ohio."

"That must have been a big change."

"It was," I agreed. "I would assume as big as coming from northern California."

He laughed easily. "Yes. Though you have snow."

"True. It doesn't snow that much here."

Morgan rolled her eyes. "It snows enough for me."

"I'm glad I never have to shovel another driveway in my life."

"I could see that," David said. "Things seem…slower here. California is always go, go, go. Do you love it?"

"Well, I would say that Wright is still go, go, go," I told him. "But Lubbock is definitely a slower pace. It has that nice small-town vibe in a bigger city."

"I've noticed that. I like it so far. Different than I expected." His eyes turned to Sutton. "And you don't work for the company, right?"

"I'm the only one," she said, though her eyes were glued to Jason where he played with Bethany and Lilyanne.

"He's adorable. Yours right?"

She nodded. "He looks just like his dad though. I had to carry him for nine months, and he came out looking like someone else. Not exactly fair."

David laughed boisterously. It was the first completely genuine look I'd seen on his face. I could see why everyone liked him.

I turned to Austin and found him joking around with Patrick. Their bromance was pretty ridiculous, but at the same time, I enjoyed it. I liked that Austin wasn't a loner. I liked everything about this situation right now.

I had just about had as much heat as I could handle before the Wright barbeque this afternoon. I turned to tell Austin that maybe we should head out when Sutton jumped to her feet. Someone was breathlessly screaming her name.

My eyes shot to a girl wearing a marathon number and flagging as she approached Sutton.

"Annie," Sutton said, "what's going on with you?"

"Mav," Annie got out. "Mav...Mav, he collapsed."

"What?" she gasped. Her body was so still. As if she couldn't process what had just been said. "Is he okay? Where is he?"

"About a mile back. They were going to send an EMT, but I just took off to come get you. They're taking him to the hospital. I don't know what's wrong. We had almost made it all the way. One minute, we were joking about hugging you with

how sweaty we were. The next, he was on the ground. You...
you need to get to the hospital right away."

My jaw dropped open at her words. Maverick had collapsed
while running, and they had to rush him to the hospital. That
wasn't normal. And Sutton was as white as a ghost.

"We'll take care of Jason," Kimber said at once, shuffling
him in with her kids.

"Thank you," Sutton gasped out before dashing from the
parade route without another word.

Morgan chased after her.

I offered her friend Annie a bottle of water. She gratefully
took it in her shaky hands and downed it.

"You can come with us, Annie," Jensen offered.

"Thank you," she said, abandoning her number, so close
to the finish line.

"We should all probably go to the hospital to find out
what's going on," Jensen said. He began apologizing to David,
who immediately fended him off.

But fear pricked at me. "Do you think he's okay?" I asked
Annie.

Tears threatened to spill from her eyes. "I don't know."

Twenty-One

Austin

Maverick was dead.

One minute, he had been there, taking care of Jason, working for the company, running a marathon. And, the next minute, he was gone.

Twenty-three years old with his entire life ahead of him. A wife and a son. Now, a widow and a boy who would grow up without his father. Just like all the other Wrights at the hospital. But worse. So much worse. He would never even know his dad. He wouldn't know the man he had been or how much he'd loved his mother. He'd have plenty of family, but no one could replace a father. I knew that firsthand.

Sutton was inside the ER room. She had collapsed onto the ground when she found out that he'd died of an unknown heart complication. Her wails could still be heard, but she screamed at anyone who wanted to come inside to console her.

There was no consoling with this.

Only empty words.

And pity.

I knew that she wanted neither of them.

The only thing that she said coherently was Jason's name. Over and over again. Like a lament.

But she'd told us not to bring him into the room. She wanted to be the one to tell him when the time was right. He was too young to know what was happening, which was its only mercy. But he wasn't too young not to know that something was wrong. I didn't blame her for protecting him. Even when nothing could make it right.

Because nothing would be right again.

We had all joked when Sutton got pregnant that Maverick had done it on purpose, that they had a shotgun wedding, and that he only wanted her money. Then, over the last year and a half, we'd all realized how wrong we were. Maverick had adored Sutton, and beyond that, he had been a great guy and a hard worker. He'd fit in better than anyone had anticipated.

That was irreplaceable.

I wished that I could do something, but none of us could. We just waited on the other side of the hospital room door and listened to our youngest sister, the best and brightest and happiest of all of us, as all of that was crushed out of her.

I found Julia in the waiting room. She had her knees tucked up to her chest with her chin resting on them. She was staring off into the distance with red-rimmed eyes.

"Hey babe."

I reached my hand out to her. She put hers in mine and then stood. I wrapped strong, comforting hands around her, holding her tight to me.

"How's Sutton?" Julia asked with a sniffle. "God, what a stupid question. I'm sure she's horrible."

"Yeah. She's not good."

Julia wiped tears from her eyes and hiccuped. "I can't imagine. I just...can't imagine."

"No, I don't think any of us can. It made me want to come see you immediately. Touch you, feel you, make sure you were still here, still real."

A tear slid down her cheek, and I gently swiped it away with my knuckle.

"That's sweet."

"It's the truth. The thought that you could be gone sent me into a panic. I can't explain it. I couldn't breathe. I couldn't think. I just needed to see you."

"Sutton will feel that every day, and when she looks for Mav, he'll be gone," Julia whispered.

"Maybe we should get you home." I worried over her distracted, glazed expression.

My Julia was locked away somewhere. Trapped deep within herself. I didn't know what to make of this, but I would take care of her the best that I could.

"All right," she whispered. "Should we say good-bye to anyone?"

"I'll just text Jensen."

She nodded, completely out of it, as she walked through the sliding glass doors. I followed her out of the hospital and into an Uber. Neither of us had driven anywhere today. We went to her place instead of mine because I wanted her to feel at home and safe.

What had happened gave me perfect clarity in the same way that it seemed to have completely messed with Julia. She was distraught. And all I wanted to do was comfort her and make it all better.

"Maybe we should get you in a shower," I suggested.

She shook her head and then collapsed onto the couch. "How is she going to be able to go on?"

"I don't know, Jules. It's not going to be easy."

"It's going to be impossible. I was there with her all day. I saw her love for that man. She was sad because she'd barely gotten a kiss before he left for the marathon. She's going to regret every single thing that happened this morning. It's just wrong."

"I know. There's nothing any of us can do for Sutton, except be there for her. And, right now...we can't do anything. So, let me take care of you. It's the only thing I can do."

She looked up at me with unblinking wide eyes. "I really want a drink."

"Okay," I said slowly. "I can do that."

"Fuck, Austin. No. No, no, no." She pressed her hands hard into her eyes. "I shouldn't have a drink. Definitely not around you. That's horrible."

I sank to my knees before this beautiful woman. "You're hurting. It's perfectly normal to want to numb the pain."

"Don't."

"I won't drink with you."

"It's mean."

"It's okay, Jules," I said, drawing her hands away from her face.

"It's not okay. None of this is okay."

"Julia."

She finally looked down at me. I kissed both her hands.

"None of this is going to get better today. Not for Sutton. Not for you. Not for anyone. Beating yourself up for how you're feeling isn't going to help anything. If you want a drink, I'll pour you one. I'll take care of you. Just let me take care of you."

"Oh, Austin," she whispered.

Her lips brushed against mine. I felt the pain in that small movement. My Julia was broken, and there was next to nothing I could do about it. But I did what I could.

I swept her up into my arms. She buried her face into my shoulder, wrapping her arms around my neck, and clung to me. I brought her into the bathroom and gently set her back on her feet. After I turned the shower on, I took my time stripping her out of the sticky clothes she'd worn to the Fourth of July parade. I kissed her once more before moving her under the hot water. She shivered under the spray as I removed all of my clothes and followed her inside. I lathered a loofah with the cherry body soap and washed the sweat off her skin.

Once she was clean, I helped her out of the shower and toweled her off. She wrapped her hair up in a towel. I saw some of the hollowness had left her eyes, but she was still out of it.

"Thank you," she whispered.

"Of course."

I urged her into bed. She disappeared under the covers. I pulled on my boxers and found a small liquor shelf in her kitchen. It had two bottles of top-shelf gin and a full bottle of Maker's Mark. My fingers itched for the Maker's.

I stood there, momentarily paralyzed. I'd told Julia I wouldn't drink with her. I'd told her that it was okay that she had a drink. And it was okay.

This was one of the most stressful days of my life. It wouldn't just be a drink to get the edge off of withdrawal. It wouldn't be a casual drink with friends. This was the day my brother-in-law died. My sister became a widow. My nephew, fatherless. It was okay to drink today. I could be strong for Jules, but I wasn't strong today.

My hand tightened around the bottle of whiskey, and I brought it down to the counter. Just one. I only needed one.

I tipped a shot into the glass and tipped it back. My hands were still shaking when I set it down. The drink had done nothing. I still ached. Nothing was numb. I'd need to bury myself in that bottle for it to fucking do anything. And I wouldn't do that to Julia. Not when she needed me right now. One would have to do.

I shoved the Maker's back on the shelf with a force that I couldn't control and made Julia her gin and tonic. Before I went back to the bedroom, I rummaged through the junk drawer until I found a pack of gum. Spearmint. I hoped that would cover the whiskey on my breath. I popped two pieces in my mouth. Then, I snagged Waffle, who was on a chair in the corner, and brought the unicorn in with me.

She winced when she saw the drink in my hand but actually cracked a smile at the unicorn. I offered both to her. She snuggled up with Waffle as she downed her drink like a professional. I would know. I wouldn't have minded a drink that size either. But not today.

I slipped into bed next to her, drawing her over to snuggle me. I didn't care that it was the middle of the day. Reality was a train wreck at the moment.

"You know, Jules, with everything that happened today, I don't want any more regrets in my life."

"Mmhmm?"

"I know we might have started out in a fucked up way. That we've had our ups and downs. But all I could think when I found out about Mav was that…they didn't get enough time. Not by a long shot. They were only married for a year and a half."

"I know," she said, sniffling again.

"Life is so uncertain. I don't want us wasting our moment."

"We're not wasting our moment, Austin."

I kissed her shoulder, feeling more secure with her pressed against me. What had happened to Sutton was unthinkable. I'd had a lot of loss in my life. More than the average person, but losing the love of her life…that was a loss I had no idea how she'd endure. I felt broken for my sister, yet my feelings for Julia had never been clearer.

Tragedy had sharpened my resolve. I was not going to let this woman go for anything. The scariest part was that Sutton had felt the same way, and look where that had gotten her.

Twenty-Two

Julia

The Wright family was dressed in black.

Black suits. Black dresses. Black heels.

A black hat with mesh to obscure Sutton's swollen red eyes.

Black gloves that did nothing to obscure her shaking hands.

Normally, this would have suited me. Black was my favorite color. But today was a day of mourning. Black, a color of death. And the funeral for Maverick Wright was under way.

I still couldn't believe it had all happened. Sutton had found a man she loved beyond words. Sure, it hadn't been easy. She'd gotten pregnant too soon, had the wedding too soon. By societal standards, she and Maverick should have never worked in the first place. I'd been at the wedding. I'd heard what everyone had said.

But they'd defied those standards. They'd laughed in the face of everyone's judgment. They'd lived and loved. Then, it had all been destroyed.

So quickly. Without warning.

Austin put his arm around my waist. "You okay?"

I shook my head. "How could anyone be okay?"

"I know."

He squeezed me a little tighter. The week since Maverick had died on the Fourth of July was somber but, in some strange way, perfect for our relationship. I'd been completely out of it, but Austin had been there the entire time. It was as if he knew exactly what I was feeling and anticipated all my needs.

It felt a little wrong that things were so right with Austin and me when Sutton had lost so much.

The service itself was short. Sutton hadn't wanted anything big. She'd insisted on a small affair with family and Maverick's closest friends. We stood outside, around a closed casket, on a Wright plot in the local cemetery. It was a West Texas sunny day without a cloud in the sky. Heat beat down on our black attire and soaked up the tears on all the faces.

Jason was too young to really know what was going on, but he seemed as quiet and restrained as the rest of us. He kept reaching up and touching his mom's face, as if to stop the tears. But she couldn't contain them. She whispered something into Jason's ear and hugged him against her.

"Sut, I'll take him," Morgan whispered.

Sutton nodded and handed her son to her sister. Morgan held Jason firm. Sutton stepped forward and set down a calla lily on top of the casket. She laid her palm flat against the casket, speaking to her husband one last time.

We all watched on helplessly as final prayers were said. Then, it was time to say good-bye.

No one was ready to leave Sutton alone here on this day. The past week had been hard enough. And there was still a wake to account for this afternoon.

Jensen finally approached her. "Sut."

"Just go," she said hoarsely.

"Sutton, come on. I'll drive you home."

"I *said*, go."

Jensen nodded for everyone to go ahead on to the house. Morgan passed Jason into Jensen's arms. They shared a look of sympathy, and then Morgan was herding everyone away.

I really wanted to say something to Sutton. But I knew that she needed to be here, alone, to mourn. Nothing I said could change what had happened anyway. Still, I had a profound need to be there for her during this.

Austin slipped his hand into mine. "Come on, Jules."

I took one more fleeting look at the scene before my heart broke all over again. Sutton fell to her knees before the casket. Jensen held her son in his arms, so she didn't have to be alone. Jensen was a better father to her than their own father. More of a father than a brother to all of them. It killed me to know that Sutton had lost both her parents and her husband before the age of twenty-three.

No one should have to endure that. It was even worse than my parents, and that was saying something.

I followed Austin from the cemetery and to his parked car, which looked ostentatious in the parking lot.

"I wasn't looking forward to that," Austin admitted.

"I'd imagine not."

"The world sure isn't fair to the Wrights, huh?" He shook his head and leaned his arms against the top of his car as he stared at me over the roof. "Sutton lost our mom when she was only one year old, just like Jason. She grew up without a mom, and he's going to grow up without a dad. Then, our dad died when she was only eleven."

"Awful."

"I always thought she was the lucky one."

"How?"

"She doesn't really remember them. She didn't have to have their shadows following her around. She's shone brighter and loved easier and felt deeper." He ran a hand back through his hair shakily. "And then this happens. How much can one person take?"

I had no answer to that. I was a testament to enduring a lot through life. I'd come out ahead, but I hadn't seen the light through the tunnel. Not for a long time. And, still, I hadn't gone through what Sutton was going through now.

"I'm really worried that she's going to lose all that brightness and joy," he said. "She doesn't know how much she's the glue to our family. The optimism to our pessimism. The idealism to our cynicism. I wouldn't blame her if she did. She's lost a piece of herself. But I hate it for her."

"She'll come back to herself," I said. "You just have to be there for her when she needs you. And she'll need you. All of you."

"And you."

"Me?"

"You were there when it happened."

"I suppose I was."

"You'll always be ingrained in the memory of that day. She'll need you, too."

I smiled sadly and slunk into the passenger side. We drove across town to Jensen's house. The wake was open to a lot more people than the funeral had been. The Wrights congregated in the kitchen, pretending to sort dishes for all the guests who had come to pay their respects.

No one spoke.

Landon and Heidi hovered over the desserts. She would glance down at the diamond ring on her finger every now and then. I could practically read the thoughts going on in her head. *What would she do if the same thing happened to her?*

Emery couldn't seem to stand still without Jensen. She kept arranging and rearranging plates and silverware until her sister showed up to calm her down.

Morgan and Patrick were standing close together. Not close enough to touch. But close enough that they almost looked like a couple. They weren't. But even they didn't realize that this tragedy had pushed them together.

Austin and I were the last ones to arrive. I picked at a plate of food and eventually gave up on eating anything. Food roiled in my stomach. Nothing helped.

Eventually, Sutton, Jensen, and Jason showed up. Everyone tittered around them like birds showering them with condolences and shared memories of Maverick. Sutton kept a strong face through all of it, but I could tell that she wanted to leave. She wanted it all to be over with.

"Let's get some air," Austin suggested.

I nodded absentmindedly and swiped a stray tear from my eye. We snuck out the back door to Jensen's massive backyard. Austin tugged me over to a park bench under a shady tree.

"You looked like you were about to hyperventilate," he said.

"Yeah. It was hard to breathe in there. I don't know how Sutton's doing it."

"Jules, I've been thinking a lot lately."

"About what?"

"Us," he said, entwining our fingers. "I wasted two years without you all because of some idiotic reason. I shouldn't have feared my feelings for you. This is what I want. You are what I want."

I smiled and gently brought my lips up to his. "You are what I want, too. I appreciate you taking care of me during the last week."

"I plan to do it for the rest of my life."

My mouth dropped open. "That's a bold statement."

He laughed at himself and nodded. "It is. It really is."

"You want to be with me for the rest of your life?"

"Yes. One day, I'm going to be the man you deserve. Then, I'm going to put a ring on your finger," he said, sliding the pad of his finger down my left ring finger. "Going to give you my name and make you mine forever."

My heart constricted at his words. *Forever.* I hadn't been able to think about forever in so long. It was only during the last couple of years that I had thought about having a future at all. And, now, I was giving it over to this man. Someone who thought he didn't deserve me in some way. It was almost laughable.

"You're already the man I deserve."

He laughed. "I assure you, I'm not. But I'm going to get there."

I opened my mouth and then closed it. There was so much about me that Austin didn't know. So much I wanted to confide in him. *How could I accept that he wanted me forever without him knowing the truth? How could I want him forever without him knowing exactly what he was getting himself into?* I was going to have to risk him hating me.

"What is it?" Austin asked.

It was as if he could actually see all the thoughts spinning through my head.

"Nothing," I finally said.

Not now. Not here. Soon.

"You sure?"

No.

"Just overwhelmed."

I needed to get my shit together if I wanted to make this work.

The door to the backyard flew open. Sutton rushed out, slammed the door behind her, and crushed her back against the brick wall. She covered her face with her hands, breathing heavily. I wasn't sure if she was crying or just trying to figure out how to breathe again.

After a minute, she removed her hands and trudged over to us. "Hey," she muttered. "Sorry about that."

Austin shrugged and patted the seat next to him. "You don't have to apologize to anyone."

Sutton sat with a huff. "I know. I just...hate all of this. I hate every last thing about it. I should feel thankful that all these people want to help me, but I don't. I feel nothing. I look around for Mav to make fun of the big event, and then I remember...he's not here. He's never going to be here again. And I don't know how to live that life."

"You don't have to entertain anyone," I told her. "If you don't like any of this, then I'll tell everyone to leave."

"It'd be rude."

"So?" I said with a shrug. "I don't mind being the bad guy. You do not have to be available right now. You have to do what's best for you and Jason. That's it."

"You'd do that for me?"

"Of course we would," Austin said, backing me up.

"Would you do something else for me?"

"What's that?" I asked.

Her eyes traveled down Austin's half-sleeve and to the tattoos I revealed in my spaghetti-strap dress.

"Take me to get a tattoo?"

Austin

"You're sure about this?" I asked Sutton for the tenth
time since we'd shown up at the tattoo parlor the next
day.

"More than sure."

She was split between excitement and nerves at the
thought of her first tattoo. I could still remember my first.
I'd gotten it the day after I turned eighteen, and my dad had
beaten my ass the next day. But I'd done it for my mom, and
I didn't care that I'd broken a rule while living under his roof.

"She'll do great," Julia said. "The first one is the hardest."

I laughed and squeezed her hand.

"What?"

"I was just thinking the same thing."

Sutton looked between the two of us through hollow eyes.

I quickly released Julia's hand. "Sorry."

"Don't," Sutton said, waving us away.

But I saw tears coming to her eyes again.

Fuck, I'm stupid. I hadn't meant to flaunt my relationship
in front of her.

"Let's just do this," Sutton said.

We walked inside and met with my tattoo artist, Nick. His boyfriend, Michael, was also there that day, lounging around and making fun of the absurd tattoos Nick had recently put on people's bodies.

"Austin," Nick said, clapping hands with me. "I was happy when you called, man. What are we doing for you?"

"Not for me," I said. "This is my sister Sutton."

"Virgin skin?" he asked.

"Yeah, this is my first," Sutton said, relaxing at Nick's easy demeanor.

"Great. You know what you want?"

She nodded. "Yeah."

"And you?" Nick asked. He eyed Julia's tattoos. "May I?"

She held her hand out, and he took it, looking at all the inked skin that I adored.

Nick whistled. "Please tell me, I get to add to this masterpiece."

"I haven't quite figured out what my next tattoo will be," she told him.

"Whoever did the rest of your work really knew what they were doing. I'd love to play on your skin."

Michael snorted down the row and kicked his feet up onto the counter. "Language, love."

"Michael, appreciate her beautiful work, and then get back to me."

"She's not my type," Michael shot back.

Nick thoughtfully patted Julia's shoulder. "You're not mine either, honey."

I just shook my head, and even Sutton cracked a smile.

Julia gave him an amused look. "That's probably for the best since I'm with Austin."

"Oh, new honey. I love it." Michael cooed from the front.

"Girlfriend," Austin corrected.

Nick's eyebrows rose. "How new and different. Now, let's focus on the sister. You know what you're in for?"

"They filled me in," Sutton said. Then, she glanced at us both before adding, "A couple of times."

Nick laughed and grabbed her hand. "I bet they did. They can't help it. Now, let's head back and get you prepped. Tell me everything about you. What are we doing today?"

Julia and I followed her into the back room where Nick worked on getting her ready for her tattoo.

"Nervous?" Julia asked.

"Yeah, but I can handle anything now."

"What are you going to get?"

Sutton glanced down at her wrist. "A dandelion. It's how Mav and I started. We'd known each other for a year before he worked up the nerve to ask me out. Said I was out of his league. Then, we were at a party. We were both a little tipsy. It was silly at the time, but he plucked a dandelion and wished on it for us. It's been our thing since then."

"It's perfect," Julia whispered, her voice choked, as if she could barely form the words.

"Yeah," Sutton said. She reached out and took Julia's hand. "Thanks for being here for me."

"Of course," Julia said.

"I'm happy for you and Austin, you know?"

I smiled and ruffled her hair. "Thanks, Sut."

"I know that I'd never be able to do this with anyone else. Thank God Jensen isn't prejudice and doesn't care what someone looks like as long as they can do the work."

"I would have been fired a long time ago," I said.

Sutton rolled her eyes. "Yeah, right. For one, you can cover your tattoos with a button-up, but Julia has hers on display. She dyes her hair. She has a nose ring. Her skin is a palette of colors. She doesn't hide who she is."

Julia squirmed at the attention. I could tell again that something was wrong. Just like the day before at the wake. She had looked like she wanted to tell me something. I could feel her holding back. A part of herself that I couldn't seem to reach. I had fallen hard for this girl, and my whole family loved her. I needed to find a way to get that through to her. I didn't want her to feel like she had to hide.

Nick returned then and started his work. Julia and I alternated with holding Sutton's hand as she got her first tattoo. By the time she was done, she was shaking. But she looked happy despite the pain she'd endured.

"It wasn't so bad," she said as we left sometime later.

Julia and I snickered.

"We're going to get you addicted," Julia said.

Sutton nodded vigorously. "I feel like I already am."

I knew this wouldn't make it up to her. Nothing ever could. But at least we'd found something to cheer her up even if it was momentary. It gave me hope that she'd pull through in the long haul. Not yet. Not anytime soon. But maybe eventually.

Life went on.

Going back to work on Monday morning felt...crazy. Like we had all been swimming through rough waters and were now expected to sit in the kiddie pool. No fires to put out. Just regular work. *How could everything go back to normal, as if Maverick had never died?*

His office was on my floor. It had been cleared out before I even got into the office. I didn't know how I felt about it. Was it a relief or depressing? That we could erase someone so quickly.

I knew one thing. I was glad Sutton didn't work for the company. We would have made her take time off anyway, but I couldn't imagine her coming in and seeing that. It'd break her already broken heart.

But we couldn't ignore work any longer.

Elizabeth Leyton would be coming in this afternoon for her interview for the CFO position. We'd moved her back from last weekend, and we had two more interviews to do before the end of July. I knew Jensen wanted to decide about the position before the end of the summer. That way, everyone could get trained into their spots, and he could work on his private architecture venture.

Everyone was moving into their dream job. Everyone, except me.

The thought of figuring out what I wanted to do with my life and everything with Sutton made me want to open a bottle. Patrick and I had thrown out all the ones in my office weeks ago, so I wouldn't be tempted. I'd seriously reduced intake just enough to keep me from feeling sick to my stomach. I knew the worst was still yet to come with all of this. Giving it up entirely was the next mission, but it had been hard enough, reducing it. I didn't think I was ready. My hands shook as the taste of whiskey flooded my mouth, as if I were actually drinking it. Sometimes, the taste would come to me so suddenly that my blood seemed to sing at the thought of having a drink.

But I had Julia. She could get me through this stress. I could make this work. I didn't need a drink.

Fuck!

I pushed away from my desk and left my office. I'd thought I was fine with all this shit. It turned out, my clarity only came from Julia. Once I stopped and thought about Maverick's death, everything hit me fresh. All the reasons I'd started drinking in the first place. All the reasons I couldn't stop myself from craving the bottle. It ate at me.

I stumbled into Patrick's office and shut the door behind me. "Do you have a drink?"

Patrick glanced up from his computer. "What the hell, man? I thought you were cutting back?"

"I am. Fuck!"

I slammed down into the seat in front of his desk and put the heels of my hands to my forehead. "I just…need a drink."

"Dude. No. You just want a drink. Is this about Sutton?"

"Maybe."

"Look, I'm like your brother. I've been there from the start. I know that Maverick's death can't be easy with your past," Patrick said. "But is having a drink really the answer?"

"Do you have one or not?" I snapped at him.

"I'm not going to fucking give you one when you're like this."

"You're a dick."

Patrick shrugged. "You've been doing really well, dude. Take some deep breaths, and get yourself back under control. Would you have gone to Julia for this?"

"Of course not!"

"Then, you don't need that drink."

"I know!" I burst out of my seat and started pacing the room. "I know I don't. But…what the fuck am I going to do, Patrick?"

"You're going to sit your ass back down and deal with it, like how everyone else does."

I sat. "How does everyone else deal?"

"With time," he said. "I know that's not what you want to hear."

"No, it's not."

"But this will pass."

I tilted my head back and looked up at the ceiling. He was right. Inherently, I knew he was right. But it didn't stop the thirst. It didn't make me feel any less crazy for wanting it so desperately. I didn't know how to explain it. I didn't think I knew anyone who could understand what I was going through.

"Okay. Yeah. You're right." I shook my head.

I don't need it. I don't need it. I don't need it.

"Are we still on for my birthday next week?"

I nodded. "I'm down. What do you want to do?"

"I'd say dinner, but Mindi and I are off again."

"Big surprise."

"I don't want to be the third wheel with you and Julia."

"Then, invite someone else."

"I guess I could see if Mor is free."

I grinned. *Was Patrick finally admitting what was between him and Morgan?*

Then, I looked at his face and realized the idiot still had no clue.

Patrick wrinkled his nose and then shrugged. "But maybe we should just go out with the guys."

"Cool, man."

Patrick stared back at his computer screen. Case closed. "You should probably stay in here until you're okay again. All right?"

I nodded and didn't move from his office for several hours.

Fuck, I'm so weak.

Twenty-Four

Julia

My back ached. *Why the fuck did I decide to wear heels to work today?*

I had no clue how Heidi did it every day. All it did was make my feet hurt and put me in a bad mood. And I'd promised to have a girls' night with Heidi and Emery tonight while Austin was out with the guys. I sure hoped they didn't expect me to stay in my heels. Not happening.

I hopped out of my Tahoe with a wince and hobbled inside to my apartment. I kicked the annoying shoes off my feet, flexing them against the carpet. With a sigh, I stripped out of my work outfit and into sweatpants. *Best part of the day.*

I was just tugging on an oversize T-shirt when the doorbell rang.

"Coming!" I called.

A man stood on the other side of the peephole. Unease ate through me.

"Who is it?"

"I have a delivery you have to sign for," the man said.

"What's it for?"

"Uh…flowers."

I released the breath I'd been holding in a whoosh. *Flowers. Just flowers. Of course. That's…logical. Not where my brain was going at all.* God, I wished that I didn't almost have a panic attack anytime someone showed up at my apartment.

"Sorry about that," I said after I slid all the locks open.

"No problem. Just sign here," the guy said.

He still looked at me like I was a lunatic. I forgot that the sign coming into Lubbock said, *The Friendliest City in America.* I probably seemed like a crazy person with all my paranoia.

I signed the paper and handed it back to the guy. He passed me a green glass vase with a bouquet of white lilies in it. My favorite.

I kicked the door closed and brought the vase inside. After setting it on the kitchen counter, I searched for the card. But there was no card.

"Seriously?" I said, glaring at the door again. Brought the flowers and forgot the card. At least it was obvious who they were from.

I grabbed my phone and checked the time. Austin wasn't leaving to go out for Patrick's birthday for another hour. That was plenty of time.

I laughed and tore out of my clothes again. Austin had no idea how much flowers were my utter weakness. They always had been. He'd done good.

I dug through my closet and found the slinky midnight-blue dress Heidi had talked me into a couple of weeks ago. I'd have to endure the heels again after all. I reached for my totally-not-work-appropriate, fuck-me strappy heels that made my legs and ass look sexy as hell. Two things I knew Austin couldn't resist. I tousled my hair and applied a thick layer of red lipstick.

My phone, car keys, and Ray-Bans went into my purse, and I tossed the strap of my leather crossbody over my head. I took one big inhale of the lilies' perfume before sauntering out of the apartment, ready to let my boyfriend know how much I appreciated the flowers.

Thankfully, Austin's house wasn't that far from my apartment. I parked on the street and walked straight through the front door without knocking.

"Austin," I called into the house.

No answer.

Hmm.

I slammed the door shut behind me, dropped my bag, and took the stairs up to his room. I could hear the shower running from the master. My mind drifted away from me, imagining the hot naked man behind that door. The sculpted abs, the sexy V, the tatted biceps, the long, hard dick waiting for me.

I pressed the door open and saw Austin's naked figure silhouetted against the glass door to the shower. My feet stopped moving, and my mouth fell open. Austin had his dick in his hand. His head was tilted back. He was working himself back and forth. Jacking off with such vigor that my mouth watered, and heat spread between my thighs. I could watch this all day.

"Fuck," I breathed.

Austin's head whipped to the open door. His breathing was ragged. I swallowed as our eyes locked through the glass… and he didn't stop stroking himself.

Oh, fuck. Oh, fuck.

I squeezed my legs together as my body ached for him. And he wasn't stopping. *God!*

While he watched me, I ran my hand up my bare thigh and under my minidress. I found that most sensitive area and stroked across the light fabric. It was wet. I pushed the material aside, swiped some of that wetness, and swirled it around on my clit. My body shuddered at the contact. I could come like this.

He'd stopped stroking as he watched me with fascination. My eyes glazed at the touch, and I let out a breathy gasp.

Finally, he pushed the door open. His eyes were dark and needy.

"You going to get your ass in here and let me finish you off?" he demanded.

"Depends," I said.

"No, it fucking doesn't. Get out of that fucking dress now, or I'm going to get it very wet."

"Oh, I get a choice now?"

Austin growled low. Then, he stepped over the threshold, his dick jutting from his body, and bodily pulled me into the shower. I laughed as all my handiwork got soaked. There'd been no point in fixing my hair or the dress or any of it. Austin hardly cared.

I held my finger up to him. "Want to taste what you do to me?"

He gripped my hand at the wrist and then took my entire index finger into his mouth. Then, he sucked me off, as if I were powdered sugar on a funnel cake.

"That what you want me to do to you?" I murmured, mesmerized by the way his tongue played with my finger.

He popped my finger out of his mouth and then found the zipper on my dress. He yanked the thing off along with my strapless bra, tossing them both from the shower without care. Then, he dropped to his knees, dragging my underwear all the way down my legs. They ended up in a corner, but I lost all coherent thought as he pushed me against a wall, drew my heeled foot up and over his shoulder, and then buried his face into my pussy.

"I love watching you touch yourself," he said, nipping at my clit. "But your pussy coming under my tongue is better."

And I did uncontrollably. Seeing him pleasure himself had gotten me so wet that the slightest provocation from Austin's tongue sent me straight over the edge.

I dropped to my knees as my orgasm rocketed through me.

"Holy fuck," I moaned.

"You're going to be saying that a lot."

My eyes locked with his. "Were you thinking about me?"

I reached out and wrapped my hand around his throbbing cock.

"Only you, babe."

"What was I doing that got you so hard?"

He panted, slamming his hand against the wall, as I drew out his pleasure. "First, you sucked me off."

I moved my mouth forward and brought my tongue all the way up his cock. Then, I sucked in the head.

"And then?" I asked.

"Then, you let me take that sweet ass of yours."

"That what you want?"

His eyes met mine as I left bright red lipstick marks all up and down his cock. That was a yes.

I could feel him tensing, getting ready to come. As if he couldn't hold out any longer. He shot sticky liquid into my mouth, bracing himself against the wall of the shower and crying out.

"Fuck, Jules! Jesus Christ! Fuck, fuck, fuck," he cried.

I swallowed his come and teetered back on my heels. "You're going to be saying that a lot," I teased.

I reached for the strap on one of my heels to take it off.

Austin's hand shot out. "Don't fucking take those off."

"Oh?"

"I'm fucking you in that. Only that." His eyes traveled over my flushed body. "I'm never going to be able to look at those heels again without thinking about you showing up and getting me off."

I blushed, pleased with myself. Austin reluctantly wiped the lipstick off his dick, turned off the shower, and then dragged me into his room.

"I want to try this," he said.

"Try what?"

He grabbed a bottle of lube, and then we walked back downstairs.

He moved me over to his couch and then bent me over the arm of it. He smacked my ass, leaving a stinging pain in its wake. I gasped and squeezed my legs together. But it was a waste. I was spread open for him and completely at his mercy. And I was soaking wet. So ready for him.

"God, Jules," he groaned as he pressed his cock against my opening.

I whimpered as he entered me, taking me in long, easy strokes. I didn't know how I was even functioning with how he was teasing me. He held on to my hips hard. I could see why he'd wanted to try this. The arm of the couch was the perfect level. And he bottomed out over and over and over again.

"Perfect. You're perfect," he said, shaking from exertion.

We were both already so close again. I could feel the early waves of an orgasm washing over me. I sank my hands into the sofa cushion and muffled a scream into the pillow.

"Not yet," he instructed.

"Please," I begged.

I felt a cold squeeze of lube over my ass. He pressed one finger into the hole and then another. I tensed around him, and then I took a deep breath and relaxed.

"You ready to come for me?"

I nodded, pushing my ass toward him. He chuckled at my desperation to have him take me like that. I wasn't ashamed that I loved it. We both did. And I was going to come so hard once he filled me.

The head of his cock touched my ass, and slowly, he stretched me around him. I gasped as my body opened to take him all the way in. It burned at first, but as soon as he fit into me, that subsided. And all I felt was pleasure as he moved in and out of me with ease. Not slamming into me, as he had with my pussy, but taking care with my ass. Knowing that every little movement shook us each to our core.

The next time Austin filled me, I came with a force. I squeezed around him, and he finished with me. My body was properly filled, fucked, and finished. Austin withdrew, and still, I didn't move. I didn't know if I could.

"That was...wow," I murmured into the pillow.

"Yeah. It really was," he said.

Twenty-Five

Julia

After a few minutes, we both moved to clean ourselves up. Another shower was in order. Then, Austin had to find me clothes of his to wear until my dress was dry. There was no hope for my hair. I was just lucky to find a hair tie, so I could slick it up into a ponytail.

I crashed back on his bed and yawned. "You took everything out of me. I could go to sleep."

Austin smirked, all proud of himself. "I'd just have to wake you up for another round when I got back."

"You'd have to convince me. This one was a thank-you."

He shot me a quizzical look. "A thank-you?"

"Yeah. For the flowers."

His expression didn't change. "What flowers?"

I shot up in bed, a stone sinking in the pit of my stomach. "The lilies you sent me."

"Uh, I didn't send you lilies."

"Wh-what?"

"Who's sending you flowers, Jules?" he asked with a laugh. "Who do I need to beat up?"

"I…" I sputtered. "Oh no."

My chest rose and fell rapidly as realization shot through me. Austin hadn't sent me the flowers. He didn't know that I loved lilies. He didn't know that flowers were my weakness. He couldn't possibly be that good of a guesser.

But there was someone who did know those things.

My blood ran cold.

"Oh, fuck," I gasped.

"Jules?"

"No, no, no, no, no," I said over and over again.

"You're white as a ghost. What is going on? Does this have to do with who sent you the flowers?"

I shook my head back and forth and then dropped my head onto my knees. "Oh my God, I'm so stupid."

"What is going on?"

"I thought I got away," I whispered. "I thought I was safe."

"Babe, you're safe with me."

I looked up at him through hollow, unseeing eyes. "I'm not safe anywhere."

"You're scaring me. What is going on?"

"My name isn't Julia Banner," I blurted.

Austin sat heavily on the bed. His eyebrows were scrunched together. "Okay. What is your name?"

"Juliana Peterson."

"I don't understand. Why did you change your name?"

"Because of Dillon."

"And who is Dillon? This guy send you the flowers?"

I nodded. "I think so." My hands trembled. "He's my ex-boyfriend."

"A serious one, I'm guessing."

"Yeah. The reason I didn't want to have the exes talk."

"So, why is he sending you flowers? Are you still seeing him?"

I laughed, but it came out choked and disbelieving. "No, Dillon destroyed my life. There's so much you don't know,

Austin. Fuck. I wanted to tell you everything. I wanted to tell you who I really was. Ever since Mav died, I wanted to spill it all, but I just…I was worried you'd hate me."

"Jules, how could I hate you?"

"Because you don't know anything about me."

He sighed and ran a hand through his hair. "I know everything I need to know about you."

"You say that now."

"Then, tell me. You have a different name. So what? I plan to change your last name anyway," he said passionately. "You can tell me."

"I met Dillon the summer before college. He was…he was bad news. I liked…like guys that way," I said, wincing, as my eyes snagged on his tattoos. "I was enamored. Dillon only showed me the parts of him that he wanted me to see. I gave up my full ride at Northwestern to stay home and go to community college. I couldn't be away from him. He wouldn't let me be away from him. I was that idiot girl. He was dealing drugs. I knew but thought it didn't really matter. You don't grow up around Akron without seeing your fair share of drugs.

"He went from being the perfect boyfriend to being possessive to being…insane. I knew it. I wasn't stupid. But I thought I loved him. I couldn't leave. I couldn't get away." I shook my head. "I got into Ohio State my sophomore year. At first, he wouldn't let me go. Then, he expanded his dealing and moved there with me. I had no friends. I had no one. I went to classes. I made straight As. But I was utterly isolated."

"That still wasn't enough, was it?"

"I managed to graduate, but the next two years of my life were hell. The only person I had was one of my professors. I put it all on the line. She got me out of Ohio, helped me change my name, and found me the job at Wright."

"You were lucky to have her."

"I thank God for her every day," I admitted. "But…I thought I could escape Dillon forever."

"And, now, you think he's found you?"

"It all makes sense," I whispered, putting all the pieces together. "He stole my jacket. He broke into my car. He probably got my car towed."

"Julia, that stuff has been happening for weeks."

"I know," I whispered.

"Don't you think he'd have approached you by now?"

"He's a psychopath. Who knows what his next move is?"

"I wish you'd told me about this shit," Austin said. He stood and started pacing the room. His hands clenched and unclenched.

"I'm sorry. I know I should have told you, but I haven't told anyone."

"I just...fuck!"

"Austin?"

"Just give me a minute."

He continued pacing, absentmindedly running his hands through his hair. I could see his brain working. I didn't know if he was trying to find a solution or if he was just pissed at me. I knew the look on his face. He wanted a drink. I was overloading him.

"Austin—"

"A minute," he snapped.

I recoiled into myself, and he sighed.

"Fuck, I'm sorry. I didn't mean that."

"It's okay."

"No, it's not. It's just a lot at once. I fucking hate this prick who hurt you. And, now, I feel like a douche. No wonder you never wanted to talk to me again when you thought I'd used you. Christ! How can you even look at me?"

"You're not Dillon, Austin."

Austin Wright might be an asshole. He might have a drinking problem. He might put himself first in most things. But no one was as bad as Dillon.

If this was already too much, there was no way I could tell him the rest. If I peeled back all the layers of Juliana Peterson, no one could love her. She was a broken, used girl. And, when I thought about Dillon, I became that scared, helpless girl again. Rather than the strong woman who'd gotten away and built her own life. And I needed Julia Banner.

"We need to go to the cops," Austin said abruptly.

I nodded, knowing he was right. "I'll go in the morning."

"We're going now."

"Austin, you have Patrick's birthday tonight."

"That can wait."

"No. Look, it's just one night."

"Julia—"

"I'll be with Heidi and Emery. Have fun with the guys. Let me deal with Dillon."

Fire burst in his eyes at that suggestion. He didn't seem to like that one bit.

"I need to tell the girls anyway. Just…be safe, okay?"

"I'm driving you there. I'm not leaving you alone."

"I'm not going to have my life dictated again," I told him.

"You just told me that some psychopath is out there, and you expect me to let you drive off alone? Fuck no, Jules."

"Okay. You're right," I said. I didn't want to fight.

I'd just dropped a lot on Austin. It was unfair of me to just expect him to be okay with something I'd been dealing with all of my adult life. Not that I was okay with anything that had happened with Dillon.

Austin seemed frazzled the rest of the time as we got ready. All the tension that had left his body from the hot sex we'd had was gone. He threw on jeans and a button-up with the sleeves rolled up to his elbows. After running product through his hair, he hustled me out of his house in my slightly damp dress. He finally conceded in letting me drive my own car, but he followed me all the way to Heidi's.

We both parked in the driveway. He hopped out of his idling car and came around to help me out.

"Thanks," I said, leaning forward to kiss him.

"Are you sure I should still go out tonight?"

"Yes, I'm sure. It's your best friend's birthday."

His cupped my cheeks and dragged me into a slow, steady kiss. "Be safe, Jules."

"I'll be fine. I promise."

He sighed and looked like he wanted to say so much more, but that was when Landon stepped out of the front door.

"Do I get to take your piece-of-shit car to the party?"

Austin flipped him off. "Watch your mouth!"

Landon snickered. "Come on. Let's get going. Patrick is going to be surrounded by those douchey gym bros you all hang with. He'll need some class."

"Then, why are you coming?" Austin asked.

Landon punched him as he passed by, walking toward the Alfa Romeo. "Can I drive?"

"Fuck no," Austin said. "No one drives my car!"

Landon slid into the driver's side anyway.

"See? You'll have a good time."

"If I don't kill my brother in the meantime."

"You love him."

"Yeah. I do."

Austin kissed me one more time before kicking Landon out of the driver's seat and zooming off toward Patrick's party. I sighed with relief. I was glad that conversation was done with. He had some time to hang with the guys and decompress. Hopefully, that would help him wrap his head around the truth bomb I'd dropped on him.

Now, I had to do it all over again with my girls. They deserved to know as well. Especially because, if Dillon was here in Lubbock, then no one was safe. Not really.

I took a deep breath and then went inside to find Heidi and Emery. Heidi was in a hot-pink sundress with her blonde hair in long, beachy waves. Emery was in cutoff jean shorts and Converse. Apparently, I'd chosen incorrectly for girls' night.

Heidi arched an eyebrow at my appearance. "Girl, what the hell did Austin do to you?"

I smiled. "Nothing I didn't ask for."

Emery snorted, next to Heidi. "I like it."

"We were thinking shopping and maybe takeout. You could borrow something of mine if you wanted to be more comfortable."

It was my turn to look disbelieving. "Since when would I ever fit in your clothes?"

"You could!" Heidi cried. "I have a dress that would fit you so well."

"Can we...can we talk before we go?" I asked.

Heidi and Emery shared one of their customary looks before nodding. We moved into the living room with the exposed wood beam ceiling and stone fireplace. It was stunning. Obviously custom built.

"What's up?" Heidi asked. "Did something happen with you and Austin?"

"Yes, but no. Nothing serious."

I frowned down at my tightly clasped fingers and then delivered the news I'd told Austin. A weight lifted off of me as I finally got to divulge who I really was to my friends. And better yet...they didn't hate me. They didn't hate me for lying and hiding who I was. Dillon had always said that anyone who really got to know me could never really like me. No one other than him, of course. It was hard to dispel that poisonous voice whispering in my ear.

"So," Heidi said, shaking her head, "how about we skip shopping and get that restraining order?"

"All in favor, say aye," Emery said.

"Aye!" Heidi and Emery said together. They raised their hands in unison.

"I'm going to go with Austin in the morning. I think he might be upset if I went without him."

"This Dillon guy really did a number on you," Emery said. "And I thought I'd had bad relationships."

"Yeah, Julia, I can't imagine what you're still dealing with," Heidi chimed in. "What you had to endure all those years."

"Giving up a full-ride scholarship," Emery muttered.

Of course she would snag on that. She'd gotten a full ride to Oklahoma and dropped out of her PhD program after her professor boyfriend cheated on her. She was now a high school teacher. I wasn't surprised that the idea of someone smart screwing up in such a spectacular way hurt her.

"Not my best move."

Not my worst either…

"Well, we don't have to go out if you're worried something could happen," Heidi said.

"I'm not, but Austin is. I just can't figure out what Dillon is up to. Why break into my car and steal nothing? Why take my jacket out of my own freaking apartment and then return it? I mean, he put it back on a hanger in my closet! Why have my car towed? Why freaking send the lilies?"

"He's playing a game," Emery said. "He wants it to all add up, to freak you out."

"Yeah. He's a manipulative bastard."

"And you can't prove he did any of that," Heidi said, chewing on her bottom lip. "Even the towing. Didn't you say that the guy had said the company called it in? He's not leaving a trail. Just terrorizing you from afar."

"Pussy," Emery spat.

"Hey, a pussy can take a beating!" Heidi said. "I bet he's more like balls. The slightest flick sends him to his knees."

I laughed at her analogy. "Either way, he's dangerous. I knew that when I got out. Having him here, in Lubbock…" I shuddered and closed my eyes.

The last time I'd seen Dillon flashed before my eyes. The way he'd held me. By my hair. The way he'd spat in my face. Literally and figuratively. The terror as he lost control. Fucked up on who knew how many drugs. Pissed at me for…God, everything. Just everything.

"Hey," Heidi said, sinking into the cushion at my side. "You are not alone in this."

Emery took the seat on the other side. "We are here. Austin is here. You have the full weight of the Wrights behind you."

"And, really, all you need is us," Heidi said, nudging me. "Em and I can fuck shit up."

Emery rolled her eyes. "Have you been taking kickboxing again?"

"It's a good workout."

"Dear Lord." Emery shook her head. "What she's trying to say is…you have us. We're sisters now. We'll do everything to make this right."

I wanted to believe them. I appreciated what they were saying. But they didn't know Dillon. And, if they did, they wouldn't want to get involved. I wouldn't want them involved.

But I smiled and nodded. I agreed to stay in and have a chill night. Emery put on *Buffy the Vampire Slayer* while Heidi found some sweats and a T-shirt that did actually fit me, to my utter shock. I suspected the pants at least belonged to Landon.

"Oh my God," Heidi said when she came back into the living room. "If we have to watch Angel become Angelus one more time, Em, I swear!"

"But it's the best season!"

"Give me some Spike! All the Spike!"

Emery muttered something vulgar under her breath with a muffled, "Team Angel," and then changed the TV to a different season.

Heidi piled up bowls full of ice cream so high, it rivaled Kevin McCallister in *Home Alone*. We all sat down and dug in.

I was with Heidi. I liked bad-boy Spike. But for me...not Buffy.

And that had been my problem for all of time. I always wanted the bad boys. It was as if I were marked or something. My mind drifted to Dillon, even as I tried to forget him. This was not how I'd wanted this night to go. Not at all.

But I was lucky at least. I had found friends who actually stuck by me. Girlfriends that I'd never had before. Not even close. And a family behind me. Not a family I couldn't even claim.

I chewed on my fingernail and promised myself that I'd enjoy the rest of this night. Dillon had his own agenda. If I let him interrupt my day, then he'd win. He wanted to throw me off and to make me feel like I was never safe.

Well, I wouldn't let him win.

Fuck that!

Never again.

Twenty-Six

Austin

Patrick's birthday was exactly what I needed right now.
Not that I could tell anyone why.

I was so utterly fucked up.

This prick had hurt Julia. For *years*. She'd been so hurt that she had to run. She'd had to become a new person to get away from him. And then, when she'd finally opened herself up to someone, it had been *me*.

And what had I done? Fucking hurt her.

She never should have given me a second chance. She had to see Dillon when she looked at me. Fucking asshole addict who used and abused her good graces. That slap she'd hit me with last fall felt so much more weighted. I'd deserved it then. I knew I deserved it more now.

Landon shot me a curious look. "You're awfully quiet."

"I don't like to listen to the sound of my own voice like you do."

"Whatever, dude. It's more than that."

"Let it go, Landon."

He sat up straighter in his seat as we pulled up to The Shack. It was the best barbeque west of Dallas. Even if my car did hate that it had a gravel parking lot.

"You want to talk about it?" Landon asked.

"No."

"All right. Well, if you change your mind…"

"Seems unlikely," I said, stepping out of the car. "We're here to celebrate my best friend. Not for you to baby me."

Landon held his hands up. "My bad, dude. Just looking out for you."

"Well, don't."

I locked up my car and headed through the front door, behind Landon. Patrick was already there with a few of the guys from the gym—Evan, Mick, and Connor. I was truly surprised it was this subdued, considering the fact that Patrick was such a life-of-the-party kind of guy. But I wasn't complaining. I'd rather it just be us anyway.

Landon and I ordered at the front. Landon got brisket while I got ribs. I was obsessed with them and would come to get them all the time if the Shack were closer to the office. I filled up a water cup and then headed for Patrick's table in the back of the restaurant, near the bar.

My eyes lingered on the shelves of whiskey. I really wanted a drink. One to take the edge off. This felt like a good reason. I'd even take a fucking beer. Anything. Instead, I sat my ass down and just stared longingly instead.

"Happy birthday, man," I said to Patrick as I waited for my food.

"Good of you two to finally show up!"

"Yeah, sorry. I got hung up."

Patrick raised his eyebrows. "Why do I have a feeling that wasn't the only thing hung in this joke?"

I laughed and shrugged. "I've got a pretty amazing girlfriend."

"Aw, my lovesick puppy," Patrick joked.

"Here we go!" Evan said, carrying four beers in his hands and dropping them on the table.

Mick had two more drinks and passed one to Connor.

"Hey, thanks, man!" Patrick said, grabbing a beer.

Landon took his, and Evan swigged back some of his.

And then there was one.

It was as if Evan had freaking looked into my brain and materialized the exact thing I wanted. But I let it sit there, in front of me, tempting, alluring. I knew exactly how it'd taste. How it'd make me feel.

"That one's for you, Austin," Evan said, pressing it over to me.

Patrick and Landon shared a look.

"I'll just double-fist it," Patrick said with a laugh.

"It's just one," I said, meeting their eyes. "No big deal. Right? It's your birthday."

"Austin," Landon muttered, "are you sure?"

My hand slid across the table and wrapped around the beer. *God, yes, I am so sure.*

"It'll be fine," I reassured them.

I could be like everyone else. I could have one drink for my best friend's birthday. This was totally possible.

The first sip brought it all back. It was an effort not to empty the bottle. It tasted so good. So fucking good.

But I felt Landon's and Patrick's eyes on me. Worry creased in every line of their face. So, I forced myself to put the drink down and grin. Some of that worry left their eyes.

Everything went back to normal. Our food came. I finished my beer. We ordered another round. We were all having such a good time that, when I went through the third beer, I wasn't even sure anyone else had noticed.

"I know you wanted this to be a small thing," Evan said after we all finished eating. "But I might have invited the rest of the guys for drinks at Flips. It's supposed to be a surprise party. So, act surprised."

Patrick laughed. "You sneaky motherfucker."

Now, Landon glanced at me. "Maybe we should head out."

"What's the worst that could happen?" I asked.

"Famous last words, Austin."

"Ah, come on, man. It's not a big deal. We'll hang out for a couple of hours and then get back to the girls."

"You sure that you're okay?"

"Fine."

We all stood to go, and I was pleased to see that I could walk just fine. If I'd felt drunk at all, I might have heeded Landon's warning, but I didn't feel drunk. I was fine. Even better than fine.

I peeled out of the parking lot of The Shack and sped toward Flips. I hadn't been in a bar since that night I was with Julia at the dueling piano bar downtown. I used to live in them.

Maybe I should have been worried that it felt like coming home.

But all I felt was relief as the group of us entered the favorite local bar.

A large group of guys that I recognized from work, the gym, and college called, "Surprise!"

Patrick laughed and moved to the center of the festivities. We were herded together. Beers were handed to us. Shots on trays appeared. Everything started to turn into a blur. Just a haze of alcohol like I hadn't had in a long time. Even Patrick and Landon seemed to have had enough that they were retreating back into that time before. Back when this had been my life.

The next thing I knew, we were walking up to the bar like fools.

"Peter," I said, tipping my head at the bartender.

"Wright."

I always thought he called me that because he couldn't or didn't want to tell us apart.

"Three rounds of Four Horsemen of the Apocalypse."

Peter's eyebrows rose high. "All right, man."

"It's Patrick's birthday," I said, clapping my best friend on the back.

Peter poured out the drinks, and I passed over my credit card to pay for it all. As a drink, the Four Horsemen was a hot fucking mess. As a shot, it was worse.

One shot Jim Beam. One shot Jack Daniel's. One shot Johnnie Walker. One shot Jameson. And then Bacardi 151 poured over the line of shots and set on fire.

"Fuck," Landon said.

"This is going to be fucking awesome," Patrick said. "Take a picture!"

He passed over his phone to Peter, who begrudgingly accepted it. I could tell he hated that request. But who fucking cared? It was one picture.

Once the three of us were lined up, Peter struck a match and touched it to the end of the line. One by one, the shots went up in flames until all were ignited. I slung an arm over Landon's and Patrick's shoulders and grinned as Peter snapped a shot.

Then, we tipped back shot after shot.

Jim Beam went down harsh. Jack Daniel's was a little smoother. Johnnie Walker was like heaven. And, by Jameson, I could hardly taste it at all.

I eased back into a seat as the burn from the liquor coated my stomach. Finally. There it was. There was that feeling I'd been missing. Numb.

This would be good. I used to drink *way* more than this without it even touching me. I was fine. I was celebrating after all.

———

My thoughts felt hazy. Everything was funny. I felt good. Really fucking good. God, I'd forgotten how good I could feel.

I moved forward, back to Patrick's side, and nearly stumbled right into Evan. "Fuck, man. Sorry."

Evan put out a hand and steadied me. "You look fucked up, dude."

I laughed. "I feel fucked up."

"Maybe you should slow down."

I passed him the beer in my hand. I'd only had a sip. "Take my beer."

Evan shook his head and laughed. "Patrick, I think you got Austin past the point of no return."

Patrick turned to look at me, but I was sure he was seeing double. "Fuck, man. I'm pretty sure I wasn't supposed to let this happen."

"Ah, come on! It's your fucking birthday!"

A vibration came from my pocket. I jerked the phone out and promptly dropped it. I picked it up and cursed violently at the shattered screen.

"Hello?" I called into the phone when I saw Jules's name on the phone.

"Austin Wright," Julia said in a serious tone, "are you drunk?"

"What gives you that idea?"

"Besides the slur?" she growled.

"I'm not slurring."

"What about the picture Patrick posted of you guys doing four flaming shots at Flips? Was that a Four Horsemen?"

"Maybe."

"Christ," she spat. "I thought you guys were going out for dinner. Not going to the bar!"

"Babe, don't worry about me. I'm fine."

"You're on a bender! You went and got fucked up!" She sighed heavily into the phone and then was silent for a few seconds. "Should I come get you?"

"You don't need to come get me." I turned to Patrick and stuffed the phone in his hand. "Patrick, tell Jules that I'm totally fine."

Patrick put the phone to his ear. "Hey, Julia. Yes. Yep. Uh-huh. Probably a good idea. Oh, I so am. It is my birthday. Yeah, I know. Sorry. Okay. Sure." Patrick handed the phone back. "Uh, here you go."

"Babe, see?"

"I'm fucking coming to get you."

Then, she hung up on me.

I stared down at the phone in shock.

"What the hell did she say to you?" I asked Patrick.

"That I was irresponsible and a shitty friend. That I should have taken better care of you, and I should be glad that she wasn't going to kick my ass."

I sputtered into laughter. "She didn't say that!"

Patrick shrugged. "Your girl is crazy. She's perfect for you."

I couldn't deny that. Julia was the best fucking thing that had ever happened to me. I'd marry her right now if she wanted to do it. Course, she deserved so much more than no ring and a dirty bar.

"Hey, guys," Evan said, reaching his hand out to Patrick. "I'm going to call it an early night. My girlfriend hates when I'm out late."

"Ha!" I shook his hand. "That makes two of us."

Evan laughed and then disappeared.

"She doesn't hate when you're out late. She hates when you drink," Patrick corrected.

"Eh. Goes hand in hand."

"You haven't even fucking sang to me yet!"

"You do not want to hear me sing."

"I already have!" Patrick said. "I think I still have *Fiddler on the Roof* on tape somewhere."

"Fuck you!"

Patrick laughed. Landon appeared then in front of us. His eyes were wary, and he suddenly seemed much more sober than us.

"I just heard from Heidi. Looks like she's on her way here," he said. He cringed as he glanced between me and Patrick. "She's going to chew me out for letting this happen."

"It's my birthday," Patrick said with a shrug. "You need another drink, Landon."

"I think we're all cut off."

"Hey, I'm not pussy-whipped by anyone. I can have as much as I fucking want," Patrick said.

"Do you want to deal with Emery, Heidi, and Julia?" Landon asked with a pointed look.

"Bring it," he said.

Landon shook his head and went to the front door to wait for the girls. It didn't take long before they showed up at the bar. Heidi and Landon seemed to be having a heated argument at the front of the room, but eventually, they moved with Emery to the bar to talk with Peter. I knew Heidi was friends with the bartender. Plus, this was really her bar. She hustled pool here like a champ.

But it was Julia who caught my attention. She was in the skimpy dress I'd stripped her out of in the shower. And she looked hot as fucking hell. Christ, I wanted my dick in her so bad right now.

"Jules," I said as she approached.

She sighed, looking resigned. "Come on, Austin. We should get you back to your place. Try to detox you again."

"Babe, I'm fine."

"Look, I'm not surprised that this happened. I figured it would happen at some point," she said. "I'm just disappointed that it did."

"Why the fuck are you disappointed? Because I'm here, celebrating my best friend's birthday?"

"Not everyone has to get wasted to celebrate a birthday, Austin."

"Yeah, well, I did."

She narrowed her eyes in warning. "No, you didn't. This is the addict talking right now. Not you."

"What the fuck would you know about it?"

She clenched her jaw. "Why are you trying to start an argument with me? Fuck, I haven't missed this."

"Come on. I know arguments get you hot."

I ran my hand up her bare arm, and she shoved me off.

"Stop it," she snarled. "I wanted you to go out and celebrate Patrick's birthday. I thought dinner and some guy time would be good for you. I thought you would be responsible. After everything I told you, I knew you wanted a drink. I fucking knew it. You were doing so well."

"Well? You think I was doing well? I was fucking drowning. Not drinking was killing me. I finally feel like my-fucking-self again."

"So…when you're with me, you don't feel like yourself?" she asked, her tone low.

I should have heeded it, but the alcohol ignored it.

"I feel like the guy you want me to be. But, if I want a drink, then I should be able to have it without feeling guilty about it."

Her eyes were hard…yet still sad. "You need help."

"Fuck that noise!"

She didn't even flinch. "You know how I know you need help? Because I've seen people just like you. I've seen my father just like you are right now. I've seen him get so wasted that he beat my mom. I dated a fucking drug dealer, Austin. I know what addiction looks like, and I know that this is a problem for you. I might not have been addicted to drugs or alcohol, but Dillon was as good as an obsession. I had nothing and no one! And I was strong enough to get out. You…" Her eyes traveled the length of me with deep pity. "You have everything and everyone, and still, you do nothing."

She waited for my response, but I had none. What the hell could I say to that?

"I want to be here for you. I needed someone to be there for me, and they were. But I had to reach out. All you have to do is ask for help, to rely on someone, anyone. We would get you professional help. We could get you past this. But you can't do that. You'd rather try to hide it. Try to bury it. All secrets come out in the end, Austin. Trust me, I know."

Then, she turned on her heel and walked away from me. My head was swimming with her words. With the cruel indifference I'd flung at her.

Here was the perfect woman for me. Perfect in every single fucking way. And she was walking out the door.

If she left, then I knew she wasn't just leaving the bar. She was leaving me.

I was running before I even finished the thought.

Twenty-Seven

Julia

What the hell had I been thinking? I had known what I was walking into. I had known that Austin would relapse. It was only a matter of time.

But the argument, the nonchalance, the entitlement.

I could be there for him. I could bring him back to the light. I could even see him through therapy or rehab. But, right now, he didn't even care. He immediately defaulted to the douche that I'd sworn I'd never get back together with. The kind of guy I'd never, ever date. Because I knew what it felt like to be used, to be manipulated and abused. I was not going to go through that again.

Maybe, when he sobered up, Austin would feel differently about his drinking and our argument. *But how long until it all happened again?*

It hurt that I'd trusted him. I'd finally confided in him. He knew the danger I was facing. And, instead of having dinner with Patrick for his birthday, Austin had gotten smashed. There would have been nothing he could do if I'd needed him.

I didn't deserve that.

That was why I'd put a stipulation on our date in the first place.

Austin was a better person when he was sober. But he was the only person who believed otherwise.

"Jules!" Austin called behind me.

But I kept walking. Straight out the front door of Flips.

I had just made it to my car when a hand clamped around my upper arm.

I screamed and jumped back. But the hand held.

And everything narrowed down to the moment when a body stepped out of the shadows by my car and materialized, fully formed, into a thing of nightmares.

"Dillon?"

"Hey, Jules," he said with a lethal, manic smile.

My heart rate ratcheted up. My body trembled under his touch. I thought I was going to be sick. I couldn't get my breathing under control. Everything was panic, panic, and more panic. My brain wasn't firing on full cylinders.

How? How could this be happening to me?

"Wh-what are you doing here?" I gasped out.

"Came to get you back, baby girl."

He ran the back of his hand down my cheek in an all-too familiar way. I shuddered at his touch and felt sick to my stomach.

"Dillon, you were in jail."

He grinned. "Got out on good behavior."

Of course he had. The bastard could charm a snake. No one had even believed me when I first came forward. Why would anyone believe his girlfriend of six years? And, even then, the sentence had hardly stuck. I'd been happy for anything to give me time to get away. I'd been desperate enough to testify against him.

"You're shaking like a leaf," he said. Then, he rubbed his hands up and down my arms. "You have to let me take care of you."

Fear held me in place. I knew that I should jerk back. That I should be the woman I'd become in his absence. But, staring into his blue eyes and that mask of innocence he wore like a second skin, I became the girl who would never leave him.

"Please," I whispered.

"Please what?"

"I can't do this."

"Do what?" he asked, his voice like a knife.

I swallowed hard. "This."

Anger flashed in his eyes, but before he could respond, Austin finally reached me. Fear sparked in me.

No! I couldn't let Austin near Dillon. I couldn't let this happen. I knew what Dillon was capable of. I knew that the charges against him were the least of what he'd done. I would never forgive myself if Austin got hurt.

"Austin, no," I said, stepping between him and Dillon.

"Evan?" Austin asked. He was breathing heavy, and he seemed totally disoriented. "I thought you left a while ago."

"Yeah, I did, but it turned out, my girlfriend was going to show up anyway."

I stared between Austin and Dillon with my mouth hanging open. A pit opened in the pavement, and I fell into it.

"No," I whispered. "No, you didn't."

My eyes found Dillon's. He gave me a perfectly blank, perfectly serene look.

"You must be Julia," he said, holding his hand out to me. "I've heard *so* much about you."

I swatted his hand away. "Stay away from me."

"Jules, I know you're pissed at me, but don't take it out on Evan," Austin said.

"This isn't Evan!" I nearly shrieked. "I don't even know who the fuck Evan is. This is Dillon." I choked on my own words. "This is…it's Dillon."

The words hung in the air, waiting for someone to crack. For the facade to shatter and everyone to realize that the game was up. Whatever Dillon had been up to while infiltrating my life, making fucking friends with Austin, and otherwise being a psycho, it was over. His stalking of me was *over*.

"Dillon…like your ex-boyfriend?" Austin asked slowly.

"Yes."

"What the hell is wrong with you? You made me think that we were friends," he demanded of Dillon.

"Aren't we friends?" Dillon asked, as if he didn't care about any of this.

"We went to the gym together three times a week. You said you moved here for your girlfriend," Austin said in horror.

My stomach twisted. *Oh, fuck!*

"I am here for my girlfriend," Dillon said possessively. "Seems you've met my Jules."

"Julia, get behind me," Austin said.

"Austin, no. Please, let's just go. Don't get into this with him," I pleaded.

Dillon laughed in Austin's face. "What do you think you're going to do? You're drunk off your ass, man."

"Don't fucking talk to me like you know me."

"I don't need to know you. I know your type," Dillon said. "Trust me, I know an addict when I see one. And you're as bad as any of them. Too bad my girl walked right into your train wreck."

"Dillon, stop it," I spat.

"He doesn't like to hear the truth? I've spent the last couple of weeks watching you. Wanted to find out if these Wrights were everything everyone had made them out to be. Every one of them is fucked up. This one, worst of all." Dillon shook his head, like he was disgusted with the sight of Austin. He was a good actor. Always had been. "You think he's been sober? He's been drinking. Check his house. Check his car. Check his fucking gym bag. You think you're his only girl? He spent the night at Maggie's place. You think he cares about you? Just take a good look at him, Jules."

I didn't want to listen to Dillon. I knew what he was doing. I knew he was manipulating me and trying to turn me away from Austin. I was pretty sure I was the only person on the face of the planet who knew the real Dillon Jenkins. He never showed the insanity behind his bravado. Only to me.

Still, I couldn't stop myself from turning hurt, questioning eyes to Austin. *Had Dillon been following him? Had he seen things that I hadn't wanted to see? He might be using them to hurt us, but they could only hurt us if they were true.*

"Is that true?" I asked. I clenched my hands into fists and waited.

"I...I, uh," Austin said, stumbling over his words. "It's not like he said it."

"But...it's true?"

"It's more complicated than that."

"Did you stay at Maggie's place?" I asked.

"Yes."

I breathed out in a rush. "Fuck you, Austin."

"It wasn't like that! We weren't together."

"And that makes it better?" I shrieked.

"No. No, that's not what I meant. Maggie wasn't even there! Just Mindi."

I shook my head. "God, Austin, are you hooking up with crazy butcher-knife Mindi now?"

"No! God, can't you see what he's trying to do? He's trying to turn you against me."

"I'm not against you, Austin! I just wanted the truth. I wanted honesty. I thought we were doing all of this together. I know he's not reliable, but we wouldn't be fighting about this if you'd told me. Have you been hiding your drinking?"

He opened and then closed his mouth. "You knew I was weaning off of alcohol."

"Yeah. It sure looks like it."

"What do you want me to say, Jules?"

I closed my eyes against the frustrations and tried to clear my thoughts. I could feel Dillon infecting us, seeping his poisonous words and toxic personality into my life again. He was Loki, the trickster god. Preying on our fears and using the weeks he'd spent watching us to sow that seed of doubt. To splinter the fragile relationship we had been building into solid stone.

"This is all your doing!" Austin cried.

He turned his undivided, drunk attention to Dillon. And then, before I could do a single thing, Austin threw himself at Dillon. He swung wildly, sliding his fist against Dillon's cheekbone.

"Austin, no!" I shouted.

But he wasn't listening to me. There was nothing I could do.

I knew Dillon had let Austin take that first swing. He'd been waiting for it. Knowing that anything that came next would be self-defense. He'd used the excuse before.

Dillon had been boxing since he could walk. It was the only thing his deadbeat dad had ever given him. He was quick on his feet and could throw a punch that I knew all too well hurt like a motherfucker.

Dillon's eyes analyzed Austin's drunk form before striking with the precision of someone who had been doing this for a very long time. I screamed as he battered Austin's face, jabbed into his ribs, and knocked him off his feet. Austin stood no chance. Maybe, if he'd been sober, he would have had a weight advantage. Austin was solidly built, but Dillon had years of experience. It wasn't a fair fight.

"No, no, no," I said. I grabbed on to Dillon's shoulder and tried to pull him off of Austin.

He shoved me backward with one hand, throwing me into the gravel. I skidded across the blacktop and felt the top layer of my forearm take the brunt of the hit. My hip connected next, and gravel buried like shrapnel into my knee.

I winced as I tried to stand, but I had to. I had to stop this fucking nightmare. Dillon could not do this.

He'd kill Austin.

Fuck, he'd kill him.

Blood spewed from Austin's face. He was curled in on himself. The alcohol in his system must at least be keeping him from the majority of the pain. God, I hoped so.

"Dillon, baby," I whispered hoarsely, "I'll go with you. I'll…I'll go with you."

He stopped assaulting Austin and turned to look at me. "What'd you say?"

"You heard me. I'll go. We…we can be together again. That's what you want, right?"

"What's the catch, Jules?"

"No catch. I left Austin anyway. He was trying to change my mind, but he can't. Let's just…let's just go," I said, my voice shaky. I needed an ounce of his bravado.

Austin groaned. I thought I heard him say no, but I had to do this. I wouldn't let Austin die because Dillon had found me again.

Dillon seemed to take in the situation and then nodded. He'd won. He was done. If Austin was a threat again, he'd kill him. I saw the knowledge of that flash in his eyes.

He reached a hand out to me. "Got to get you cleaned up."

I nodded. No mention that he was the one who had done this to me.

"I'm ready to get back to the way things should be."

"Me, too," I lied.

Then, I followed him, trembling, as I tried hard not to look at Austin. As I followed the man I'd sworn I'd never let rule me again. As I entered my own personal hell and prayed I'd be able to come out on the other side.

Twenty-Eight

Austin

"Austin! Austin!" a voice shouted over me.

"Fuck!" someone else cried.

My mind was fuzzy. Everything fucking hurt. My ribs, my face, my head. God, I felt like my head was about to rip in fucking two.

"Whaaaa…" I slurred.

"Oh, fuck, he's okay," the voice said.

I opened a puffy eye and saw the person standing over me. "Heidi?"

"Yeah, Austin, I'm here. We're all here. We called the cops and an ambulance. They should be here soon. What the fuck happened to you?"

"Jules," I got out. Then, I spat, and blood landed in a wad on the floor.

Floor? Hadn't I been on the pavement? I looked around and saw that I was back inside Flips, lying on top of the bar. They must have carried me in here without me knowing. That meant, I must have blacked out.

"What happened with Julia?" Heidi asked frantically. "Is she okay?"

"Austin, man, take it slow. Tell us everything you know."

I looked up into the face of my brother. "Landon."

"Yeah, I'm here. Patrick and Emery are here, too. Jensen and Morgan are on their way."

"Don't tell Sutton," I muttered. She'd been through enough.

"Okay," Landon said hesitantly. Guilt swept his features. "Why don't you tell us what happened. Is Julia okay?"

I winced and tried to sit up. But everything ached, and I crashed back onto the top of the bar.

"Whoa. Take it easy," Heidi said.

I could see she was worried. Everything felt so far away. I tried to grasp on to what had happened outside, but it kept slipping through my fingertips. Suddenly, nausea hit me over the head. I turned my head and threw up all over the bar floor.

"Fuck," Heidi groaned, turning away.

"That looks like a concussion. Fuck," Landon said. "Sorry, Peter."

"Not the first time. Not the last."

I closed my eyes and tried to remember all the details. I didn't know why everything kept slipping away. *Is it the alcohol? Did I have a concussion? Fuck!*

Then, it hit me.

And my blood chilled.

"Dillon," I spat.

Heidi froze. "Julia's ex-boyfriend?"

"He's Evan."

"Um, what?" Heidi asked.

"Evan is Dillon, and Dillon is Evan. Evan's been my friend, but he's not. He's—" I cut off as a wave of disorientation hit me.

"Isn't Evan the guy you go to the gym with?" Landon filled in for me.

"He's Dillon. He took her."

"Evan or Dillon?" Landon asked, clearly confused.

"Oh no," Heidi gasped. "I think I get it. Dillon has been pretending to be Evan. And he took Julia tonight?"

"Who is Dillon?" Landon asked.

"Long story. We need to be out there, looking for her. We need the cops out there, looking for her. She's in a lot of trouble."

Heidi rushed off to go talk to Emery and Patrick. I slowly eased into a sitting position against Landon's better judgment.

"Did this Dillon-slash-Evan guy do this to you?" Landon asked.

I nodded and regretted it. I cradled my head and winced at the pain. "Yeah, he did. He beat the shit out of me, and I couldn't do anything. I couldn't get to Julia. And she left with him. I don't know what she was thinking. We need to find her, man."

"We will," Landon assured me.

But I could see that he had no clue how to do that. For once, the Wrights didn't have a plan. We didn't know how to fix this. My girlfriend, the love of my life, was out there, somewhere, with a psychopath, and I couldn't do a damn thing. I couldn't even walk yet.

If I hadn't been drunk, then none of this would have happened. If I'd told Julia everything, then she wouldn't have been pissed at me. If she could have trusted me with her story, maybe I never would have fallen for Evan's bullshit.

Instead, I'd stepped right into his trap. We'd done exactly what he wanted. And, now, he had Julia.

I couldn't stand for that.

I might have messed up, but she hadn't left of her own free will. She'd done it to save me. After what she had told me about Dillon, I knew that she wouldn't have gone willingly. She hated him. And that wasn't about to change in a matter of hours. Even if we weren't together, she wasn't going to run back to the guy she'd run from in the first place.

231

That meant, there was only one course of action. I had to get out of this fucking bar, and I had to get my girl back.

Twenty-Nine

Julia

I'd saved Austin's life.

That was what was important here.

If I hadn't left, Dillon would not have stopped. He would have left Austin a bloody, dead pulp on the pavement. It had been bad enough, witnessing Dillon fuck him up, but dead? No, I couldn't even fathom that.

We were in a nondescript pickup truck that I was sure he'd stolen. Adding grand theft auto to his record was nothing. I'd seen him jack a car he needed for the business. He never got caught. Not before I'd ratted him out at least.

And, if it wasn't stolen, then he'd really gone to extreme lengths in setting up this Evan personality. That was even more terrifying. The premeditation. He'd planned this all out. Weaseled his way into my life and Austin's life and Lubbock life so seamlessly. Instead of approaching me as soon as he'd gotten here, he'd subsumed himself into a whole new identity.

"Where are we going?" I asked, picking gravel out of my arm with a wince.

"Your apartment."

I startled. "Why?"

"Got to pack up your shit. I know you want that jacket."

I held back my shudder at the violation. In his twisted mind, he probably didn't even think that he had done anything wrong. I was *his*. And that was all that mattered. It was all that had ever mattered to him. Not how I felt or what I wanted. Only his desires and obsessions. I just happened to be the person who had gotten stuck in the middle of his insanity.

So, I needed to tread very carefully around him. He thought I wanted to be here. I'd left freely. And I needed him to think that was the truth.

"I love that jacket."

"I know," he said.

We pulled up to my apartment. He hopped out first and met me on the other side. "Come on. Let's make this quick."

I nodded and then hurried for the front door. *Okay, I could do this. I could figure out a way around this.* A stop at my apartment meant that I had a chance to escape this. A chance to get away. I needed to focus on that now. I'd saved Austin. No one was coming to save me. I had to save myself. As always.

Dillon grabbed my purse before I could dig through it, and he removed my keys. I longingly looked at my purse for a second before turning away. My phone was in that purse. He had to know that I wanted it. Maybe he even guessed I'd been planning to call the cops.

He slid the key into the lock and opened each of them individually. Not that they had done me much good in the end. Nothing had kept Dillon out of my life.

He snagged my wrist hard enough that bones ground together. I was careful not to cry out. He hated that, and it set him off. Most things did. Then, he tugged me inside and closed and locked the door behind us.

"Nice flowers," he said, grinning at the lilies he'd sent me, still on the counter.

I hadn't been home since I realized they weren't from Austin.

"Do you know how long I've been thinking about this moment?"

"No," I whispered, stepping back once.

"Years. But planning? I've been planning for months. I had to find you first, of course. Changing your name?" He laughed, but it held only madness. "Changing your name was smart. It made my game a little harder. But I found you. I thought, when you dumped that first guy, that it was our time. I knew it was coming to that, so I snuck over and took your jacket. I thought I'd surprise you. But then...then it didn't go as planned. You started with the alcoholic."

"Dillon," I pleaded. I knew he liked to hear himself talk. The mastermind behind all of his plots. But I didn't want to know. I really didn't want to know how he'd infiltrated my life so easily.

"Right. Packing."

He turned to face me, and I swallowed. The full weight of his attention was never a good place to be.

"Come here."

I took a step forward, toward him. His blue eyes critically assessed me. He gently slipped my red hair off my shoulders. I tensed. When he was gentle, I knew it was going to be worse. Much worse. He grabbed my hair at the bottom and then wound it around his hand until it was in a tight fist.

"You could never be with anyone else but me, Jules."

"I know," I said hoarsely.

His grip on my hair tightened, angling my head backward so that I stared up at him.

"Ever."

"Yes."

Harder. I felt some of the hair pulling from the roots. Tears came to my eyes. He was hurting me. All that time I'd spent learning to protect myself, and still, he was hurting me.

"Don't forget it again," he said.

"I won't," I gasped out.

Then, he smiled a chilling smile and firmly pressed his lips against mine. I knew resisting him would only mean something bad for me, and he already had the control. Swallowing back the bile rising in my throat, I opened my lips to him. He kissed me with the ferocity that came from a three-year absence. I felt nothing. Not a thing in his lips. Once, he'd been my world. I would have given anything for any kind of reaction from him.

But, now, I hated him. *Fuck, I hate him!* For everything he'd done to me and all the pain he'd caused. For the fear I couldn't escape. For forcing me…into everything.

"Let's go," he said, shoving me off of him.

My hand went to my head. I winced at the tender touch. *Fuck. Fuck. Fuck.*

Dillon nodded his head toward the bedroom, and I anxiously entered ahead of him. He shoved me into the closet and pulled out a suitcase. He knew exactly where it was.

"Pack," he said.

"Dillon?" I said in that soft, submissive voice I knew he loved. "Do you think you could get me something to clean up my cuts and maybe some ibuprofen?" I carefully met his eyes.

"On one condition."

"What's that?"

"Let me see it," he said.

I was frozen. "See what?"

"My name."

Fuck. Oh, fuck.

When I was twenty, Dillon had convinced me to get his name tattooed on my body. He'd said it was more permanent than marriage. A fucking piece of paper didn't mean shit to him. He'd already owned me. Putting a permanent reminder on me had just sealed the deal.

But the first thing I'd done when I got out was, I'd found the best fucking tattoo artist in the state of Ohio to tattoo over it. Dillon was right. It had been a constant fucking reminder of him. And I'd wanted it gone.

My hands were shaking when I slid up the front of my dress and showed him the navy-blue thong I wore underneath. I tugged the material down just an inch and showed him the delicate flowers and vines that covered up his name and wrapped around my hip. He could only see half of the masterpiece that started at my hip, snaked up my ribs, across the outside of my breast, and up to my shoulder.

He knelt before me and traced his finger over the sensitive skin where he'd insisted I get tattooed.

"We'll have to fix this," he said. He leaned forward and nipped at the skin.

"We'll do it when we get home," I said, forcing excitement into my voice.

He grinned. "Finish packing."

I nodded and started haphazardly throwing clothes into the suitcase. But, as soon as he left the closet, I bolted for my safe. It was my only chance. I had to try for it. I didn't know how much time I had or how familiar he was with my bathroom and where the medical supplies were. But I had at least a minute, maybe two if I was lucky.

I typed in the combination on the lock. I held my breath as it clicked open, and then I was in a race against time. I would not be a victim. Not with all the time I had spent at the shooting range. Not with all the time I had spent becoming a new person and getting away from Dillon. I was *not* going back to Ohio, to that life and that person. No way in hell.

I grabbed my Glock out of the case. My fingers didn't fumble. I didn't hesitate. I ejected the empty magazine, loaded bullets as efficiently as I had practiced time and time again at the range, reinserted the magazine, and pulled the slide back to chamber a round.

"Jules, I didn't find the ibuprofen," Dillon said as he entered the closet.

I whirled around and held the gun level with his chest. Bigger target. I could hit his head, but if I only got off one shot, I wanted to make sure I didn't fucking miss.

"What the hell are you doing?" he demanded.

He was angry. Fiery fucking angry. Ballistic, going-to-kill-me kind of crazy angry.

"Dillon, why don't you back the fuck up right the fuck now?"

"Jules," he said, as if he could reason with me.

"Now! Out of my closet, out of my bedroom, out of my fucking apartment."

"Think about what you're doing."

"Don't give me a reason to use this."

"You're making a huge mistake," he growled low and deadly.

But I was the one with the gun.

"You were the one who made a mistake when you came here."

"Jules, just put the gun down. Don't do anything fucking stupid." Dillon took a step toward me.

"Don't come any closer," I snarled.

"You're not going to shoot me," he said, taking another step forward.

"I have every right to shoot you right now, Dillon. And, if you've been watching me as closely as it seems, then you know I know how. I won't miss. Now, step back!"

He took one more step toward me. He was almost close enough to grab the gun if he wanted to. I couldn't let that happen. This was my only fucking chance. I aimed and fired at his foot. He jumped backward just in time to miss me shooting him.

"I said, back the fuck up."

Dillon reassessed me. I didn't know who the fuck he'd thought he was dealing with this whole time. But I was not the stupid girl he'd manipulated. Maybe he'd thought, because I'd ended up with an addict, that not much had changed. Maybe he'd only seen as much as he wanted to see. But he was seeing me for who I really was now.

Finally, as if he realized he'd lost the edge, he stepped backward, out of the closet. I followed him at the exact same pace. He never turned his back on me. He watched me, as I'd seen him watch many opponents in the past.

"You know this isn't over, Jules. The next time I find you, you won't have your little toy. We will be together."

"Go fuck yourself," I spat. All that confidence had returned to me while I held the only thing keeping me from a miserable existence.

We made it out of the bedroom and to the front door.

"And, if I can't have you, Jules, then no one can have you. I'd rather kill you myself than see you with that asshole."

I shivered at the intensity of his words. He really believed it. He really believed that, the next time he saw me, if I didn't go with him, he'd kill me.

"I hope you burn in hell," I told him.

Dillon shot me a cocky grin. He liked that he'd gotten under my skin. He liked knowing that, anywhere I went, I'd be thinking about him, wondering if he'd show up, wondering if he'd kill me.

He had to turn to slide the locks and open the door.

"I will never be yours, Dillon," I told him when he was finally on the other side of the door. "And I'm not afraid of you. If I see you again, I won't fire a warning shot."

"Big threats, Jules."

"Not a threat," I said. "A promise."

I slammed the door in Dillon's face and hastily locked the place back up, not that I felt safe here anymore. He'd been here. He'd been inside. Every inch of my safe space had been violated.

My knees gave out, and I sank to the floor with my back against the door. All the strength I'd held on to, to face Dillon left me. The hand holding the gun was shaking so violently, I had to put the gun down.

I'd fired it. Oh, fuck, I'd actually fired it.

My breaths started coming out in short gasps right before I burst into tears. *What the hell am I supposed to do now?*

Thirty

Julia

I didn't know how long I'd sat on the floor and cried.

By the time I found the strength to get up, I had seventeen missed calls from Heidi, Emery, Landon, and Patrick. Not one from Austin. My mind immediately went to the worst. Maybe I'd left him dead on the pavement. I hadn't looked. I hadn't checked. I'd just walked away.

I called Heidi back first, holding the phone in one hand and my gun in the other. This little hunk of metal had saved me from a fate worse than death. I wasn't about to let it go anytime soon.

"Julia!" Heidi nearly screamed into the phone. "Oh my God, Julia!"

"How's Austin?" I asked.

"He's fine, Jules. Are you okay? Where are you? Where did that psycho take you?"

My heart restarted. *Austin is fine. He isn't dead.*

"I'm at home. I'm okay."

No. No, I'm not. I was about as far from okay as I'd ever been. And that was saying something.

"Oh my God. Okay." I heard Heidi turn away from the phone and repeat what I'd said. "Em and I are going to come get you. The guys are giving statements to the cops about Dillon-slash-Evan, trying to give them information to find him. Austin has to finish up with the EMT, and then he'll come over, too—"

"No," I said abruptly. "No, uh, tell him not to come over."

"Julia, there's no way in hell I can tell him that," Heidi said with a sigh. "He's totally messed up. His face looks like he got hit by a train or some shit. I think he has a concussion and maybe some broken ribs. I don't know."

"Fuck," I whispered.

"But he doesn't give a shit about himself. All he's been talking about since he regained consciousness is you. His phone died or broke or something, so he couldn't even call you. The fact that we're going to see you before him is going to be hard enough. I know I won't be able to convince him to stay away."

I sank into the couch. Of course she was right.

"All right. I'll just…be here."

"Oh no, do not get off the phone with me."

"I need to call the police," I told her.

"Emery is already on it. She called 911 when I told her where you were. The cops are going to meet us at your place."

"Oh," I whispered. *Is this what it's like to have people take care of you?*

"Just stay on the phone with me, okay? This whole thing scared the shit out of me. I want to know you're safe."

And I never would be again. The last two years had been an illusion anyway. I'd never been safe from Dillon. I never would be.

We stayed on the phone until Heidi and Emery showed up at my apartment. Even though I knew they were outside and I'd just hung up with Heidi, I still startled at the knock on the front door. My heart beat through my chest. I felt like I was going to be sick. It could be Dillon. I knew it wasn't…but it could be.

"Julia," Heidi called, "you can let us in."

"It's all right. We're here to help," Emery said.

I took a deep breath, turned the locks, and then opened the door. My girls stood there with terror in their eyes.

"Oh, Julia," Heidi whispered when she took in my appearance.

"You have a gun," Emery noted.

"Why are you holding a gun?" Heidi asked.

I glanced down at the gun in my hand. It felt nice. Weighted and secure. Even with the barrel pointing toward the ground.

"Maybe you should hand that to me," Emery said.

Emery stepped forward and gently extracted the gun from my hand. I felt empty without it. Like I needed the feel of it in my palm again. It was my new security blanket.

"Julia," Heidi said, "why don't we go sit down as we wait for the cops?"

I nodded. "Yeah. Sure."

Heidi wrapped an arm around my shoulders and eased me back into the living room. Emery carefully popped out the magazine and set it down on the table. This was not the first time she'd done that.

"Can you trash the flowers?" I asked.

Emery gave me a curious look and then did as I'd asked. I hadn't been able to touch them. But I was glad they were gone.

She came to sit next to me.

"Do you want to tell us what happened?" Heidi asked.

"I'd really like to tell it only once. So…can we wait until the cops show up?"

"Sure," Emery said. "Just…take a few deep breaths."

"Do you need anything? Water? A change of clothes?"

I shook my head, and we sat in silence with just their presence working to pull some of the tension out of me.

The cops showed up a few minutes later. It was a tall female cop with cropped brown hair and an overly muscled guy whose eyes swept the apartment, as if expecting Dillon to pop out at any second.

"Hello, I'm Officer Matthews," the woman said. "This is my partner, Officer Curtis. We came over about a complaint of an assault and a kidnapping of Miss Julia Banner."

"That's me," I said, concentrating entirely on Officer Matthews.

"Why don't you start from the beginning?"

"Okay," I said. Then, I started from the beginning. The very beginning.

The cops took some notes and asked some questions along the way. Heidi and Emery gasped in all the right places. I had to show them the gun and where I'd fired the warning shot. They took pictures of everything and collected the shell.

Officer Curtis went back to the police car while Officer Matthews inspected my place. We were almost through with everything when another car pulled up in front of my apartment.

We all waited apprehensively. I ached for the gun once more. I might have finally told them the whole story, but that didn't mean they understood. Then, Landon appeared, helping Austin through the doorway.

My stomach sank when I took in Austin's appearance. His face was battered, almost beyond recognition. He had a tender split lip, and one of his eyes had already started to swell closed. His hand held his side. Broken ribs, Heidi had said. He looked...horrible. Dillon had done this. I wanted to cry.

"Jules," he said, reaching for me. He tugged me into a hug, groaning at the impact. "You're safe. Oh, fuck, you're safe."

I carefully wrapped my arms around his waist. I breathed him in and brought all of his warmth against me. I knew it would be the last time, and I wanted to remember the way I perfectly fit into him.

Then, I took a step back and dropped my arms.

"And you are?" Officer Matthews asked before I could say anything.

"Austin Wright."

"And you were the one assaulted?"

Austin pointed to his face. "What do you think?"

I frowned. Not the time to joke. "Yes, he was."

"I was cleared by an EMT and another officer already," Austin said. His eyes darted to me. "Or else I would have already been here."

Officer Curtis came back inside then. "Looks like this Dillon Jenkins has a warrant. He skipped his parole in Ohio and has been missing for a few weeks now. This is the first tip to his location."

Officer Matthews nodded. "We're going to get you an emergency protection order in place against Dillon. We recommend you take it in and file for a more permanent restraining order against him. We're going to do everything we can to find him and stop this from ever happening again. It would be in your best interest if you stayed with a friend for a while. Also, you'll need to keep us informed if anything else happens."

When the cops finally left, the room felt much too small for all the people in my apartment.

"Can I stay with you?" I asked Heidi.

Her eyes widened in surprise, but she nodded. "Of course. You're welcome anytime."

"Jules," Austin said.

"Do you think we could talk?" I asked, glancing around at my friends. "Alone?"

Everyone made a hasty departure, leaving me alone in the apartment with Austin. Standing here made me feel horribly exposed. I hated this place. I would be happy if it burned to the ground.

"Jules, about what happened," Austin said, stepping forward.

I held my hand out and tried not to break down in front of him. "Please, don't."

"I feel like an idiot. He got into my friend circle. I thought...I thought he was my friend. I never expected any of this to happen."

"I know. Dillon is a master manipulator. I should have been paying more attention. I should have known he was out on parole and that he'd come for me. I thought I was safe. That the name change and the huge move would be enough. But I was wrong."

"That's not your fault."

"It is my fault," I said, looking up into his face. His beaten, bruised, swollen face. "All of this is my fault."

"This is Dillon's fault. Not yours. He did this, Julia."

"I brought him here. I let my guard down. I thought I could live a normal life, Austin...and I just can't."

"Yes, you can," he tried to assure me. He took a step forward.

I shuddered and pulled away. All the anger welled up inside me. All the things I'd learned about Austin. Everything he'd been keeping from me. I couldn't do this.

"Don't touch me," I said, my voice low.

"Jules," he groaned. But he was still drunk. He'd still be drunk for a while. "Don't pull back from me. Don't let him win."

"It's not about winning or losing. It's about what I can handle. And, right now, I can't handle this."

"This?" he said hollowly.

"Us," I corrected.

"Are you breaking up with me?"

I looked him square in the eyes and saw the man I'd fallen so desperately for. The man who I'd needed today. And he hadn't been there. He had lied—to me, his family, to himself. I couldn't be with a man like that.

"Yes," I finally said.

"Julia, I know you're upset with me about the drinking. I know I shouldn't have done it. But I am not stepping back from you because of your past."

"No, you're not physically stepping back from me," I said, raising my voice. "You just emotionally abuse everyone around you. My past is my past. But what we're fucking dealing with, Austin, is your present! Your argument is that, because you know now that you shouldn't have done it, I should roll over and ignore the bullshit."

"Jules—"

"Don't call me that!" I shrieked. "Didn't you hear him call me that? Don't you understand why I can't hear it?"

Austin cringed. "I know. Fuck!"

He ran a hand back through his hair. It was hard for me to even look at his face.

"I don't want to lose you over this."

"You don't get a say," I told him.

"I damn well do!"

I winced at his raised voice and wrapped my arms around my body. In that moment, I felt like a victim again. I'd managed to stand up to Dillon, and Austin was freaking out on me now. No, I couldn't do it.

"Fuck," he groaned, turning away from me and pacing. "I'm sorry. Please, tell me what happened. Tell me how I can fix this."

"You can't." I shook my head and stared off into my bedroom where the remnants of the bullet I'd fired still remained in the carpet.

"I can," he insisted.

"I don't know what you want me to say," I said. "I've made my decision. Now, get out of my apartment."

"No. Watching you walk away with him was the most terrifying moment of my life," Austin said. "I can't let that be the end of us."

I straightened at his declaration. "You didn't hear what the fuck happened here, Austin. But I had to back Dillon out of my apartment with a gun. So, don't stand there and fucking tell me that you won't leave when I tell you to." I shook my head and crossed my arms. "You fucked up. You stayed at your ex's place, hid your alcohol use, and then went on a bender. Actions have consequences. And, right now, they prove to me that I was delusional for thinking you were serious about us."

He stammered over his words as shock registered.

But I couldn't stop. He didn't understand. He didn't get what had happened to me.

"Dillon might be a piece of shit, but even *he* told the truth, and you didn't. It proves that I can't rely on anyone else. You were drunk, and you couldn't help anyone, Austin. I helped myself. I can rely on just one person, and that's me."

It was always just me. And maybe a part of me wanted to hear Austin's words, to give in to what he was offering, but the other part of me, the part screaming in my ear, was saying to back out. To take care of myself and save everyone else from equal misery.

"Julia, please…"

"I don't know what I deserve in a relationship, but it isn't this. It's not a drunk or an addict or a liar. I can't do this again. So, just…let me go."

I brushed past Austin, on my way out the door. His hand reached out to touch me, to stop me, but he let it drop.

I'd accomplished what I had to do. I just wished I didn't hate myself so much for doing it.

Thirty-One

Austin

What the fuck had just happened to my life?
I stood alone in Julia's apartment. She'd just left me. I couldn't believe it. After everything…she'd walked.

Landon cleared his throat behind me. "Hey, man."

I didn't say anything. I was still in shock. Dillon/Evan hadn't been as shocking as Julia breaking up with me.

How could she have done it? She had to know how I felt about her. Not that I'd come straight out and said it, but I'd sure acted like it. Then, one fucking fuckup had torn the house down.

"Austin," Landon said, putting his hand on my shoulder, "let's get you home."

"She left me."

"I…I know." Landon sighed. "She's going through a lot. Just give her some time. She'll come back around."

"No," I said softly. "You didn't hear her. She was certain. This was it."

"I know that's probably how she sounded. Trust me, I've been there. I never thought Heidi would talk to me again after the whole thing with work, but I gave it time. It worked out."

"This isn't some work bullshit that we can throw money at to fix the issue. This is a fucking ex who did a number on her so much so that she doesn't think she deserves to be loved. She just remembered what that feels like. She's not going to change her mind in the morning."

"Why don't we wait until the morning to find out?" Landon said reasonably. "You can sleep this off."

"I can sleep off the alcohol, and I can sleep off the pain, but I'm not going to wake up and suddenly be back with Jules. Not after everything that happened tonight."

Landon sighed. "Maybe not. But you need to heal. So, we need to get you to bed. You can come to our house, too, if you want."

"No, she doesn't want me there."

"Okay. Then…your place."

I didn't argue with him. I just got into the Uber he'd called and let him drop me off at my house. Landon followed me inside just to make that Dillon didn't happen to be there. But it was empty. A little too empty.

"Call me if you need anything. And, Austin?" Landon said.

"Yeah?" I said, staring, unseeing, at my empty house.

"I'm really sorry about tonight. I knew that you shouldn't drink. I could have stopped it. I should have stopped it, and I should have seen what was happening. This is my fault. Patrick and I feel really awful that this all happened."

"Don't go blaming yourself. Either of you. There's plenty of blame to throw around, but none of it is yours. I took the beer from that fuckface. I walked right into his plan. He might have been the catalyst, but I was the idiot who fell for it."

Landon nodded seriously. "Are you sure you don't want me to stay?"

"No concussion. Just a fucked up body. I'll be fine. Go home to your girl and…and take care of mine, okay?"

Landon sympathetically touched my shoulder once before departing.

At least Landon's place had a state-of-the-art security system. Julia should feel safe there. Or safer at least.

Safer without me.

———

The next morning, my face was the size of a balloon, and I couldn't tell where the pain started or ended. After a delirious, pain-riddled phone call, Jensen showed up bright and early. Thank fuck he was a vampire.

Jensen whistled when he saw me passed out on the couch. "You look like shit."

"Thanks," I said, dripping with sarcasm.

"Much worse than last night." Jensen said. He'd shown up around the same time the cops had gotten there and dealt with the aftermath at the bar.

"Are you just here to make fun of me?"

"Isn't that what older brothers do?"

I flipped him off and then winced, reaching for my fractured ribs.

He laughed. "Come on. We need to get you to a doctor. Noah's at the hospital today. He said he'd fit you in."

"Great. Can we go see Julia on the way?"

"Let's get you something to help with the pain first. Figure out Julia after."

I grumbled but let him help me off the couch and into his huge truck. Noah was Emery's sister's husband. He worked at the Texas Tech Medical Center and was an all-around great guy. I liked him. I liked him even more after he stopped prodding at my injuries.

"We could do an X-ray, but that rib is definitely fractured," Noah said. "You'll need a lot of rest and ice. Try not to breathe too shallowly. We want to make sure this doesn't turn into something worse."

"Rest. My forte," I said with a sigh.

"I'll write you a prescription for the pain. Your face has to feel horrible."

"You're telling me."

"Kimber told me what happened," Noah said with a shake of his head. "I hope you're pressing charges against that guy."

"Oh, I am. As soon as they find him, I'll do everything I can to see him behind bars for what he did to Julia."

"No less than he deserves."

Noah handed me the prescription, we shook hands, and then I headed out. Jensen was still waiting for me, talking to one of the nurses he knew. Jensen knew fucking everyone.

"Ready?" he asked.

"Yeah. Let's get this filled. Fuck."

We finished the rest of the errands, and as soon as I popped a pill, I felt the worst of the bite of the pain subside. With a couple of weeks' recovery staring me in my destroyed face, I was glad to have the pills.

"Be careful with those," Jensen said.

"I'm using them as indicated."

"Make sure you do."

I rolled my eyes as he drove me to Flips to collect my car. "Austin…"

"What?" I asked, halfway out of the truck.

"Be careful with Julia. She might need some time."

"I'll give her all the time she needs. But she went through one of the most traumatic experiences of her life. Would you have let Emery walk away after that?"

The answer was written all over his face. No, of course not. We were Wright men. We didn't back down from anything, and we certainly didn't walk away from our women just because they were hurting.

"Let me know if you need anything."

"Sure, man. Thanks," I said. Then, I shut the door and headed to my car.

I made it to Landon's house in record time. I tried the door handle and was glad to see it was locked. I didn't want Dillon to show up here and have easy access to Julia again.

Landon appeared a couple of seconds after I rang the doorbell. He wiped his hand down his face and yawned. "Hey. It's early."

"Yeah, Jensen picked me up at the ass-crack of dawn. How's she doing?"

"She hasn't come out of the guest room."

I started to cross the threshold, but Landon put his hand out.

"She's a guest here, Austin. If she wants you to leave, then you're going to have to listen to her."

"I'm your brother."

"And, as your brother, I'm telling you not to do anything stupid to that broken girl in there."

"I'm not going to do anything stupid," I told him.

Landon gave me a disbelieving look, but he moved his arm. Heidi came out of the master bedroom in one of Landon's golf T-shirts and short shorts. Her eyes were wary as they followed my progress toward the guest bedroom. It seemed that everyone thought it was a bad idea for me to talk to Julia.

I knocked twice and waited for her to say something. But there was no response. Maybe she was still sleeping.

"Julia?"

"Go away," she said through the door.

"Can we talk?"

"What do we have to talk about?"

"Last night."

"No," she said firmly.

I sighed in frustration. "I'd prefer to talk to your face than through a door."

"Go away, Austin."

"Please, Julia."

No response came from the other side of the door. She wasn't going to talk to me. After everything, it was as I'd thought. She really meant what she'd said last night.

Then, slowly, the door cracked open, and beautiful dark eyes stared back up at me.

"You have five minutes," she said. Then, she opened the door for me.

I could work with that.

Julia shut the door behind us once I was in the room. She went and sat down on the bed, but I could tell that sitting next to her would be pushing it.

"How are you feeling?" I asked.

"Tired."

"Didn't get much sleep?"

"No."

"Have you heard anything else about Dillon?"

"No."

Okay…one-worded answers. I needed a way to draw my Julia out of there. She looked so run-down and bedraggled. I'd be shocked if she'd slept at all. And, still…she was everything I wanted in one package.

"I want to make this right between us. Tell me what to do. What do you want me to do?"

She'd been staring down at her clasped hands. A million thoughts seemed to be running through her mind at once. Finally, she looked back up at me. "Leave."

"Why do you push me away? Why can't you accept that someone is going to be here? Because I'm here. I'm not going to just go away," I said. I wanted her to fight me, to fight back, to show some ounce of life. "You said I wasn't Dillon, and you're right. Show me you're more than that girl who got hurt by him."

"I don't have to show you anything," she said quietly, calmly. "We're not together."

"I can't accept that," I said, dropping to my knees in front of her. "I'd take that beating a hundred times over if it meant that it didn't end where we are right now. You're fire and energy and passion. You're not...dead inside."

She turned her face away from me. No emotions clouded her eyes. I wasn't even sure if she was in pain over my words. She seemed so resigned. As if the night had solidified everything that she'd said to me, as if she'd set cement.

"Your five minutes are up."

"Julia, you're not even listening to me."

She held her hand up. "You're trying to start an argument with me, Austin, and it's not going to work. I made my decision last night. I'd appreciate it if you respected it. You told me once that love and hate were powerful emotions. You said that you had to work for indifference. So...that's where I'm at."

I stared, slack-jawed, up at her.

I'd always felt like, even when Julia and I had been apart, there was this link between us. That, when I could get her riled up, I knew she still had feelings for me. But, overnight, that had all disappeared. She wanted nothing to do with me, and I didn't know how to fight for something that wasn't there.

A vibration from the side table fractured her attention. She immediately lunged for her phone and answered it, "Yes. This is Julia." She listened on the other end for a few seconds and then gasped. "I'll...I'll be right down."

"What happened?" I asked once she hung up the phone.

She looked sick to her stomach. "The police found Dillon."

Thirty-Two

Julia

I was going to be sick.

Definitely, definitely sick.

I was standing outside of the police station with Landon, Heidi, and Austin. They'd already called Jensen and Morgan, and Jensen had assured them that he'd have his attorney there as soon as possible. I knew that he'd said I shouldn't say anything until the attorney got there, but I worried. *What if something had happened? What if I was somehow at fault?*

I couldn't shake the feeling. Dillon could charm the cops. Sure, he had a warrant out for his arrest and now had aggravated assault and battery charges from Austin. They wanted to press for kidnapping and domestic violence for me. *But is it still kidnapping if I had gone willingly? And would the assault charges hold up if Austin had hit him first?*

I wouldn't put it past Dillon to have already figured a way to get out of all of this.

"Are you ready?" Heidi asked, coming up to my side.

"Yeah. I think so."

My eyes darted to Austin's for a split second before I walked through the front door. I could do this. I didn't need to think about what had happened with Austin last night or the desperation in his voice this morning. I was hurting him. I didn't want to. But I couldn't seem to stop.

We spoke with a man at the front desk before he directed us to a detective's office. I had Heidi, Austin, and Landon wait outside the office.

Heidi squeezed my hand and nodded. "We'll be right here," she said, pointing at a group of folding chairs across the hall.

"Thanks, Heidi."

"Of course. Good luck."

I nodded and then entered the room. The detective was an athletic woman with frizzy ginger curls and freckles. She had a shrewd appearance about her. I wouldn't want to fuck with her.

"Uh, hi. I'm Julia Banner. I'm here about the Dillon Jenkins arrest."

"Of course, Miss Banner," she said, "please take a seat. I'm Detective Taylor."

"Thank you, Detective," I said, sitting.

"We want to thank you for your confidence in this situation and everyone's help. The information about Dillon Jenkins led us straight to a place on the east side of Lubbock. He was arrested with the possession of a stolen vehicle, and his premises, where he was illegally living under the false name of Evan Brown, had cases of cocaine stashed, presumably after crossing the Mexican border."

I sighed. Of course he hadn't just been harassing me. He'd been working, too. Setting up a run between the Mexican border and probably going all the way back to home.

"You don't seem surprised," she said.

"How can I be? He just got out of prison on good behavior. They couldn't crack him for dealing drugs even though he'd been doing it since he was twelve."

"I read your statement. You were very brave, coming forward," she said, rifling through a stack of papers. "You have a long history with this man."

"Yes. Where is he now?"

"Jail. And he'll stay there. I can't think of a judge alive who would let him out on bond. Maybe if it had just been the violation of probation charge, but with everything—"

"I...I don't have to see him? To identify him?" I gasped out.

The detective looked at me, startled. "No, we found him in record time. We just wanted to speak with you and let you know the details since you were under a temporary order of protection."

I breathed a sigh of relief. "That's...that's really good."

Another knock came from the door, and a squat man stuck his head inside. My lawyer, I presumed.

"Detective, I see you're speaking with my client."

"Jake," the woman said with a sigh. "And I thought you only worked for the Wrights."

He shrugged. "Seems she's a Wright."

I frowned. No, I certainly was not.

"Come on, Julia. Let's go somewhere else and talk."

Jake hauled me out of the detective's office and started speaking a million miles a minute. But my head was spinning with just one solid fact—Dillon was behind bars. And, if we played our cards right...he could be there for a very long time.

A sob caught in my throat. It was far from over, but he wasn't on the loose anymore. He wasn't going to find me and kill me. He wasn't going to go after all the people I loved here. He might have runed so many things, but he wasn't going to take this new life from me.

I spent a few hours in a secluded office with Jake McCarty, going over everything that had happened. By the time I finished, I felt like I'd been wrung out.

"How much is this all going to cost?" I asked finally.

Jake grinned and put a reassuring hand on my shoulder. "I'm on retainer for Jensen. I wouldn't worry about it."

But I did. I didn't want to be indebted to the Wrights. I knew it was impossible to be rid of them, considering I worked for the company and each of my closest friends was dating a Wright brother. But it worried me that this was all related to Austin…that I never would have gotten this otherwise. And, if that was the case, then I'd rather just pay my own legal fees if need be.

At the same time, I was unbelievably grateful. I never would have known where to start finding someone. Certainly not someone like Jake McCarty.

"We have a long road ahead of us, Miss Banner. But I can assure you that I'll do everything to see that Dillon Jenkins is behind bars for life. It would give me great pleasure to know that he could never harass you again."

I gave him a little half-smile at the notion. To be rid of Dillon forever? It seemed impossible.

"Thank you."

"My pleasure."

I left the room and found that only Austin was still waiting for me. God, he really looked fucked up. His face was a wreck. It'd been cleaned up some, but, Christ, it couldn't be safe for him to be driving, could it?

I wanted to be indifferent, like I'd told him I was, but I wasn't indifferent to Austin. I was crazy about him and still brimming with anger. But the more I showed either of those emotions, the more he would think we could get back together. I wasn't ready for that. I didn't know if I'd ever be ready for that.

"Hey," he said, rising to his feet.

"Hey."

"Can I take you back to Landon and Heidi's?"

I chewed on my lip and then nodded. I needed to get out of this police station. When we were back out in the hot, dusty Lubbock air, I finally felt like I could breathe again. It made no sense.

"Where did Heidi and Landon go?" I asked.

"I think they wanted to get a bite to eat and pick up the Tahoe from Flips." He shrugged as we approached his car. "Apparently, Heidi snagged your keys earlier."

"That sounds like her."

"How do you feel? With Dillon back where he belongs?"

I shrugged. "Numb."

"Yeah."

"I know it should feel like a victory, but it feels more like a joke."

"How so?"

"Like I'll wake up, and thinking I'm safe from him is the punch line to a joke."

"I don't think that's going to happen."

"Doesn't change how I feel."

I walked around to the passenger side of his shiny red car. But he paused before opening the door. He stared down at his keys and then tossed them across the roof of the car. I caught them with one hand.

"You wanted to drive her, right?"

I stared at him, momentarily in shock. "You never let anyone drive your car."

"I know."

That was all he said as he walked around to the passenger side of the car. He dropped a kiss onto my forehead and then sat down.

I pulled myself out of the trance. *What the hell was happening? I was getting to drive the Alfa Romeo?*

I sank into the driver's seat and adjusted the seat for my short legs. He laughed when I had to pull the mirror all the way down if I was going to have any hope of seeing out the back. I thanked my dad for teaching me how to drive a stick the one time he'd been sober in my teen years. Then, I flew out of the police station.

Landon and Heidi's house was further out in the country, so I got to take her on long stretches of flat land. She really opened up then, and for those blissful minutes, I felt free.

When I pulled into the driveway, a smile was plastered to my face. "Now, I get the car."

"Exhilarating, right?"

"Like flying without the fear of heights that comes with actual flying."

Austin leaned across the seat as the soft rumble of the car sounded beneath us. His hand went to my cheek, and I flinched. He sat back.

"I don't understand, Julia. Dillon is behind bars. You're safe again. You can move on with your life. You don't have to be tied to his shadow."

"You know why I'm afraid of heights?"

He looked intrigued by my change of direction. "No."

"Well, I always was. But it was really more the fear of falling. I had dreams of falling endlessly, like Alice when she went down a rabbit hole. But Dillon found out about my fear, about how much I hated heights. Then, he spent the next couple of years terrorizing me…apparently, in a way to get rid of my fear. Fear is weakness and all that."

Austin's jaw clenched despite the pain I could see on his face.

"What put me over the edge the day that I decided to get out was because he took me to the top of our apartment building at the time and dangled me there by my wrist." I met his angry eyes. "My broken wrist. The wrist he'd broken."

"Fuck, Julia."

"My fear didn't go away just because he'd dragged me up to the top of the building. My fear of Dillon isn't going to disappear just because he can't reach me anymore either."

"I understand that."

"Do you?" I asked. "Because I don't think you understand. I don't want us to be together."

"You're right. I don't understand that, Julia."

"Just because Dillon is behind bars...doesn't change any of the other reasons I broke up with you. I wish it did, but if I'm not going to be the victim anymore, then I have to apply that to all things in my life. I'm sorry." I choked on that word. "I really am sorry."

I tried to get out of the car, but he grabbed my hand. "Julia, please don't go."

"Austin..."

"It's really over?"

His eyes searched mine for a flicker of hope. But I didn't give him one.

"Yeah...it really is."

I wanted to feel good about walking away and taking control of my life. But, when I entered Landon and Heidi's house without Austin, I just felt empty. I wanted Austin. But I wanted him sober, honest, and without an ex-girlfriend who just might show up naked at his place. I couldn't make him want those things. And he hadn't proven to me that it was even possible. Knowing all the addicts in my life who had failed over and over and over again, I doubted it ever would be.

Thirty-Three

Austin

I stared at the half-empty bottles of liquor still in my house. I'd gotten rid of almost everything. Patrick had become the new owner of the whiskey and scotch that I was only able to get directly from the distributor. I hadn't been able to throw those out. I'd cut back so much that I had nothing left in the cabinet in my house. I'd once had a fully stocked wet bar. I could have made a Bloody Mary any hour of the day.

God, I'd kill for a perfectly made Bloody Mary.

But I'd have to settle for this.

I took out all the bottles. A halfway-filled bottle of Maker's Mark. A quarter of Johnnie Walker Blue. Some Grey Goose. A shot-sized bottle of Fireball that I hadn't been able to part with. Basil Hayden's and Four Roses were down to the last dregs.

I could work with this.

I popped two pain pills and chased them with a shot of Maker's. Julia had left me. There was no coming back from that. None at all.

She'd been dead inside when she delivered the news. She wouldn't take me back. We couldn't fix this.

I couldn't fix anything. That was Jensen's forte. He was the family fixer. He would have been able to make this work. Even Landon had fucking figured his shit out with his crazy ex-wife to land Heidi. I was the only one who found it impossible to keep a girlfriend. Then, I'd put myself out on the line, and she'd walked.

And, fuck, how could I blame her? Would I want to deal with my train wreck?

I wondered how much I would have to drink to forget about Julia. *Is there an amount of alcohol that's capable of that?* I didn't know, but I figured I'd give it a try.

I spent a solid hour binge-watching whatever the hell was on TV at that time while taking shots. At some point, I stopped even recognizing the show. I stopped recognizing anything. There was just the alcohol and then the buzz that quickly converted into being full-out drunk.

Not that I planned to stop there. I was still thinking about Julia. Trying to figure out how the hell I had let this shit happen.

"Fuck. Fuck. Fuck!" I screamed as anger ripped through me.

I stood, stumbling around the living room. I kicked the coffee table across the room and smashed the lamp off of the side table. I grabbed the bottle I'd been finishing and threw it hand over fist into my mounted seventy-inch TV. The screen splintered and looked as fucked up as I felt. The glass had exploded on impact and scattered across the room.

I wheezed and clutched my ribs. Even the alcohol couldn't stop the pain there, it seemed. *Motherfucker.*

My ass crashed back down on the couch, and I clutched my head. I needed more. More alcohol. More everything. Something to make me forget.

No, not something.

Someone.

My phone was in as shitty shape as my TV was, but it still miraculously worked after I plugged it back in. I'd need to replace it, but right now, it did the trick.

"Austin?" Maggie said warily.

"Mags," I breathed.

"This is a surprise."

"Come over."

"Are you drunk?"

"Not drunk enough."

She laughed a low throaty thing. "I thought you were dating someone."

"Do you want to get fucked or not, Maggie?"

"Has that ever been a question?"

"Then, get your ass over here."

I hung up on her before she could respond.

She'd show. She always did.

The way I'd treated her at the Parade of Homes was the outlier in our relationship. She'd been shocked by my behavior because I'd never treated her poorly. Even though we didn't have an official thing, we'd always had fun.

And, God, I could use some fun. Forgetting. Just fucking forgetting.

Fifteen minutes later, a knock at the door roused me from my melancholy. I yanked open the door.

"Maggie," I slurred.

She looked like sin itself. Her dark hair wild. A blood-red dress. High heels.

"Austin," she gasped. "What happened to you?"

She reached out and tentatively ran her manicured nail down my cheek and across my split lip. I'd almost forgotten that my face was a road map of bruises.

"Julia's ex's fist found my face."

"Christ," she whispered. "I hope you got in a few hits yourself."

I laughed, which turned into a cough, which hurt like a bitch. "I don't want to talk about that."

She shrugged, as if to say, *Suit yourself.*

I stepped forward and ran a hand down her side, over the silky material of her dress. She leaned into the touch and seemed to be searching my face for something.

"I wasn't sure I'd show," she said.

"Why?"

"Because I thought you'd gone soft, Wright."

"Why don't you find out?" I suggested.

She laughed, as soft as a purr. "There'll be time for that. But maybe you should let me inside first."

I shoved the door open, and she strode in.

Her feet stilled after only a few feet. "What the hell happened to your house? Did Julia's ex do this to your house, too?"

"Don't worry about it."

"Don't worry about it?" she asked, whirling around on me. "This is fucked up. Tell me what happened."

"I got pissed off."

She arched an eyebrow at me. "You've lost it."

"Don't," I ground out. "I didn't call you here for therapy. I thought you were the only one left who wouldn't lecture me."

"Whatever," she said, kicking the broken lamp and stepping over a piece of broken glass. "I wasn't expecting a construction zone."

"Bedroom is still clean," I said with a smirk.

"I see the Maker's is all over the floor. Anything else for me?"

"Got some Goose and a shot of Fireball."

"What the hell?" she said as I followed her into the kitchen. "Where is the rest?"

"Gave it up."

She snorted. "Sure looks like it, Wright."

I leaned heavily against the counter as she popped open the Grey Goose and downed it straight, like a lady.

She smacked her lips together and shivered. "Yum," she muttered.

"Want a chaser?"

"Do I look like a pussy?"

I grinned and swept eyes down her.

She held her finger up and wagged it in my face. "Easy there."

"No intention of going easy."

I strode toward her, backing her into the counter. Her nails dug into my T-shirt, and she dragged me hard against her.

"I don't have to know what's going on with you, Austin." Her hands slipped under my shirt, and her nails scraped across the waistband of my shorts. "But I know something is."

"Does it matter?" I snapped.

She shrugged. "You didn't call me for therapy, right?"

My hands gripped the back of her thighs and hoisted her onto the countertop. I gasped in pain as my ribs seized under the pressure. *Holy fuck!*

"Are you okay?" she asked, her eyes wide.

"Fine, Mags. Just…shut up."

I grabbed her face between my hands and crushed our mouths together. She was still for only a second before returning the kiss. Her legs wrapped around my back, tugging me closer. And I tried to will all the anger I'd been drowning in into that kiss. *Fuck everything else going on in my life.*

I wanted to forget. I wanted someone to help me forget.

But I wasn't forgetting.

Because that name still rattled around in my head. The brown hair wasn't red. The blue eyes weren't brown. Her lips didn't taste like cherry. She wasn't covered in ink. Her body didn't match mine.

I tried to force it. I didn't need feelings with Maggie. We never had. I just needed one night. Then, maybe I'd learn how to move on. Learn how to be as dead inside as Julia was.

Here's to hoping.

Thirty-Four

Julia

"I have looked at seven thousand new apartments today, and I hate them all." I pushed my computer back and slumped into the couch.

"You'll find the one," Heidi assured me. "What about this one?" She pointed to the last one I'd looked at.

It was on the first floor with a security plan and a fence with code access to get inside and, and, and...

All the features I wanted. Yet none of them fit.

"No, I don't like it."

"Well, you don't have to get a new place right away."

"I don't want to impose," I said at once.

"You're not imposing. We have plenty of house, and it's no trouble at all."

I still felt bad. Even though it hadn't been very long since everything went down. It didn't help that I couldn't seem to sleep. Not without nightmares jolting me out of bed in a cold sweat. I was exhausted and had no energy. I wanted this all to be over.

Heidi seemed to notice that. "Let's look more tomorrow. We should relax until Landon gets up. He really likes his beauty sleep."

I shot her an appreciative smile. "That sounds good."

"I could make us omelets. Landon is the better cook, but eggs, I can do."

"Sure."

I'd go for anything that didn't involve people looking at me with pity. I knew I was pitiful. I didn't need to see it when everyone looked at me. I might have saved my own life, but I still felt like the victim. And it didn't help that everyone was treating me like one.

"Great!" Heidi hopped up and started getting things out for the omelet.

I grabbed my computer again and flicked through a few more apartments. Not that anything was jumping out at me.

The doorbell rang. My head popped up, and I stared at Heidi with frightened eyes. Fuck, even the doorbell was freaking me out.

"Don't worry. I got it," Heidi said. She went to the door and pulled it open. "Austin, what a surprise."

"Hey, Heidi. Is Julia still here?"

"She is."

"Can I talk to her? It'll only be a minute."

Heidi's head swiveled back to me. "Julia?"

I breathed in deeply and then stood. Man, I was not looking forward to this again. I didn't care how persistent Austin was; I wasn't about to change my mind. Not with things the way they were.

"It's fine," I told Heidi.

She nodded and brushed my shoulder as she went back into the kitchen.

"Let's go outside," I suggested.

"Okay. But it's not going to take long. Jensen is waiting for me."

He pointed his thumb over his shoulder, and I saw Jensen's giant truck idling on the street. *Strange.*

"Still having trouble driving?" I asked as we stepped outside.

"No. I'm leaving."

My head snapped up to him. "You're leaving?"

"Yeah. Jensen is taking me to rehab. I'm going to be gone for the next three months at an inpatient facility. Jensen set it all up. But I wanted to see you. I, uh…" He glanced off for a second, as if arguing with himself. "I wanted to tell you some stuff before I went."

"Okay," I said hesitantly. "You're…you're really going to rehab?" I couldn't keep the disbelief from my voice.

Austin had rejected the idea of getting professional help from the start. He'd never thought it would be helpful or that he needed it or that he even had a problem. He'd just done whatever he wanted, never really improving. It was almost too good to be true to think that he was actually doing this.

"Yes, I am." He gestured for us to sit on the outdoor furniture in front of Landon's house. "Jensen didn't even think that I should stop and talk to you before going, but I had to."

"Even though we're broken up?"

"Especially because we're broken up."

I didn't know how to take that. "Well, I'm glad you're going. I think it's a really good idea. I hope it helps you."

"Me, too. Because you were right."

"About?"

"Everything." He ran a hand back through his hair. "You and Jensen and my family and everyone. You all saw me for what I was and what I was doing to myself. I didn't really realize until this morning. I'd thought I did, but I was fooling myself."

"What made you see the light?"

He winced. "Just…hear me out."

I braced myself because I had a feeling whatever he was about to say was not something I wanted to hear.

"What did you do?" I asked low, worried.

"I emptied the rest of the bottles in my house last night and mixed them with the pain pills I'd gotten from Noah. It was stupid, but I just…" He shook his head in frustration. "I defaulted to how I always acted. I was so fucking hurt. After I'd gotten the shit beat out of me, you broke up with me. Just abandoned me."

"Austin—"

"No, no, I'm not mad at you. Well, not anymore. I get your reasons. I get why you did it. I get why you don't trust me. I don't trust me." He looked like he wanted to reach out for me, but he didn't. "I wanted to go back to not feeling. I didn't know how to feel this intensely. I didn't know how to react to what I felt without finding the bottle." He shrugged and glanced off. "But that isn't why I'm here. I'm just…fuck, I really want to avoid this conversation."

Tension vibrated through every muscle as I waited for the news, and I didn't even know what it was. "Tell me."

"When I got drunk, I invited Maggie over."

I froze and stopped breathing. "Wow."

"Julia—"

I shook my head and stood up. "Go fuck yourself, Austin."

"No, no, no," he said, running ahead of me to block my path.

"Get out of my fucking way. You don't get to come here and throw that bullshit at me."

"I'm not," he insisted. "I didn't sleep with her."

"And you expect me to believe you? *Again?*"

"I'm not asking you to get back together with me, Julia. I'm not even asking you to forgive me. I hardly forgive myself for even inviting her over. I'm asking you to listen. You can call Maggie yourself if you want. Though you're probably not her favorite person right now."

"I'm not *her* favorite person?" I nearly shrieked.

All of that cool, calm I'd felt toward Austin shattered, and I was left reeling. *What the fuck?*

"No, you're not. Because I invited her over. We…made out," he said with another well-placed wince. "And I thought that being with her would make me forget you. But she was all wrong. Nothing could make me forget you. No one else could ever be you. I realized too late that you are perfect for me. Perfect for me in ways I hadn't even known."

"That doesn't make up for what you did. We'd been broken up for a day!"

"I know, I know. It was stupid. I got wasted, like I always did, and did shit that I had done back when I was so fucked up all the time. But I didn't sleep with Maggie. I feel bad enough that we even kissed. That I even thought that I'd be able to get you out of my head." He reached for me but stopped before his hand met my arm. Then, he regretfully dropped it. "I told her to leave. I told her how I felt about you. That I never had feelings for her. That I'd never have feelings for her, and all of this was a mistake. I wasn't particularly eloquent, as I was drunk off my ass."

"I don't even know why you came here to tell me this," I said, seething. "Why you even bothered."

"Because I wanted the truth out there. I didn't want to hold out on telling you and you find out from someone else. For you to think the worst."

"Too late," I spat.

"Yeah, I deserve that," he said. "You were right about me. And, when I woke up, hungover and alone, this morning, I realized that I had proven every fear you had about me right. That I was a drunk, lying addict."

"Asshole," I finished for him.

"That, too. You have every reason to hate me. I am all those things, and you deserve better than me."

"So, you're going to rehab to try to be the man I deserve?" I asked with a sarcastic bite to my voice.

We all knew how well that would fucking work.

"No, I fully understand that this might be the last time I see you. I don't want to accept that, but I can eventually if that's what you really want. But I'm going to rehab for me. To be the man I want to be...that I need to be."

I didn't know what to say to that. I wanted to believe every word he'd said. I hoped he had all the best intentions, but I'd been burned so many times. It was hard to stand there and hear him say the same bullshit I'd heard from my dad...from Dillon.

"So, I guess I'm going to go," Austin said.

His eyes were so intent on mine that I couldn't pull myself away even if I wanted to.

"I'll be out of here for the next ninety days at least. Plenty of time for you to figure out if you want anything to do with me. But just don't forget about me, okay?"

"Austin, I'm not giving you any promises."

"I don't want you to. I want you to know that you're the most important thing in my life." He took a step forward and dropped a soft kiss onto the top of my head. He sighed heavily. "I'm sorry I realized that too late."

Then, he pulled away from me without a good-bye. It was as if he might never leave if he stayed another moment.

I watched Jensen's truck barrel down the road, carrying Austin far, far away from here. I was shaken. I didn't know where to start. Part of me was fucking furious that, after everything, he'd gone and gotten fucked up and then hooked up with Maggie. But the other part of me was just so happy he was going to get help. He needed it. He really fucking needed it.

Heidi's head popped out of the front door. "Did he just leave?"

"Yeah," I said distantly.

"Everything all right?"

I could see Landon standing behind her with a worried expression on his face.

"Jensen is taking him to rehab."

"Oh, wow," Heidi said.

"Are you serious?" Landon asked, coming fully out of the house now.

I nodded. "Yeah. Can I ask you for a favor?"

"Of course," Landon said. "What's up?"

"Will you get me Maggie's number?"

He frowned. "Uh, why?"

"Because I need to make a very important phone call."

I didn't give two fucks if Maggie hated me. The feeling was mutual. But I wanted all the fucking facts about what had really happened. I wanted to hold on to my anger and not trust everything he'd said. It was easier than thinking that maybe, just maybe, Austin had realized his mistakes. Easier than thinking that we might have a shot at this if he really did get the help he needed.

Thirty-Five

Austin

When I'd asked Jensen to take care of it, I hadn't quite expected this. We were in Malibu, driving up to an enormous and gorgeous rehabilitation facility. It was the best in the country and had the price tag to prove it.

"I can't believe we just flew to California for this," I said.

"Well, it's not a vacation," Jensen said as we moved through the gated doors.

"Of course not."

"I got you the best treatment available. This is where all the top celebrities go because it offers them the privacy they need to get better. You deserve nothing less than that."

It was on brand with the Wrights. Jensen did what he could to protect the family and the company.

"Thanks, Jensen."

The car stopped in front of the giant building, and we were brought inside.

"Mr. Wright," a man said, approaching us.

"Yes, Austin," I said, shaking his hand.

"And you must be Jensen."

"That's right."

"I'm Bartholomew. We're glad to have you here. Right this way, and we'll get you checked in and settled into your new villa."

Villa?

I raised my eyebrows at Jensen, and he just shrugged.

"We want you to be as comfortable as possible. We think treatment shouldn't be in a hospital-like setting where more stress could fracture your recovery. We just want to help you succeed, and everything we do here is focused on that goal."

"Great," I said skeptically.

The man laughed. "You'll fit right in here. Everyone has that same tone when they first get here. But, while it might seem luxurious, your days will be packed with activities and therapy to get you on the right track."

When Jensen realized I wasn't going to say anything, he smiled at Bartholomew. "That's excellent. I'd expect nothing less."

"You do want to get better?" Bartholomew asked me, ignoring Jensen and staring at me straight in the face.

Did I?

Fuck.

I wanted to say, *Yes.* I wanted to say, *Of course.* I wanted to say so many things. But the truth was, the thought of professional help scared the shit out of me. What if I was a lost cause? What if, despite the six thousand dollars a week that Jensen was going to fork over for this insane rehab center, I couldn't get my shit together?

"I'm ready to try," I finally said.

Bartholomew nodded with a kind smile. "That's all we ask. We can help you with the rest."

Julia

Austin hadn't slept with Maggie.

I'd actually made that phone call even though I was terrified to. I'd thought that maybe he'd told me to call Maggie as a bluff. He hadn't thought I'd actually call her. But, hey, I'd pulled a gun on my ex-boyfriend. One phone call couldn't be that bad.

Maggie had admitted that he had stopped at a kiss, that he'd gotten all mopey about me and then tried to apologize for using her. She'd laughed, as if she was using him. Then, she'd threatened me within an inch of my life if I ever called her again and hung up on me.

But I believed him now. Didn't make him inviting her over or that kiss any better. But he'd been honest. It was a step in the right direction. Even if I wasn't ready for a relationship... and had no clue if I ever would be again.

He'd found the honest bone in his body and then fucking left.

He'd really, really left.

Landon told me that he was at some ritzy rehab center in California with security that even paparazzi couldn't get through. The program he was in required no outside contact for the first thirty days. He'd start family therapy after that, and Landon was excited to get to go to California and see him. I was sure he was also interested in taking a vacation, but I didn't say it.

Not that I was checking up on Austin or anything.

Okay, maybe a little.

It was really quiet around here without him. But I was kind of glad that I had time to process.

Plus, it helped that, two weeks after Austin left, I finally found the most perfect apartment ever.

"I am so sorry I stayed here for so long," I told Heidi and Landon on moving day.

"I'd be more okay with it if you helped move this couch," Landon grunted.

"Shit, sorry," I said, jumping into action.

"We really should have hired someone," Heidi said.

"My back is going to love this," Landon grumbled.

"Aw, poor baby," Heidi cooed.

"Can you keep your lovey-dovey bullshit to yourselves until after we get this couch out the door?" Patrick groaned.

Heidi laughed. "No apologies from me."

Morgan wrinkled her nose. "Just keep all this shit to a minimum when Sutton gets here."

"She's coming?" I asked in shock. I ran my back into the doorframe and dropped the couch. "Fuck!"

"Yeah, Jensen and Emery are bringing her. We're trying to get her out of the house some. Kimber said she'd watch Jason," Morgan said.

"Wow," I muttered. "How has she been?"

Morgan shook her head and glanced away.

Eesh. That bad.

"Julia, couch," Patrick grumbled.

Somehow, I felt more like I was part of the Wright family than ever despite the fact that Austin was gone. I didn't know if they were doing it out of obligation because of him or if they just liked me, but I was grateful. It was hard not to feel loved when these amazing people reached out to me.

Jensen, Emery, and Sutton showed up when we were already almost finished with my old apartment. I didn't have that much stuff. Especially after burning half of my clothes, including that damn bomber jacket. Sutton looked like a hollowed-out version of herself. Since Mav had died a month earlier, she'd lost at least ten pounds. Her cheekbones jutted out of her face, and her dress hung off of her. She didn't say much, just started picking up small boxes and taking them to the moving truck.

By the time we done unloading at my new studio apartment downtown, it was lunchtime. The selling point of the place was that it had the gorgeous space for my art. And I figured, if Austin was getting the help he needed, then I was going to help myself, too.

Sutton came to stand at my side in the art studio. All I had in there were a few boxes of supplies and an easel.

She stared at the blank easel. "Do you love my brother?" she asked.

I turned to face her, but she wasn't looking at me. She was somewhere very far away.

"I don't know if it's that simple."

"I heard how much of an idiot he was." She finally met my eyes with her sad, sorrowful ones. "But, if you love him—and I assure you that he loves you—and you let him go because of his relapse, then you're the idiot." She sighed. "I'm just saying…you never know how much time you have together. Forgiving someone is easier than living without them."

I watched her retreating back with a rapidly growing ache in my chest. Sutton had firsthand experience in the matter, and it had drastically changed her from the silliest of the entire Wright bunch to…the wisest.

And her words were wise.

Austin

"Austin!" Morgan said with a huge smile. She threw her arms around me and squeezed me tight. "Man, I've missed you. I didn't realize how quiet it would be without you cutting up."

I laughed and released Morgan. "I'll take that as a compliment."

"You look good," Landon said.

We clapped hands, and then he pulled me in for a hug.

"Not good but better," I told him.

They were all here. In California. Jensen, Landon, Morgan, and even Sutton.

"Hey, sis," I said, pulling my little sister toward me.

She was a shell of her former self. I couldn't believe how tiny she was. She'd never been a big girl, but now, she was a rail.

"Are they feeding you? Because I have a personal chef here, and he's the shit."

She cracked a smile. "I eat. Don't worry about me. We're here for you."

Jensen reached out and shook my hand last. "I think I like this place even better than when I dropped you off."

"It grows on you."

It had grown on me. In the month I'd been here, I'd started to love the Malibu center. The first week at least, I'd hated it. Well, I'd hated everything and everyone. Detoxing my body from all the alcohol I'd consumed over the years was more painful than I'd ever imagined. I was right when I'd thought that going cold turkey would kill me. It probably would have without the right people looking over me. But, now, I was into the actual rehabilitation part. That also meant, visitors. Eventually maybe even approved weekend trips, but I wasn't going to hold my breath.

"No Patrick?" I asked.

"He couldn't make it," Morgan said. "He has a big work project. His boss is a bitch."

I laughed. "You're not a bitch. You're just efficient."

"He'll be here next time. Don't worry."

"Good. And...Julia?" I managed to get out.

I'd talked about Julia a lot in therapy. Thought about how I'd treated her, how I felt about her, where to go from here.

Not that therapy gave anyone answers. Just a hell of a lot more things to think about. And Julia was constantly on my mind.

All of my siblings were stone-cold silent though.

Finally, Landon spoke up, "She's doing good. She's just still…I don't know."

"She needs more time," Sutton finished. "But she misses you."

"She said that?" I asked hopefully.

"No, but I know she does."

"Oh."

I supposed that was a start. I didn't expect her to ever forgive me…or even miss me. So, if she did, I'd take it.

"Well then…why don't I show you around?"

I took my siblings on a tour of the facility. If I weren't here for rehab, I would think this was a resort. It had heated pools and private tennis courts, a spa, horseback riding, and even a fully equipped art studio. I would have loved to show that to Julia. If I had an artistic bone in my body, I would take some classes. But I'd leave that to her.

Morgan leaned forward on the balcony and yawned. "I could just take a nap. I'm so tired."

"I bet."

"Work is…a mess."

"Have you hired a new CFO?"

Being isolated meant that I didn't know anything that was going on in the world and even less about the company.

She frowned. "We put out an offer to David Calloway this past weekend. I'm sure we'll have to negotiate the contract, and then he'll start next week."

"You made the right choice. David seems like a great guy. I really liked him when I met him."

"You're not upset?"

"That I'm not the CFO?" I laughed and shook my head. "No. No, I'm definitely not. I was stupid to think that was what I wanted in the first place."

"No, it wasn't stupid. We're Wrights. We are the company. Jensen knows that."

I shrugged and leaned forward. Jensen, Landon, and Sutton had gotten into suits and were hanging out by the pool. Maybe they needed this visit as much as I did.

"I wasn't ready for that job. Jensen knew that, too. I'd rather you have someone like David, who already knows his stuff, and you can train him. It'll be easier than working with me."

"A month in here, and you're this sensible?" she teased. She poked me in my finally-healed ribs. "Who will you be when you come out?"

"Same me."

"I don't believe that for one minute."

"Sober me," I suggested.

"What are you going to do when you get out?"

"I don't know. Will I still have my job?"

Morgan arched an eyebrow. "Do you still want it?"

"If I've learned anything from this experience so far, it's that I didn't appreciate a goddamn thing about my life before this. That job was a godsend, and I treated it like a joke. I felt entitled to whatever I wanted without having to work for it. That isn't real life. But I love that company, Morgan." I turned to face her. "Maybe as much as you do. I always have."

"Then your job is waiting for you when you get back."

"Thank you. I know I probably don't deserve that, but I do appreciate it."

We both stared down at the pool.

"You want to change? Or are you going to take that nap?" I asked.

Morgan stepped back into my villa, as if debating on what she was going to do. "Let's join them."

"All right. I'll get a suit."

"Austin?"

"Hmm?"

"What are you going to do about Julia when you get back?"

I smiled. I'd thought about that a lot. "Appreciate the fuck out of her."

Thirty-Six

Julia

My hands were covered in paint. Drop cloth obscured the hardwood floor of my studio. Canvas took up every open space.

It was perfect. A messy perfection.

Just like me.

Something had taken over me ever since I moved in. I couldn't stop painting, drawing, sketching. I'd even tried my hands at sculpting. Art infused my body and my mind. It made my soul sing.

It was like I'd found my muse.

My eyes moved to the only one hundred percent finished painting in the whole room. It was the naked picture of Austin I'd painted in art class this summer.

Nina had called me to come pick it up even though I wasn't taking any more classes. She'd been impressed with my work and asked me to come back. She'd introduced me to the art community in Lubbock.

And, suddenly, I'd come alive. I had a naked muse in my studio and a group of people encouraging my art in a way I never had before. It felt right. Wright even.

The doorbell rang, and I actually didn't jump. I'd destroyed a few good paintings that way. But art had become my therapy. With it, I was finally de-stressing, post-Dillon.

I wiped my hands off the best I could on a red towel and then gave up. I was in leggings and a tank top that used to be white before I covered it in paint. My hairdresser, Lisa, had dyed my hair into a rose-gold ombré, so it was lighter on the top before it faded out into the red I'd had for so long. I liked the new look. Not that anyone could see it in the messy bun I had on the top of my head.

I looked out the peephole and didn't see anyone there. After deactivating the security system and unlocking the door, I pulled it open. I warily looked around before realizing there was a giant box on my doorstep.

My eyes rounded in confusion.

"What the…"

I hadn't ordered anything.

I checked the shipping address. It was from somewhere in California. *Huh.*

It wasn't heavy when I kicked it inside. I found a pair of scissors in a drawer in my coffee table and tore into the packing tape. The box was covered from top to bottom in little green Styrofoam peanuts.

"Jesus," I muttered.

I dug my hand in, up to my elbow, before I came across whatever was in the box. I wrapped my fingers around something soft and tugged. In a shower of peanuts came a shiny pink-sequined unicorn with a ribbon tied around its neck and a letter attached to it.

I burst into laughter when I saw Waffle.

I'd known that the unicorn had ended up at Austin's house, but I'd thought he'd just forgotten about it. And maybe about me, too. He'd been able to have outside communication for three weeks, but he hadn't reached out to me.

𝒯𝒽𝑒 WRIGHT MISTAKE

With excitement that I couldn't explain, I plucked the letter off of Waffle's neck and placed our unicorn on my kitchen island. I ripped open the envelope and stared down at the neat print of Austin's handwriting.

Dear Julia,

I've wanted to write to you every day that I've been here, but my therapist and I agreed that it was better for you to have space. I'd asked you not to forget me, yet I had to give you room to if you chose. So, in the event that you continue to want nothing to do with me, feel free to stop reading and throw this in the trash.

I'm going to assume...or maybe just hope that you're still reading. If that's the case, here's your damn unicorn. Waffle got me through the hardest parts of detox. But, since we share custody, I thought it only appropriate that you got her for a while. That way, I stop getting jabs from my brothers about having a pink-sequined unicorn in my room.

Why the snail mail? I'm sure you're probably wondering. I could have called you or emailed or whatever. You could come visit even. But, strangely enough, I found that I can articulate how I'm feeling best when I write things down. I apologize for my penmanship in advance.

Anyway, all I really want to say is that I'm sorry. I took you for granted and didn't listen to you or appreciate you. If I could go back, I'd fix things. But I don't have that ability. I have to accept that I hurt you and that what I did might be irreversible.

But...if there's maybe a small chance that you might be willing to meet a new Austin Wright—not perfect but maybe better—I'd be the luckiest guy in the world. If that's something you are interested in, then write me back. You can send it to the address on the envelope, and it'll get to me.

I'll be anxiously awaiting your letter. And, if I don't get one, then...I understand.

Still yours,

Austin

I read the letter three times. Each time, my smile grew bigger and bigger. After the last time, I found my own piece of paper and started writing.

Austin

Julia's letter showed up three days after the package was delivered.

It had taken fifteen different sheets of paper before I got the wording right on mine, and even then, I'd thought it sucked. I hadn't wanted to send it. And, at the same time, I'd been dying to send it. I thought I had been more worried that she'd ignore me. I wouldn't have blamed her, but a guy had to have hope.

Dear Austin,

I might be interested in a new Austin Wright.

Just not totally new. Maybe one more like that guy who "won" me Waffle in the first place. Or who walked me through the First Friday Art Trail. Have you seen him lately?

I'm glad you're in therapy. I've had my own brand of therapy. Found a muse, which is nice because I converted a bedroom in my new apartment into an art studio. Finding my art again...you know? Waffle likes the studio, too. She might not be just pink anymore.

Anyway, I talked to Maggie. I don't think you actually expected me to, but I did. So, I believe you. I'm still upset about what happened. That anything happened at all. Maybe my moral high ground should say that I have no right to be upset, considering we were broken up at the time, but that doesn't stop me from feeling it. I want to move past that, but even after talking to her and her yelling at me about you, I still feel panic at the thought of you two.

Phew. Okay, had to get that off my chest.

I don't know where this leaves us. Maybe I don't have to figure it out right now. Write me again, and I'll keep thinking about it.

Julia

P.S. I like the snail mail, and your handwriting doesn't totally suck.

I answered that letter. And the next. And the one after that. Every three days, I had a letter from Julia. I thought we'd talked more in the weeks I was away than we had when we were together. Without her sexy body in front of me and the weight of the alcohol abuse clouding everything, I found that I always had something to say to her.

The fact that I hadn't just picked up a phone or emailed or flown her out to see me made the anticipation so much more intense. No instant gratification in that. With each passing day, I ached for her more and more. Ached for her like I hadn't known was possible.

But I had a long way to go. Another month of rehab before I could even get out of California. Who knew what would happen when I was finally back in Lubbock? All I knew was that I'd do anything to make up for what had happened with Julia.

One of the things that the center really pushed was family therapy days. It helped the therapist connect to the entire situation. And mine was always trying to get to the root of the problem. What had caused me to be this way?

I insisted I had always been this way. He smiled and assured me that I didn't come out of the womb as an alcoholic. It might run in my family, but that didn't mean I had to succumb to it.

We were in one of those sessions when Jensen leaned back in his chair. "I wonder if some of this goes back to the fact that you were there when Mom died."

"You were there when Mom died?" Sutton whispered. Her voice was as light as a feather caught in the wind.

"Yeah," I said, angling away from that particular conversation. "I was with her…or…well, yeah."

"Tell us more about that, Austin," my therapist said. He pointed his pen toward me, as if to say, *Go on.*

"About Mom?"

"I didn't know you were with her either," Morgan said.

"Me either," Landon admitted.

My eyes found Jensen's in a panic.

He nodded and patted my back. "It's okay. We're not Dad. We can talk about Mom."

I swallowed and nodded. "Okay. Well, I hadn't known how sick Mom was. Dad didn't like to talk about it, and Mom tried to hide it. She was the perfect wife and mother. She was still cooking, cleaning, and taking care of us kids through chemo. It was a pretty traditional marriage by that standard, I guess."

I reached for the glass of water in front of me and took a long drink. I was off on a tangent. That wasn't what they wanted to know about anyway.

"I didn't even know about the pancreatic cancer until she died when I was nine. Maybe you did," I said, gesturing to Jensen, "but I was in the dark."

"I guessed," he said. "It definitely wasn't what Dad had said it was, but he wasn't ever honest with us."

"No, he wasn't," Landon muttered.

"She wasn't even supposed to have it," I continued. "She was so young. Only thirty-five. With five children, ages twelve to one."

"That had to be hard," the therapist said.

"It was."

My siblings nodded. I could see that they were all remembering their version of what had happened after Mom died. Jensen had taken over. Life had gone on, but it was never the same.

"I was watching her one day. Dad had told me to stay with her. She was sick and got into bed. I remember telling her that I wouldn't nap with her because I didn't want to catch her cold. I went out to play instead of staying with her, and when I came back, she was gone."

"Oh, Austin," Morgan said softly. "That isn't your fault."

"I agree with your sister," the therapist said. "As a nine-year-old boy, you were not responsible for the care of your terminally ill mother. It's perfectly reasonable that you wanted to go outside and play."

"Logically, of course, I know that. But I wasn't logical. I covered up my distress as a kid and through my teen years. I looked adjusted. Maybe I was adjusted."

"Of course. It sounds like you internalized the issue. When did you start drinking regularly after that?"

"After Dad died."

"Tell us about that," the therapist continued.

"I was twenty and in college at Tech. I was at a bar when I got the news," I said, as if that memory had just dropped into my mind.

"So, you were around alcohol when you found out about the death of another parent?"

"Yeah," I muttered. "I remember thinking about all the stuff that had happened with my mom, and suddenly, I just…I couldn't cope. Not that any of that is an excuse. I suppose it's my reason."

"Shit," Landon said.

"That's awful," Morgan said.

Sutton's eyes were red, and she was looking down at her hands. She looked like she might burst into tears at any point.

"I didn't realize," Jensen said. "All this time, you were self-medicating over Mom's death, and you weren't even responsible."

"This feels like a breakthrough," the therapist said. "Something we can work with from here on out."

I looked around at my family in shock. Deep down, I'd known that Mom's and Dad's deaths had affected me, but I hadn't ever wanted to believe that I was drinking to cover up that hurt. Now that it was in front of me, it felt like a hurdle I could overcome. And maybe it would help all of the Wrights to finally deal with it.

Julia

Dillon's trial had been moved up.

I'd been dreading this day for a long three months. But I was also glad that I could deal with this before Austin got back. I kept his last letter in my pocket through the entire ordeal.

> *Dear Julia,*
>
> *You are the strongest person I've ever met. I can't imagine how it must feel to testify against Dillon, but if anyone can do it, for a second time, then you can. You held him at gunpoint in your apartment. You got away from him twice. You can do this.*
>
> *My only regret is that I can't be there, too. I'd be the best moral support you could ask for.*
>
> *I'll be thinking about you, worrying over you, anxiously awaiting another letter to find out how it went. I have faith that the judge will make the right decision.*
>
> *Counting down the days until I see you again.*
>
> *Always yours,*
>
> *Austin*

Having his words with me helped.

Dillon was a shadow of himself after spending three months behind bars again. He looked like a wreck. And that helped, too.

When the jury came back and found him guilty, I nearly stood up and cheered. The judge gave him thirty years in prison for a laundry list of crimes. And, just like that, I was free. Finally free.

Heidi and Emery were waiting for me when I left the courtroom. They threw their arms around me, jumping up and down at the victory.

"How do you feel?" Heidi asked.

"Amazing."

"God, I'm so glad that asshole will be behind bars for the rest of his miserable life," Emery said.

"You and me both."

"If you're so happy…then how come you don't exactly *sound* happy?" Heidi asked.

"I don't know." I bit my lip and pulled out the letter from Austin. "I need to write to Austin."

Heidi and Emery shared one of their looks.

"What did he say this time?" Heidi asked.

"And how aren't you swooning over these letters?" Emery added.

I let them read the letter, and they both sighed dramatically.

"*Counting down the days until I see you again*," Heidi read aloud. "Is he for real? Jesus, these Wright men."

"I wish he were here," I said, finally admitting the feeling that had been building in me over the last couple of weeks.

"He's going to be out of rehab soon. What are you going to do when he gets out?" Heidi asked.

"We'll have to see when he gets here, won't we?"

"But…do you want to get back together with him?" Heidi asked.

"God, Heidi, so nosy," Emery muttered.

"Don't act like you're not dying to know!"

"Well, yeah, I am. But I'm going to wait for her to tell us."

I laughed. "You two are so ridiculous."

"Truth." Heidi smacked Emery's ass and grinned wickedly.

"Hey!" Emery groaned.

"So…Julia?" Heidi prodded.

"It's been three months since I've seen him. The letters are…everything. I just won't know though until I see him."

Thirty-Seven

Austin

I left rehab with one suitcase and a box of letters.

It had been the longest ninety days of my life, yet... it had flown by. I'd been skeptical when I first arrived. How could ninety days change my life? But it had. In more ways than I could even articulate.

For the first time in a decade, my thoughts were clear. I had a foundation to continue my path and grow into the person I'd always wanted to be. Instead of the drunk I'd become. I still had a lot to make up for. Relationships that I'd splintered, work that I'd neglected, and trust I needed to build up again.

But one step forward.

One step at a time.

Jensen had sent the private jet to pick me up from the facility, and I flew from Malibu to my home alone.

In some way, it was fitting. I might have shown up to rehab with Jensen, but my road to recovery had been a long one, and I'd had to do it all by myself. After all my time away, I needed to prove I could return home on my own, too.

The plane touched down at Lubbock International Airport in the middle of the afternoon on the day before Halloween.

After months with an oceanside vista, Lubbock looked flat as a pancake and lifeless. Yet…it was home.

This was the longest I'd been away since that one summer I was an intern in California. Apparently, California was the place I got away. Not that I was in any hurry to get out of here again.

I carried the box of letters off the plane and was handed my suitcase after disembarking. My eyes flickered over the empty tarmac in disappointment. I'd thought one of my siblings would have at least come to get me. I'd been gone for three months!

Then, I heard an engine revving behind me. I whirled around and found my shiny red Alfa Romeo idling. *Fuck, I'd missed that car.* It had been weird, not driving. I was more than ready to get behind the wheel and take off.

I laughed and headed for the car. Man, it was good to be home.

I had almost made it to the driver's side when the door popped open, and out came a vision. The girl I'd been dreaming about seeing for three very long months.

"Julia," I said in awe.

I drank her in. She'd changed her hair. It was lighter and shone in the fading afternoon sun. And that wasn't the only change. She looked…happier. A coy smile touched her lips, and her dark eyes lit up. She was in black skinny jeans and a black V-neck T-shirt that hugged her curvy features. Paint smudged her fingers. It looked like it belonged there.

And she was still the most beautiful woman I'd ever seen.

"Hey, Austin."

"Are you driving my car?" I asked with a raised eyebrow.

She laughed. "You gave me permission."

"That was one time!"

"Well, she handles like a dream. I might even keep her." She patted the roof. "Red really is my color."

"Fuck, I missed you," I said, stepping up to her.

"Oh, yeah?" Her eyes twinkled in delight.

"Every day."

"I missed you, too."

I set the letters down on my suitcase and left it behind as I approached Julia. She leaned back against the car and tilted her head up to look at me.

"That's really fucking good to hear."

"How was your last week?"

"Long. I was ready to come home."

"But you needed to stay?"

I nodded. "I needed the whole time. And probably years more of outpatient treatment to make sure I don't relapse again."

"You think that's going to happen?" she asked, worry in her voice.

"Not if I have anything to say about it."

"I like hearing that."

God, I wanted to kiss her. I wanted to feel her lips against mine and taste that cherry flavor and get lost in her. I wanted so much. But we hadn't made any promises in all of our letters. I hadn't even known that she'd be the one picking me up today. It had been a long game of waiting to find out if she'd forgive me for what had happened. Not forget it because no one could forget, but learn to move forward. I'd done all of this for me, but I'd be lying if I said I didn't hope that it'd helped my chances with Julia.

"It's really good to see you," I told her instead.

I wasn't going to press. If she wanted this, she'd let me know.

"I know. I'm glad you're back." Then, her eyes rounded, and she started laughing. "But you have a runaway suitcase."

I whipped around and saw that the wind had carried my suitcase and the precious box of letters away from me. I dashed after it and scooped them both up. Julia was cracking up, laughing, when I returned.

"Oh, that was good to watch."

"Thanks for the heads-up."

She leaned down into the car to pop the trunk, and I placed my suitcase inside and fit the letters next to it.

"I brought you a present," she said when I came back around to the front.

"What's that?"

She tossed Waffle at me. I caught the pink-sequined unicorn in both hands and stared at the designs that Julia had added to our unicorn love child.

"I've had custody for two months. I think it's your turn to pitch in. Don't want to be a neglectful parent."

"Wouldn't dream of it."

"So, back to your house?" she asked.

"Actually...I sold it."

"You what?" she gasped. "You didn't tell me!"

"I had Jensen hire someone while I was gone."

Her eyes were wide. "You loved your house!"

"I know. I still do. It sucks. But I bought that house, gutted it, and redid it because it was walking distance to all the bars. I thought being that close to temptation wasn't going to be healthy."

"Wow," she whispered. "That's really...responsible."

I laughed. "It's more like playing chess. I have to second- and third-guess every choice I make to see if it could somehow coincide with the life I lived before or if it might trigger a reaction that would send me over the edge again. I'm still learning to manage those triggers."

"So, where are you staying?"

"Jensen said I could stay with him."

She nodded. "Smart. Well, are you ready to take her out for a ride?"

My eyes met hers. "More than anything."

Julia's cheeks heated. She knew I didn't really mean the car.

We both got inside, and I turned over the engine. It purred to life. Then, I was pulling away from the airport and off onto the country back roads that would take me into Lubbock. The windows were rolled down, Julia's hair whipped in the wind, and it was a perfect sort of freedom.

How had I taken this for granted before?

I had my car, my girl, and my freaking unicorn. Maybe I could have a life again.

We pulled up to Jensen's house, and I parked in the driveway. I still didn't know what I thought about my decision to stay with Jensen. I loved my brother, and he had a freaking mansion, but it wasn't *my* place. I knew it was the right decision to get rid of the house. It was not the best place for me right now. Especially considering the last time I'd been in it and what had happened. I didn't want those memories. It definitely wouldn't assist my recovery.

"Let me help with the bags," Julia said.

She grabbed the box where I kept all of her letters. It popped open when she adjusted it in her hands. Then, she froze, and a slow grin stretched her face. "Are all of these… mine?"

"Did you think I'd gotten rid of them?" I asked.

She shrugged. "I didn't know."

"They were the only other things of value I had with me. My therapist got me the box as a going-away present. It's from a Buddhist healing temple or hippie community or something. Not sure, but it's handmade."

Julia laughed. "It's perfect. Your therapist has good taste."

"He knew how important the letters were to me." I paused before adding, "How important you are to me."

She smiled shyly, as if this were the first time I'd ever said something like that to her before. She touched my arm just briefly. I wondered what she was thinking. *Was I pushing her? Going too fast?* I felt like I was going slower than our snail mail. I didn't want to fall back into old habits, but I would do anything to crash into her all over again.

"I kept all of yours, too," she finally said. Then, she turned to walk through the front door.

A thrill ran through me. I felt like she was slowly acknowledging where this was going. When I followed her through the front door, suitcase in hand, my heart nearly beat out of my chest.

"Welcome home!" the roomful of people cheered.

She whirled around to stare at me with her mouth open and hand over her heart, as if to say that she hadn't known either.

I laughed and dropped the suitcase as I took in the scene before me in awe. A giant Welcome Home sign was slung from one side of the living room to the other. Blue and green streamers hung from the fan way up above. A sheet cake was on a table in the center of the room with *Welcome Home, Austin!* in big blue and green letters. A handprint took up one side, and I noticed that Jensen's son, Colton, had icing on his face.

And the best part of all, of course, was that my entire wonderful family was all together. Jensen had his arm around Emery, trying to restrain Colton. Kimber and Noah were standing together, holding a sleeping Bethany. Lilyanne was laughing at Colton's face, and I suspected she might have had something to do with it.

Landon and Heidi were lounging on the couch with giant smiles on their faces. Patrick stood by Morgan. Neither of them looked as if they'd admit that they were drawn together. Next to Morgan, I was surprised to see the new CFO, David Calloway, in attendance. I supposed anyone that high up in the company was now a member of the Wright family. I hadn't seen him since the Fourth of July when he was interviewed, but we'd been so caught up with Maverick's death that I didn't get that much time with him.

Then, my eyes landed on Sutton. She was still a shadow of her former self, and I knew no amount of therapy would help her with Maverick's death. Her only link to her husband was toddling around at her ankles.

"Thank y'all so much. This means a lot to me," I said to the crowd.

"We're glad to have you back," Jensen said. "We thought it would be nice to have everyone here to grill out and relax tonight."

"I think it's a great idea. Feel free to start with the cake," I assured them. "I'm going to put my suitcase away."

I hurried up the steps and found the guest bedroom. I stashed the suitcase in a corner and then sank onto the bed. Fuck, I loved having everyone together, but fear crept through me. Events like this had always involved alcohol. Not that they would now, but…it was hard not to worry. Not to wonder.

I'd prepared myself for this kind of thing. But it was a bit much.

"Knock, knock," Julia said, leaning into the guest bedroom. "You okay?"

I opened my mouth to tell her that I was fine. But I wasn't. "A little overwhelmed actually."

"I can see that. Don't feel bad for taking a minute. They all care about you and won't mind." She set the box of letters down on a dresser and then came to sit next to me.

"I feel like recovery has really just begun. Today, there's a party, and tomorrow is Halloween. It's a lot all at once."

"You're being hard on yourself. You've come a long way. The first weekend might be a challenge. Hell, it might always be a challenge," she said, reaching out and threading our fingers together. "But you have people who care for you… people who want to help."

My eyes bore into hers with all the intensity from our time apart. She bit her lip and then glanced down at my mouth. I was about to respond when she leaned forward and pressed her lips against mine. It was tentative at first. As if she couldn't believe she had done it in the first place. Then, her hand knotted in my shirt, and she pulled me closer. My hands went into her hair, and I cupped her face.

Every day that I'd spent without her, I pushed into that kiss. Fear that I'd lost her forever. Regret that I'd probably deserved it. Hope that she'd changed her mind. Despair that I hadn't thought she would. Lust…so much lust. And more… so much more.

I didn't want to ever stop kissing her. She tasted like cherry and turned my world upside down. The way she used her tongue heated my blood. Her body under my practiced hands sent shivers up her skin.

This was paradise. Nothing more than that one perfect kiss.

When she finally drew back, pink-cheeked and breathless, she smiled and dropped another hasty kiss on my lips. "I've wanted to do that since I picked you up."

"Same," I admitted, just as short on breath.

"Then, why didn't you?"

"I didn't want you to think I was pushing you. I thought that maybe you didn't want me at all."

"Oh, Austin." She leaned her forehead against mine. Our breath mingled in the short distance. "Our second chance destroyed us. I thought I wouldn't want you…that I couldn't want you again. But then…something happened."

"What happened?"

"You and I…we've healed. Not completely," she said, pulling back to look into my eyes. "But I'd rather work on fixing all those wounds with you than without you."

"I want that with you, too. I want everything with you."

"How about we just start over?"

"Do you think we can do that? After everything I did?"

"I don't like how you reacted when you hit rock bottom or that I was hurt when you did it. But I can't ignore that you've done everything to make yourself better, and that includes with me. I wasn't sure how I felt, and then I saw you. Now, I know that I want to try again."

"I'm going to be a better man for you, Julia," I assured her, pulling her in for another kiss. "That's a damn promise."

Thirty-Eight

Julia

"I can't believe you made me wear this," Austin said.

We'd just pulled up in front of Sutton's house. He got out of the car and tugged on the Captain America T-shirt I'd gotten him for Halloween when I went out that morning, looking for something to wear.

"Shove it, Wright. Walk around naked if you prefer."

He laughed. "I just think I'm more of an Iron Man guy myself."

"Of course you are," I droned sarcastically.

"But maybe we should have gone with the Hulk. Doesn't he end up with Black Widow?"

His eyes scanned the black leather pantsuit I'd stuffed my body into. It all fit once everything was in place, but it'd been ridiculous, getting to that moment.

"All right. Take off your clothes, and I'll paint you green."

He laughed as we walked up to Sutton's front door. "Captain America, it is."

"Smart choice."

I knocked on the door, and I heard Sutton yell, "Coming!"

She pulled open the door to the house she and Maverick had lived in together. I couldn't believe that she still lived here with all the memories. Or maybe she just couldn't let go of it yet.

"Thanks for showing up, y'all," Sutton said. "I'm still trying to get Jason into his costume. He loved it when he picked it out at the store, but now, it seems he'd rather be a streaker."

"We're happy to be here," I said, pulling Austin inside.

We'd volunteered to walk Jason around the neighborhood with Sutton for Halloween. I'd known that she needed the company and that it would be hard for Austin to come right back to life in Lubbock on a party night. Halloween had always been a night to get wasted unless you had kids. So, the whole thing worked out for us.

"Yeah. I'm excited to steal some of Jason's candy," Austin said.

Sutton waved him off. "Be my guest. I don't want to eat it, and he'll be bouncing off the walls with all of that."

She disappeared into one of the bedrooms and appeared a few minutes later with Jason decked out in a bright yellow Minion costume.

"Oh, he's adorable," I gushed.

Jason's eyes lit up when he saw Austin and me. He toddled over to Austin and held his hands up. "Up!"

Austin laughed and pulled Jason into his arms. Seeing them like that made my heart swell. But one look at Sutton's face, and I saw all the happy what-ifs flash before her eyes.

"Why don't we get going?" I suggested.

"Your outfit is cute, Julia," Sutton said. "I look like a mom. No time to do my hair or anything."

"We can watch him if you want some time to get ready before we go," I suggested.

"Who do I have to impress?" She turned away from us and took a steadying deep breath. "Okay, let's go."

She got out Jason's stroller filled with goodies for him and a bag for the candy, and then we were off. Jason made it through three whole houses before being too tuckered out to walk. Austin threw him up onto his shoulders from there, and Jason squealed in delight at the attention. This was how it was supposed to be. This was how an uncle was supposed to act with his nephew.

By the time we made it to the last house on the street, Jason was fast asleep in the stroller with a bagful of candy that he'd never eat.

"He's going to sleep so well tonight," Sutton said.

"And then he'll have a sugar high all day tomorrow," I said.

"Oh, yeah, I'm so looking forward to that."

Sutton got Jason into bed before coming back out to the living room.

"I just…I'm glad someone else was here for that. I didn't know if I could do another thing alone."

"Well," Austin said, "if you ever need anything, even just a night off, then give me a call. You deserve it."

"Really, we'd love to do it," I said.

"I appreciate it. Most days, it's okay. But holidays are the worst. So, it was good to have you here. I think I'm going to try to crash some while he's actually asleep." She sighed. "Pretty lame, huh?"

"Nah," I said. "You sound like a good mom."

Sutton beamed at that. At this point, it was all she really had. "I'm going to take y'all up on babysitting. I could use a day off for real."

We laughed and nodded before leaving Sutton's house. Both of us sagged as soon as the door closed.

"That was…hard," I admitted.

"I feel so bad for Sutton. I wish we could do more."

"Time. That's what she needs right now."

"Yeah. And for us to be there for her."

I nodded my head. "Agreed."

"Also, that barely took any time at all," Austin said as we walked to his car.

"Why don't we…go back to my place?" I suggested hesitantly.

"We can do that," he said. "If you want."

"Yeah. Let's do it."

I tried not to second-guess inviting him into my personal space. I wanted him there. I wanted us to work. It was almost a little scary, how easy it was to be with him again. Almost as if his absence had made me fall for him even harder. Not to mention, there was the box of letters I had in my apartment. Those had brought us together more than anything else ever had. And I loved exploring the man those letters had helped me find.

We made it to my apartment fifteen minutes later. I quickly turned off the security system and then reactivated it once we were inside. Austin was quiet as he surveyed my new place.

"What?" I asked self-consciously.

"Oh, nothing. I like it. My head was just elsewhere."

"Want to talk about it?"

"It's not serious or anything." He turned to face me.

I felt a sudden rush of emotions. Austin was here. In my apartment. We were together. Sober. Three months ago, I never would have thought that was possible.

"You know, you can still talk to me."

"I was just thinking about Jason," Austin said.

He took a seat on the couch, and I followed him, sitting next to him. He wrapped an arm around my shoulders and held me close.

"What about Jason?"

"If I hadn't gone to rehab, I never would have gotten tonight with him. I would have had some other stupid plans that involved getting drunk. I wouldn't have remembered the night either. And…I wonder how many other things I missed because of alcohol."

It was a sobering thought. He'd been a high-functioning alcoholic for so long that he definitely missed a lot of those kinds of moments.

"Even though I was present for shit, I only remember those things through a haze of alcohol. Like Sutton's wedding. One of the most important days of her life, and I don't have a recollection of anything past the ceremony."

"That has to be hard."

"I knew it would feel like this. Or at least, I was warned about it. But it's one thing to talk about it in rehab and another thing to experience it in person. Just something I have to live with."

"At least you're making an effort to make new memories. Sober memories."

"Yeah, I feel like I wasted most of the last ten years. I don't want to miss anything else."

I tilted my head up to meet his dark eyes. There was remorse there. True remorse. What I'd seen from him in the last two days wasn't an act. Of course, I hadn't thought it was. But seeing him torn up like this showed me how much he'd really changed. For him to even think about all the experiences he'd missed out on because of alcohol was self-reflective in a way that the old Austin never would have come to terms with.

"I'm so glad you're here with me," I whispered. My lips hovered an inch from his.

"Me, too." His eyes darted to my lips and then back up. "You know something?"

"What's that?" I whispered, aching for a kiss.

"I love you."

My heart stopped, and butterflies erupted in my stomach. "You do?"

He nodded. "Should have told you that a long time ago."

"Well, you know something?"

"No. What?" he asked, brushing his nose against mine.

"I love you, too."

No other words had to be spoken. We'd both been holding that in for so long, neither willing to really dig into our feelings, that it was as if a dam had broken.

Austin and I cleared the distance between us at the same time. Our kiss was full of the love we'd been denying. His lips were soft and inviting. His tongue promised all the dirty things my mind drifted to with him this close. His hands roamed over my tight bodysuit.

He leaned me backward on the couch, covering my body with his. I wrapped one leg around his waist. Our hips pressed tightly together, and heat rushed through me.

"Fuck," I groaned as he started to circle his hips in place against me.

All coherent thoughts fled my mind. There was just the feel of him against me and the desire to be in a hell of a lot less clothes.

One hand slid down the side of my suit and then reached around to grab my ass. He broke off the kiss to trail his mouth down my neck and across my collarbone. I could feel him, thick and ready for me, through his jeans. I couldn't help myself as I pressed my pelvis up. He pushed back, sliding his dick against the thin material covering my body.

"How the hell do I get this off?" he asked. He slipped his hands up and down my sides, hoping to find an easy way to get me out of this suit.

I laughed and tossed my head back in exasperation. "This is the worst outfit ever for this."

"It's hot as fuck, but I'll cut it off if I have to."

Austin gripped my arm when I offered it to him, and he pulled me up off the couch. I dragged him into my bedroom and showed him the tiny zipper in the back. He tugged it down. He whistled softly through his teeth when the zipper rounded over my ass.

"Julia," he groaned.

His lips touched the base of my neck and then slowly worked down my back, vertebra by vertebra. Then, he kissed my tailbone and lower. His hands splayed over my ass cheeks as he thoroughly kissed each of them.

I tugged my arms out of the sleeves of the suit in my haste to be naked. He helped me drag it the rest of the way down my body until it was in a crumpled pile on my floor.

He turned me back around to face him. "I missed everything about you while I was gone. But this body..." He shuddered. "You are my undoing."

His thumbs brushed against my nipples until they hardened into points. Then, he took one in his mouth, sucking on it, until I writhed beneath his touch, and when I was purring in his grip, he moved to the other one.

"We're...we're going to have to get you out of that shirt," I muttered, trembling from his touch.

My eyes dropped on that Captain America shirt. It showed off those biceps and that chest. But, fuck, I couldn't wait until it was off.

"I...I think I didn't get you the right size anyway."

He laughed. "It's a bit tight."

"Um...yep."

"Guess I'm not a Captain America guy after all." He stripped the shirt off over his head.

And then...*yes*. I trailed my nails down his pecs, down those abs, and to that V. Then, I hastily removed his remaining clothes and saw all my other favorite parts of him that I loved to run my hands down.

Austin threw his head back and moaned when I palmed his cock in my hand.

"God, I want to get inside you," he said. "Want you to know just how much I love you."

I licked around the head of his cock before popping it into my mouth. His hand went through my hair, tightening ever so slightly. I released him from my mouth with a smirk and then crawled back on the bed. He followed after me, his cock jutting out toward me.

Austin settled down between my legs, hiking them up around his hips. He leaned forward onto his elbows to stare down at me. I gripped his biceps as he eased inside me, stretching and filling me to the hilt.

His gaze was intent on me as he pushed my hair out of my face. He didn't move at first, and I squirmed under him.

"What?" I whispered.

"It's different this time."

"Better."

"It was always amazing," he said, "but this time, I just feel more connected. I've…I've never felt like this before, love."

"Me either. It's a little scary," I confessed.

"I'll take it slow."

He leaned forward to kiss me and then started moving, keeping to his word. I couldn't even describe how good it felt. His body pressed against mine. His cock sliding in and out of my pussy. Our breath mingling in the space.

There was no rush. We had all the time in the world. And, still, he barely had to move as our bodies eased together and then apart and then back together. We weren't just fucking, like we always had before. For the first time, we were really making love.

While I liked both options, when we finally came apart at the same time, my orgasm hit me relentlessly. I saw stars. My mind went blank. I probably could have spoken in tongues.

Nothing compared.

And I realized that nothing ever would with Austin.

Being away from one another for those three months was the best decision of our lives. I'd found my art again. Austin had stopped drinking. We'd both healed. It had been necessary. Without it, we never would have gotten to where we were right now. We never would have been able to move on. It had taken that time to show that we were strong enough separate...but better as one.

We might be works in progress separately.

But, together, we were complete.

Epilogue

Austin
Five Months Later

"Do I finally get to see what you've been working on?" I asked Julia as we drove to the First Friday Art Trail. "Maybe," she said coyly.

She'd been hinting at a big event that she had been working toward for months. But nothing I'd said or done—and, trust me, I'd tried—could get her to change her mind. She was set on me finding out with everyone else. Because of that, I hadn't been allowed to step foot into her art studio at her apartment. I'd respected her privacy, but it had been killing me not to know.

Julia had a parking spot for the event this time, so she wouldn't have to park in a tow zone. I hopped out of her Tahoe and followed her around the corner to one of the warehouses already crowded with people.

"Are you ready?" she asked.

I took her hand and kissed the palm. "I can do anything when I'm with you."

She laughed. "Oh, boy. Well, here we go."

Julia walked me to the back of the exhibit, and when I realized what I was looking at, I stopped dead in my tracks. Julia shot me a worried look. And then I burst into laughter.

"Austin!" she gasped.

"You put up the naked picture of me?" I said through my laughter.

"It's kind of the centerpiece of my exhibit."

"Oh, Jules," I said, sliding back into that nickname. It had taken a long time before she decided that I could start calling her that again. I was glad. I didn't want her to associate anything with that douche.

"You're not mad?"

I wiped a tear from my eye, and then I scooped her up in my arms and twirled her around in a circle. "How could I be mad at you?"

She giggled when I set her down. "Well, I don't know. Everyone in Lubbock can see you naked."

"Everyone is just looking at your talent."

"Well, I could have had the space for this months ago. Nina told me to do it whenever I was ready. It took longer than I'd expected to get there. I'd started on a lot of these while you were away, but I didn't get them just right until last month." She bit her lip and then glanced around at the fifteen canvases that showed the range and depth of her abilities. "It's kind of an ode to our relationship and the struggles we've overcome."

I could see it when I knew what I was looking at. A watercolor of Waffle. A collection of letters. A charcoal of water. And so many more that I recognized. It was perfect.

"I love every single one."

"One more surprise."

Then, she handed me a piece of paper. I glanced down at it and beamed.

"All proceeds are going to the foster care system in Lubbock?" I asked in awe.

"It was the first time that I really saw how there was so much more to you. I thought it was only fitting. I have a full-time job. The money I make from the pictures should go to something worthwhile. I'd rather make a donation."

"You're amazing," I told her. "I love you."

She beamed. "I love you, too. I was really worried you'd hate it."

"How could I when you put so much effort and love into it?"

I leaned down and drew her into a kiss. A throat cleared behind us, and I whirled around to find Patrick standing behind us.

"What the hell is that?" he asked, pointing at the naked picture of me.

I laughed at his astounded face.

"When Julia invited me, I didn't know I'd have to look at your naked ass."

"Can't you appreciate art?" I asked in mock seriousness.

"My eyes are bleeding."

A minute later, the rest of my family showed up with David in tow once more. He had Jason on his shoulders, and Sutton actually seemed not to be miserable at the gesture. That was something at least.

Jensen's and Landon's eyes rounded in the same way that Patrick's had when they saw the naked picture of me that Julia had painted last summer.

"So…how exactly did you get into doing that?" Landon asked.

"I volunteered to sit naked for an art class I signed Julia up for. It was full, and that was how I got her in."

Jensen raised his eyebrows. "You know, when you came to me last summer and I told you to lay it all out there for Julia…I didn't actually mean *everything*."

Julia snort-laughed, and I couldn't keep my laughter in. I clapped my brothers on their backs.

"It's tasteful," I insisted.

"If you say so," Landon said as he wandered over to look at the picture of Waffle.

Heidi came forward and hugged Julia. "I'm so proud of you!"

"It's really freaking amazing," Emery agreed.

"Especially that middle picture," Heidi added with a wink. "Pretty impressive."

Emery tilted her head as she stared at the picture. "Well... now, I've seen all the Wright brothers."

"Emery!" Julia said, covering her face.

"It does run in the family," Heidi added.

It was my turn for my face to turn beet red. "Jesus, y'all are worse than us guys."

"Duh," Heidi said, swishing her blonde hair off her shoulder.

Emery just shrugged. Her eyes glanced down to my shorts once, and then she laughed. It was Julia who finally herded them away. I could hear them chatting and giggling. As thick as thieves, that trio was.

We spent the rest of the First Friday camped out near Julia's exhibit. She sold three pictures while we were there, but I thought she was more excited about the experience of the whole thing. To use her art for good, no matter what money it brought in.

When I could see she was flagging, I finally drew her away from the warehouse and out to the food trucks to grab something for dinner.

"Lemonade?" I guessed.

"Don't act like you know me," she teased.

"Oh, but I do."

I got her the lemonade and both of us barbeque. My eyes drifted to the red Solo cups everyone was carrying and the signs for alcohol. Several months ago, I wouldn't have even been able to come to First Friday. It was a testament to the fact that I was now eight months sober and that I was able to be here for Julia. It wasn't easy. There were times when I thought I'd never make it, but it was the right choice. And, as we moved to an empty picnic table amid the chaos and I sat across from Julia, I knew that it was worth the effort.

"I'm really proud of you, you know," I told Julia.

She flushed. "It feels good to be doing what I love again."

"Will you move in with me?"

Julia's eyes flashed up to mine. "What?"

"You know…move in with me."

"Your house isn't even done," she said with a laugh.

"I know. We have another month or two. That means, you will get final say on everything. You can decide which room you want your art studio in, paint the walls, decorate, choose the details that you're good at. I want you in my life. I want my house to be your house. I don't want it to feel like a bachelor pad. I want everything to have your touch on it."

"Austin, that's a huge step."

I grinned. "That's why I'm asking you now. So, you'll have a couple months to get used to the idea."

She laughed and shook her head. "That's not what I mean."

"What do you mean?"

"I mean…it's a huge step, and I'm excited to take it with you."

"You are?"

She nodded and then laughed. She jumped up from her side of the picnic table and then threw herself into my arms. Exactly where she belonged.

Our road hadn't been easy.

In fact, at some points, I'd thought we were never going to make it.

But Julia was my forever. Full stop.

One day, I'd put a ring on her finger, give her my name, have her carry our children. But, today, knowing I had a future with her was enough.

She was enough.

The End

Note from the Author

This book was one of the hardest I've ever written. Loving an addict is hard. Loving an addict who refuses to get help is even harder. And I know so many of you out there have had to deal with family members and friends who have substance abuse problems. You're not alone. We're all here for you.

Austin's road through alcoholism was brutal, and in the end, it all worked out. He had a support network, loving friends and family, and the will to keep going. Unfortunately, that isn't the case for everyone. So, if you or someone you know is suffering from drug or alcohol abuse, please get them help. Let Austin and Julia's story be the push you need to help those that you care about in any way that you can.

Toll-Free Drug or Alcohol Hotline
1-888-509-2504

Alcoholics Anonymous
(800) 396-1602
www.aa.org

Resources to get help:
www.samhsa.gov
www.recovery.org
www.drugabuse.com

Acknowledgments

Thank you to all the people who helped make this book come to life. I was on a crazy deadline and was pretty manic through the whole thing. And you all only thought I was half-insane…okay maybe ¾ insane. But, also, for helping me make Austin's and Julia's struggles realistic. All around being the best friends ever. So, thanks—Anjee, Rebecca, Katie, Polly, and Lori.

Mindi—for letting me make you a butcher-knife wielding psycho and for reading my cop scenes for accuracy. Lauren—for all the help with guns and the firing range.

Sarah Hansen—for the gorgeous cover. Eric Battershell—for the hot picture of Austin that made me fall out of my seat when I saw it. Danielle Sanchez—for helping me make all the hard decisions. Kimberly Brower, agent extraordinaire—for all your brilliance and for already getting this book in audio! Jovana Shirley—for the wonderful editing job and formatting, especially on a tight deadline. I owe you one.

Finally, my husband, Joel, and our two puppies, Riker and Lucy! You're the ones who have to deal with my vampire schedule. I love and appreciate you!

About the Author

K.A. Linde is the *USA Today* bestselling author of the Avoiding Series and more than twenty other novels. She grew up as a military brat and attended the University of Georgia where she obtained a master's in political science. She works full-time as an author and loves Disney movies, binge-watching *Supernatural,* and *Star Wars.*

She currently lives in Lubbock, Texas, with her husband and two super-adorable puppies.

K.A. LINDE

Visit her online at www.kalinde.com and on Facebook, Twitter, and Instagram @authorkalinde.

Join her newsletter at www.kalinde.com/subscribe for exclusive content, free books, and giveaways every month.